Influence

by

Andrew Snadden

Dedicated to my Family, Friends and the Police Service

Without Fear or Favour
Chapter One

"Oh shit, it's the filth!" A sense of urgency and fear reverberated in the middle aged man's voice.

"We're screwed lads, he's coming! What are we going to do?!" said one of the four men sat around a circular table in a poorly lit room inside a disused warehouse, whilst another hurried to cover up the large amount of white powder that was in the centre of the table.

A tall, slim, middle aged man wearing a tailored suit walked forcefully into the room. He was there for business, and he meant it. As he walked up to the table there was a sense of apprehension in the room that was almost tangible. These five men had a lot to lose, and this man represented the very thing that could snatch it all away from them; an officer of the law, a police detective.

The suited detective's footsteps grew louder as his weight caused the worn floorboards beneath to flex, creating that familiar and annoying creak, the type of creak that someone needed to repair but had never had the time or inclination to bother.

"Why the guilty faces lads?" the detective enquired, knowing full well what these guys were about and what they were up to. The question was met with silence as the five faces stared back at him defiantly, unwilling to provide him with an incriminating answer.

"Come on, the game's up" the detective shouted at them as he pulled a badge that signified his power from his right jacket pocket and threw it down onto the table.

"What are you waiting for? Come on, share it with me!" he said with an air of satisfaction and a Cheshire cat like grin on his face. Suddenly the five men burst into laughter.

"And use my warrant card to cut my line!" he said without any sign of remorse.

1

The detective took a seat at the table as one of the males cut him a line of the white powder using his police identity card. He pulled an appreciative smile before he leant down and snorted the whole white powdery line with expert precision; this was certainly not the first time he had taken cocaine. The detective finished the line and leant back in his seat rubbing the remnants of the powder from his nose.

"Good to see you, it's been a while. Done any police work recently? Or are you still hiding behind that lovely desk of yours?"

Brothers in Arms
Chapter Two

Inside a large briefing room in the City's HQ, two teams of black clad Specialist Firearms Officers with enough equipment to invade a small country, sat waiting for a last minute operational briefing from a Firearms Silver Commander who would be in charge.

"For God's sake, I should be eating a kebab right now instead of waiting for another shit job as usual" said PC Dave Allen, a slightly chubby officer, who somehow managed to look like he hadn't visited a gym in years despite actually maintaining a high level of fitness.

"I know, don't get me wrong, I'm hanging out for a decent job too but why they've called a last minute operation, I'll never know. Could be a good crack though" answered PC John O'Keeffe, an athletic looking officer in his early forties whose use of military slang could be hard to fathom at times for those who were not fluent in 'squaddy talk'.

"John, Dave's right, this is going to be a load of bollocks" interjected PC Steve Evans an officer in his early thirties with an average build. "It's a Saturday and I should be at home with the wife and kids"

"Count yourself lucky then" Allen said to Evans.

"Why is that Dave?" Evans asked with a confused expression on his face that was shared by O'Keeffe too.

"Because if I had a wife that looked like yours, I wouldn't be rushing to get home!" Allen said whilst trying not to laugh at his own joke. If there was one thing you could count on with Allen, it was that he thought he was hilarious, even if others didn't.

"Piss off!" Evans said as he shook his head and turned to face the front of the room, in attempt to ignore Allen.

Suddenly another voice came from over their shoulders,

interrupting the idle chit chat and stating what should have been obvious to the specialist officers.

"They've called it because it's their job, and believe it or not, it's our job to respond to it without question! And besides Dave..........you're a fat bastard who could do with laying off the kebabs for a while; Oh and by the way, at least Steve's wife wants him at home!" the pointed remark caused both O'Keeffe and Evans to burst out laughing as Allen shook his head with embarrassment before laughing himself.

With a pleased look on his face, the officer leant back and slumped into his chair with a feeling of satisfaction derived from his sharp and witty put down. The officer, Anthony 'Jodie' Foster was a rugged but good looking man with a powerful athletic build, five foot eleven tall and with brown hair fashioned in short and smart cut. His nickname, Jodie, was the result of sharing his surname with the famous Hollywood actress Jodie Foster. If there was one thing that the officers on the unit could be counted on for, it was inventing nicknames for their colleagues, no matter how obvious or silly they may have been. Foster had joined the 'job', slang for the police service, at the tender age of twenty one and was now celebrating his fourteenth year in the service. He loved being a copper but still had a work hard and play even harder philosophy on life which revolved around his job, women and partying. And as a result of this sometimes wild persona, Foster was seen as a 'good old boy' by his colleagues on the unit, which in a nutshell meant that he was well liked and accepted within the elite group of officers. From an outsider's point of view, you would have been forgiven for believing that the four men were not on friendly terms because of the highly offensive and personal humour, but the reality, as strange as it may have sounded, was that they were all incredibly close. The way the members of the unit saw it was; if you don't like the humour, you had best piss off somewhere else.

"Alright lads, pipe down" ordered Sergeant Kevin Marriot, a tall, dark haired man in his early forties.

As silence fell around the large room, a youngish looking Chief Inspector got up out of his seat and took centre stage at the

4

front of the lecture theatre. He switched on the tape recorder and identified himself before stating the time, date and location of the briefing.

"For those of you who don't know me, I'm Chief Inspector Ben Murray, and before we move on to what we're here for, I would like to apologise for the last minute operation, I know some of you were looking forward to an after shift kebab! The time is 18.00hrs hours, the date is 10th October 2011 and this briefing is taking place in the lecture theatre of City Police's HQ, the operation's name is OP Barrier".

As a rule operational briefings were always taped in the event of a post incident Independent Police Complaints Commission (or IPCC) enquiry where the recording would provide a deeper insight into what information had been provided to the officers and why. The IPCC, not above controversy itself, didn't seem to have to adhere to the same level of accountability when it came to their own work.

"Great, he heard me talking about the Kebab!" Allen whispered under his breath to Foster and O'Keeffe.

The Chief Inspector swiftly moved on to the point of the briefing. "Right, I'm going to cut to the chase, this ain't a crap job, I know you've all heard that before but this one is the real McCoy! A few hours ago one of our Intel handlers was told by a snitch who has links to Ahmed Mahood's extremist group that Ahmed is beefing up his terror operation and plotting an attack in the UK, the City to be precise." Murray said, catching the attention of everyone in the room.

"Firearms have been seen at the target address so it would seem that Mahood is serious about doing it. The intelligence is that the attack is imminent, possibly within the next few days, so we can't just sit around waiting, we need to act now; tonight!" Murray continued.

The subject, Ahmed Mahood, was a wealthy Syrian immigrant who came to England to study, hardly your average suicidal terrorist. He was an elusive man with a high level intellect, and barring an assault charge, he had barely put a foot wrong, which made him appear as a normal member of the public. That was until he popped up on the radar of MI6 by sheer coincidence after a Special Forces operation that was conducted in Afghanistan, uncovered a number of laptops that contained a wealth of information on their hard-drives, some of which made for very interesting reading.

"Sir, what intel has the snitch provided and is it sound enough to call an operation like this on short notice" asked Evans.

"I was just about to get to those bits Evans; if you'll let me" Chief Inspector Murray replied with a put out expression.

"Right shall I continue? Ok, Mahood is said to be planning an Active shooter style attack, we don't know when or exactly where yet, but we do know where he is. Last night our snitch discovered that Mahood along with a team of five are planning to drive six cars onto the Motorway, a mile south of the City's airport, where they will stop their vehicles at an agreed designated point on both the North and Southbound carriageways, and bring the traffic to a complete standstill. Once a huge traffic jam has developed, Mahood and his team will exit their cars in possession of assault rifles and walk down each lane of gridlocked vehicles and............" Murray looked around the room with a serious face before finishing his sentence. "And walk down each lane of traffic, executing every single person in the vicinity that doesn't manage to escape. I guess it doesn't take too much of an morbid imagination to work out what would happen if this tactic was carried out at rush hour, it would be a very, very bad day. The word is that the attack could happen any day now, who knows, maybe even tomorrow. Listen guys, we have an extremely unique opportunity here to prevent this attack from taking place, rather than the usual picking up the pieces after it's happened, surely that's the most important point here; questions?"

A stunned silence filled the room, something unprecedented in tactical firearms briefings due to the number of characters the unit possessed. "Sir, is Mahood definitely in possession of these assault rifles yet and if so how did he get hold of them?" PC Calum MacNeil, a Scottish officer in his early forties enquired.

"Mahood has a wide range of contacts in the middle east and Somalia, most notably high level rebel commanders in

Mogadishu, Somalia and a few terrorist cell leaders in Afghanistan. These contacts were established when he attended training camps in the two countries for a number of months; please don't ask why this information wasn't passed to us! And if you haven't had your head buried in the sand for the last five years you'll be aware that piracy in Somalia is at an all-time high which means that the Royal Navy are very busy looking for them and not the smugglers, making it easier for them to enter the Med. Well because of this, Mahood's weapons, along with other terrorist paraphernalia, have been smuggled through the Med into Algeria then France and across the Channel right into............believe it or not, the City's Marina! Like I said, please don't ask why this wasn't mentioned to us earlier!"

The briefing continued for a further thirty minutes with details of the Mahood's current address and its layout, further intelligence and the usual reminder about use of force legislation being read out to the officers. The latter being the most boring as every firearms officer knew exactly what they could and couldn't do with regards to using force. Chief Inspector Murray finished up the extensive briefing by thanking everyone for their attention before he walked out of the lecture theatre, followed by PC Ian Phelps who was Murray's Firearms Tactical Advisor. Phelps, prior to his own departure gave the room a rude gesture and a bow, causing the other officers in the room to give him the middle finger in return. Tactical Advisers were firearms officers themselves who worked with commanding officers to advise them on the unit's tactics and policies. Although they were still part of the unit, the operational officers saw them as overtime snatchers who sat around drinking tea in a nice warm room with the brass while they froze their backsides off outside in the elements. The reality was quite different of course but coppers being coppers, they weren't happy unless there was someone to slag off or moan about. Even if it was the result of financial jealousy.

Sgt.Marriot waited for the Chief to walk out before continuing with the tactical phase of the briefing, which most certainly was not taped.

"Sarge, are they being serious? I think an operation this serious needs a little more planning than a few hours, it needs planning, and planning again. This is stupid!" PC Mark Collins remarked from the back of the lecture theatre.

"I know, I know Mark, but what can we, or I, say that will change their minds? This is last minute intel that needs to be acted on as soon as possible, nay, now! We can't wait, you know that" Marriot replied, although he agreed with Collins, he couldn't be seen undermining the command.

Collins slumped back into his seat while gesturing to PC James Simpson across from him that he wasn't happy with the unfolding situation, he knew full well that the 'Op' had to happen immediately but he also knew that a lack of decent planning could bite them.

"Sgt, I understand what you're saying but this is high end stuff with the assault rifles being involved. Are the brass fully aware of what could go wrong with such little planning? Now I'm all set with the old 'better to be judged by twelve than carried by six' but in reality the 'twelve' aren't always pro Police and if this does go wrong, we really could be on the defendants side of the courtroom being judged. Simpson said, being a little more constructive than Collins.

O'Keeffe and Simpson had both served on a Special Forces unit in the British Army and seen active service around the world and on the Counter Terrorist Unit in Hereford. After becoming fed up with the army lifestyle they decided to join the City's Police Force and had settled into the unit very quickly, appreciating the down time between jobs that just wouldn't have been afforded to them in the 'mob' that was the Special Forces.

"Look, Command understands the risk but they also know what the ramifications of waiting too long would be. I've been assured by the Gold Commander Superintendent that no matter what happens, we will have the force's full support" Sgt Marriot said trying to reassure his team.

Allen gave him a sarcastic thumbs up, he and the others knew full well that if the shit hit the fan, they would be alone. Sgt Marriot rolled his eyes, the others may have had concerns but as the third in Command, if things went south, he would be the one answering a lot of questions in any subsequent enquiry; a hell of a lot more than the PCs. Whether he was concerned or not, the show had to go on. Marriot directed his team's attention to a smart board where details of crew information and individual tasks were highlighted on a Powerpoint presentation. The plan was that the twelve officers in the room, would be separated into two teams of six, Blue and Red team. Blue were tasked with entering the building through level one, while Red team would split into two further pods of three to allow them to enter the first floor of the house via the front and the rear bedroom windows using ladders and the unit's armoured Land rover as a platform. Both Red and Blue teams would use an array of Stun grenades and explosive devices to force and secure their entry, and to distract the subjects inside, creating an element of surprise and maximising the safety of all those involved. In support of the two teams there would be three pairs of Snipers and six Authorised Firearms Officers who would help create a secure perimeter for the team to work within.

With all their questions 'answered', the two teams stood up and began filing out of the theatre to head back down to the unit's office in the basement of the main HQ building. O'Keeffe stood up from his seat, turned to Foster and said "You, me and Calum through the main bedroom window from on top of the armoured land rover, doesn't get better than that. All we need now is a bus full of Swedish cheer leaders to play with our 'wangers' and we've got the perfect night" He said

"Are there any brunettes on that bus" Foster asked.

"Just loads of different kinds of chicks" O'Keeffe explained while letting out a dirty laugh.

"Then I'm game mate. OHHH SHIT, I DON'T BELIEVE IT! John, I was meant to be meeting Amy at six"

"The beautician with the nice arse that you've not stopped talking about?" O'Keeffe enquired.

"Yes, that one John!" Foster replied with his right hand covering his forehead in frustration.

"Well you're up the creek then mate, six o'clock is long gone and isn't this the second or third time that you've stood her up? Come on, we best crack on, lots to do" He replied with a grin whilst patting Foster hard on the shoulder in a pseudo sympathetic manner. Foster's problem was something that all coppers would learn at some point in their career; relationships and police work don't always mix; if at all.

Purposely hanging back from the others, Foster switched on his phone to try and make a quick apology call to Amy. Before he even dialled her number, the phone vibrated in his hand.

"Beep, you have one new message, message received today at six forty.................YOU COLD HEARTLESS BASTARD, DON'T EVER BOTHER CALLING ME AGAIN, YOU'RE AN ARSEHOLE!" a female voice boomed from the speaker, filling the corridor.

Foster's anti-social habit of playing all of his answer-phone messages on speaker as opposed to putting the mobile up to his ear meant that everyone around him would hear his various conquests voice's at the same time he did. Seriously pissed off, he walked through the doors and onto the stairs that descended down towards the TFU office.

"AHHHHHHH Gutted!!!!" The members of Red team called out on seeing him come through the doors. The volume of his phone's speaker allowing everyone within a mile to hear what Amy's angry banshee like shouting was for! Foster stopped and rested against the wall as the others ran off down the stairs. He peered down at his phone and considered calling her before realising that he would never have been able to think of a good enough excuse for why he had stood her up again, it wasn't as if he could tell her the real reason. Foster had blown it and he knew it. The anger started to boil up inside of him to the extent where his hands were beginning to shake, he grasped the phone and squeezed it tighter and tighter in his palm until cracking noises could be heard coming from it.

"FUCK" he shouted out before launching the phone towards the lift door in front of him with the force of a tomahawk missile, causing it to smash into a thousand pieces on impact. With the rage inside him yet to be consoled, he charged towards the elevator door and punched it as hard as he could in an attempt to rid himself of the cortisol building up in his brain. Just as he was about to hit it again, he paused, suddenly realising that he had created a moon like dent in police property and also risked injuring his much needed hand. Foster fell back against the wall and slid down it until he was seated with his hands cupping his face not knowing whether to scream or cry in anger.

Unknown to his colleagues, Foster hadn't always been the fun loving 'good old boy' he was considered to be. Prior to joining the 'job' he was an off the rails teenager who had displayed a dark and violent temper on more than one occasion that could have had him arrested, or worse. However since joining the disciplined environment of the police service he had been provided with structure and focus which helped him put to rest his troubled past and distract him from his personal demons. However, in this moment, the discipline that had quelled his previous out of control ways had well and truly left him, and he was now lost in tidal wave of rage, his thoughts racing around his head with the speed of the Japanese Bullet train. It wasn't the first time that Foster had suffered with similar racing thoughts. After a recent problem with his mortgage payments increasing, he had been under a lot of stress that had prevented him from sleeping due to the unrelenting worries and thoughts bouncing around inside his skull, there had even been a few occasions where he had lost a sense of himself for short period of time, almost feeling as though he was someone else. The situation with Amy he had just been presented with was hardly going to help matters.

Ten minutes passed as he sat there motionless, lost inside his blurred thoughts until the voice of O'Keeffe that could be heard coming from the bottom of the stairs, snapped him out of his trance like state. He wiped his face hard whilst sharply inhaling in through his nose and then shouted out to O'Keeffe below that he was coming down. Foster hurriedly collected the larger parts of his smashed phone before noticing the large dent he had caused, with a lack of CCTV in the hall, there was no way he was going to report the damage. How would he explain it anyway.

At the bottom of the stairs he was met by O'Keeffe who

looked at him with a smile and said "Mate we're on a massive job and your hiding and worrying about some chick. I called you, why didn't you answer you loon".

"Oh right!? Erm; I think my phone must be playing up" Foster replied with a sense of embarrassment as he felt the remains of his phone in his pocket.

Three hundred yards into Poland Lane, just outside of the City's boundary, the lights of a detached house illuminated the dark eerie country style lane it inhabited. However this particular lane was definitely not located in idyllic rural surroundings.

Number 12 Poland lane, a Victorian era house, was less than five hundred metres away from the City's airport; one of the busiest in the country, and less than half a mile away from the large busy industrial site of Highfield. It may have been noisy at times, but there was one positive to the property's seemingly manic surroundings, and that was that no one would have believed it was there, unless they were really looking for it. The lane, though close to busy factories and the airport, still managed to exude a sense of being disconnected, which is just how the deed holder liked it; and needed it.

The owner, a one Adam Jennings was an unassuming type of guy, almost boring. Well that's what any of his colleagues at Pritchard's estate agents would have said about him. No girlfriend, no known friends and a refusal to attend any work related social functions made him appear quite unequivocally dull. His appearance didn't help much either, beige trousers, beige jackets; beige everything, a thirty eight year old man who may as well have been in his sixties. And that was the point, it made him nigh on invisible to everyone around him. Jennings, unbeknown to his colleagues harboured a dark secret. He wasn't a secret sadist with a passion for chains and whips, a heavy drinker or drug fiend, nor a devil worshipper; he was an extremist!

Jennings' conversion to Islam had taken place during a backpacking trip in Morocco, where, after being in the country for just a few weeks, he had been attacked by a group of westerner hating thugs. Laying there badly injured, he was saved

13

by a local Muslim man who took him to a hospital and then nursed him back to health in his family home, displaying the famous Islamic tradition of being compassionate and hospitable. Foster pretty much converted the day after he was taken in by the man.

However, on his return to England his new found religion was not well received by his friends or family who branded him a 'Paki lover', lamenting at how he could have become a Muslim when the large influx of 'them' had ruined Bradford. And as his family pointed out, it had not been the first time he had been influenced by someone and led astray, it had been happening continuously since his secondary school days and was an inherent weakness in his character. But what made it worse this time around was that the influencer had been a foreigner, a bloody Muslim. His parents gave him an ultimatum.......grow up, stick with your 'own' or move to Paki land and never come back, no son of theirs would ever wear a damn Turban or Burhka. The ultimatum and lack of cultural accuracy reflected their racist and ignorant views.

Upset and deluded with the bigoted views expressed by his family and friends, Jennings moved south to London where he managed to secure a lucrative career in estate agency. Unfortunately the bright city lights and financial rewards of being a successful salesmen in the affluent Richmond area of Greater London had done little for keeping with new found faith's teachings. Yet again, he had been easily led by those around him and set about drinking and shagging his way through the next few years, practically forgetting that he had ever been a Muslim in the process. Jennings was out of control and he knew it but he just didn't have the confidence to say no to the peer pressure, bowing down to it like a Cleopatra era slave.

One night after bedding an attractive but 'loose' girl, he contracted an extremely painful sexually transmitted infection that felt as though he was passing razor blades through his urethra the following morning. The extreme discomfort meant that he wasted no time in rushing to the closest GUM clinic. With his head held low and still slightly drunk, Jennings walked, or rather

14

fell, into the clinic. To his dismay he saw that a large proportion of the people sat in the waiting room were Chavs and lowlife scum who had probably been on their third or fourth visit that month. The realisation of how he must have looked caused him to develop a deep sense of shame and dirtiness, the type of dirt that just couldn't be washed away with a bit of the Body shops 'Tea tree' hair and body shampoo in a hot shower. Smelling of alcohol and still dressed in the same clothes he had partied in the night before, he left the clinic and swore to himself that he would never shroud himself in such shame again. He needed to repent his sins as soon as he possibly could, so he drove to the nearest Mosque in Kingston, Surrey less than four miles away to seek salvation and forgiveness.

Like in Morocco, he was welcomed with open arms and given a shower and some fresh clothes to wear. Jennings felt a profound sense of spiritual healing when the head of the Mosque, the Imam, compassionately hugged him and called him brother without judging him. From that moment, he attended the Mosque on a near daily basis, making new enlightened and kind friends from the local Muslim community. These were the type of friends he needed, not the sinning ones currently in his life who just wanted to party and whore themselves. As a result, it didn't take long for Jennings to shun his work colleagues and become aloof and somehow disconnected from his previous life and career. The drinking stopped and the idea of being intimate with a disease riddled western girl made the vomit rise up into his mouth. In his eyes he had been saved from an afterlife in hell.

As the months passed, Jennings' views on how the British and the West lived, started to become more and more distasteful to his fellow Muslims at the Mosque, to the extent where after two years of daily worship he was asked to leave. The Imam citing that his hatred for British people and anyone who did not follow Islam was not what they taught. There was no place for hatred and bigotry in their Mosque.

Distraught and feeling lost once again, Jennings reluctantly left the Mosque at the behest of the Imam, wondering how good Muslims could have rejected him in such a way. As he began to

15

walk out, Jennings heard an argument break out from behind him. When he turned around to see what all the commotion was about he saw a well-dressed, handsome Middle Eastern man remonstrating with the Imam. Jennings had seen this man a couple of times before, although only in passing. He wasn't a regular at worship and his relationship with the Imam had appeared strained, almost hostile at times whenever he was in the Mosque.

"ALLAH FORBIDS IT, YOU ARE TO STAY AWAY FROM HIM" The Imam shouted.

Jennings, unable to catch the rest of what the Imam had said, assumed that he had meant that no one was allowed to speak to him as a result his ejection from the Mosque.

"UNLIKE YOU, HE IS A TRUE BELIEVER. ALLAH CURSE YOU FOR YOUR ACQUIESCENCE OF SINNING!" the man angrily shouted back at the Imam.

Jennings walked out of the Mosque's doors and onto the busy Kingston street feeling vulnerable and in need of guidance when suddenly his right shoulder was gently gripped by someone from behind him.

"My brother, the Imam is wrong. A man who sees the sinning of the west like you do should never be cast out of a place of worship. Come brother, come with me, let us leave these cruel men behind and discover Allah's true will for ourselves. My name is Ahmed, Ahmed Mahood!" the man said. His expensive and intoxicating aftershave combined with his swathe good looks and seniority made Jennings feel instantly in awe of the man, which meant one thing; he was going to be vulnerable to his influence.

"Adam, the name's Adam Jennings, it's a pleasure, a real pleasure brother" Jennings replied with a huge beaming smile.

That first encounter had taken place six years before and during the time that followed it, the two men had become more like brothers. However the downside to this strong bond was that Jennings' already skewered views about his fellow Brits had now become a little more sinister due to inordinate amounts of brainwashing about the West's sinning ways that had been dished out by Mahood. His ideology was somewhat ironic, considering

16

that on his arrival from Syria in the late eighties, he had set about sleeping with as many western women as he possibly could and taking cocaine by the truck load, not to mention making a little money off selling the white stuff himself. But after a few racist attacks, his long term girlfriend leaving him for another man and the start of the Anglo-middle eastern wars, Mahood had developed a contempt and hatred for the west after his pride had been damaged.

As a result of his hatred, Mahood had always been on the lookout for new recruits to follow his anti-West ideology, but up until that point he hadn't been too successful in finding someone intelligent enough to be of that greater service; that all changed when he met Jennings. After a period of establishing whether he could trust Jennings, Mahood asked him to attend training camps with him in Somalia and Afghanistan, an opportunity that Jennings leapt at. The only problem with travelling to such places and having connections there, meant that at some point someone would get suspicious, although in his arrogance Mahood would never had believed or let that sort of thing worry him.

Mahood should have been worried though, because after a raid on a terrorist training camp in Afghanistan by the British SAS and American Delta Forces, documents were found on a laptop that linked him to the camp and its leader. With a bit of field interrogation that was inflicted on one of the enemy soldiers for good measure, the special forces operators had gained some vital intel regarding an attack that was being planned in the UK, although they were not able establish a location or name which meant that it could have been any one of the large proportion of British men who had attended the camp during the year. However when the snitch with links to Mahood had informed Special Branch that he was in possession of assault rifles and planning an attack in the City, the Force had consequently informed the intelligence services who were finally able to confirm who their terrorist was, and demanded that he be instantly apprehended, hence Op Barrier came rapidly into existence.

In the kitchen of number 12 Poland Lane, Jennings was cleaning one of their six AK47 assault rifles for the hundredth time that night which made Mahood ask him why, as he couldn't understand his gun cleaning obsession. Jennings answered that he wanted to make sure that the weapons were kept in tip top shape before their 'Jihad battle'. The answer made Mahood burst out laughing which drew a sickening puppy dog like expression from Jennings.

"It's close Adam, don't worry. Just a few days left to wait now!" Mahood said after he stopped laughing.

While the two men chatted, the four middle eastern men that completed Mahood's terrorist group were sat in the front room watching the football highlights. Unlike Jennings and Mahood, these four lacked any real intelligence which was probably the main reason behind Mahood finding it so easy to recruit them. All he needed to do was to sell them the myth about receiving forty virgins in the afterlife and they would be happy to fight to the death for him. One thing that could be guaranteed with Mahood though, was that there was no way he would be willing to meet Allah any time soon; the virgins would have to wait. Regardless of what Jennings may have believed about him, Mahood was a coward who would escape out of the country after the attack the same way the weapons had come in, and more importantly; alone! Jennings, who was still tending to the rifles began filling a magazine clip with 7.62 calibre rounds, expertly pushing each one down into the clip with his callous covered right thumb, the result of repeatedly loading the same type of magazines in the training camp. Once there was no room left to place any more rounds, Jennings took hold of the clip and offered it up into the magazine housing of the Russian made Kalashnikov AK47 (the weapon of choice for African rebels and terrorists, freedom fighters in some peoples mind) and pushed it home. The rifle with its six hundred and fifty rounds per minute rate of fire was a gun straight out of a Rambo film and if the plan worked, would send searing hot bullets sonically tearing through the flesh of hundreds of victims with nothing to stop them.

Tired, Mahood left the kitchen to go for a rest upstairs, leaving Jennings with the parting words of "Adam, for goodness sake don't cock that weapon and accidentally fire it or the police will be here within minutes! Anyway it's twenty five to three, you and the others should go to bed too". No way, Jennings thought to himself, not while the weapons needed checking, and definitely not when those other morons would soon get bored and look for something else to do; like playing with the guns. Jennings just nodded back before continuing with what he was doing.

The Final Assault
Chapter Four

A couple of miles north from Poland Lane in the car-park of the Airport's dedicated police station, a white panelled van and black armoured Land Rover were parked up, filled with twelve nervous members of the Firearm unit's Red and Blue teams. In front of the two vehicles rested a number of BMW X5s that contained pairs of Armed Response Vehicle officers and snipers, who would close nearby roads and provide support to the two teams that would dynamically enter the house.

The plan had been developed and refined over the previous hours with floor plans of the house being taped to the HQ sports hall floor and room entries practised a hundred times over before the kit was checked. It might have been a short notice operation but this wasn't the first time these guys had been on such a last minute job; albeit without the AK47 wielding terrorist threat they were facing this time. Although they may not have had the time that was normally afforded to them to effectively plan, they had still done a pretty decent job, and besides, operations could still go bent even after weeks of planning, it was just the nature of the game. At least they would have plenty of support from the ARV officers with their G36 5.56 calibre rifles and the Snipers with their HK 417 7.62 sniper rifles, the teams reflected.

"Fifteen minutes from now I want the teams moving up to their FUP" said Chief Inspector Murray over the radio.

The FUP or Form Up Point was a location where the team would stand by (wait) until they were given the green light to move to their FAP or Final Assault Point where there would be no going back and the raid would start from.

"Assault coordinator, that's received boss. Red team do you copy?" Marriot enquired.

"Red team received and standing by" Simpson responded.

After letting go of his radio transmitter attached to the top of his tactical vest that housed stun grenades, Taser and spare mags, Simpson reached up and switched on the Land rover's red interior lights to illuminate the sealed rear of the vehicle.

"Thank God for that, I can stop using my torch to locate and attach Foster's Glock retention cable to his seat" Allen joked.

The Glock 17, 9mm handgun was the weapon of choice for police services and Swat teams around the world because of its ease of use. On the British firearms units the gun was carried in a holster on the officer's leg and used as a secondary weapon to either the HK MP5 9mm or the HK G36 rifles. In order to keep the weapon attached to the officer at all times there was a flexible and coiled cord attached to the handle of the gun and the officer's holster. It hadn't taken long for this safety measure to become one of the unit's favourite wind up pranks that consisted of an offending officer sneaking up on their unsuspecting victim, removing the cord clip from their gun and attaching it to something that would end up being dragged away as they walked off. Although it was highly immature and they complained when the joke was on them, it didn't stop any of them from doing it.

"Bloody hell Dave, now ain't the time to be screwing around you nob!" an annoyed and nervous Foster snapped.

"I would've removed it when we got to the FUP" Allen said, laughing along with Evans.

Foster shook his head at him prior to turning around to finish his conversation with MacNeil and O'Keeffe. As the second in command to Marriot, Simpson the consummate professional he was, sat going over the assault plans again and again to make sure he was fully switched on should he have to take over the Assault Coordinator duties from him.

O'Keeffe, Foster and Arthur discussed their plan of action when the assault would begin, as part of Red team's second section they had been tasked with crashing their way inside through the main bedroom window at the front of the property, utilising the ladders that were located on top of the armoured Land rover. Simpson, Evans and Allen would simultaneously use a hand held ladder to gain access to the rear bedroom.

Foster began winding up O'Keeffe, making reference to him scaling the ladder with his fear of heights; something that was ironic given his experience as a Special Forces Operator. O'Keeffe laughed and wittingly replied that at least he wasn't the one going in first. Foster pulled a false smile back at him, knowing that he had indeed drawn the short straw after being tasked to go in first once MacNeil had blown the window out.

Red and Blue team made their way to the Form Up Point located within a pub car park less then quarter of a mile away from the target address. The snipers and ARVs were already in their support positions having been directed to move covertly to hidden points prior to the teams moving forwards to their Final Assault Points. This tactic made sure that the teams could move in knowing that none of the targets were outside the address or made aware of the approaching teams. After ten minutes, Chief Inspector Murray ordered the SFO's to move forward to each of their respective Final Assault Points. To prevent being compromised the team would have to move slowly and stealthily to their designated spots, creating a slight but totally necessary delay before the entry could begin. Generally speaking the FUPs would usually be closer to the FAPs. However, because of the house's position in the lane, it meant that this would have proven difficult and risked them being compromised. On this occasion the team's fitness and light footedness would have to serve them well, as clambering around quickly and quietly in heavy kit was not an easy undertaking, especially if you had been lazy with recent physical training.

"Right lads, Resi's on then" Simpson said to the others inside the back of the armoured Land Rover, referring to the respirators and helmets SFO's wore to protect themselves from smoke and other debris that could fly around a room during such a raid. In the back of the van parked next to them, Blue team were doing the same thing. It was time to step into the 'breach' once more! Foster looked at O'Keeffe and said "I'm so jacked up with adrenaline that I can barely think straight, I hope I don't screw anything up", his words betraying his alleged cool demeanour. Although Foster had attended his fair share of planned and spontaneous firearms operations since arriving on the unit, he had never been on this kind of high stakes job. O'Keeffe on the other hand with his Special Forces background had carried out a number of similar high level operations in far shittier locations around the world, which meant that he was as cool as a cucumber on the inside as well as on the outside.

"Mate you're fine, don't sweat it, seriously. We'll get these fuckers out of the way and go for a pint tomorrow night" he replied in a calming voice that made Foster take a deep breath and re-focus his slipping thoughts.

As planned, Blue team joined by Simpson, Allen and Evans, had been tasked with pulling into Poland lane and quickly alighting about three hundred meters shy of the target address from where they would move stealthily into their assault positions at the front and rear. While a short way back Foster and co would wait a minute before moving as close to the property as they could without compromising themselves using the Land Rover, in preparation of receiving the green light to charge forward and secure access to the main bedroom. It all sounded quite simple!

"Silver, all units respond if you are in position, Black side containment? White side containment......?" Chief Inspector Murray enquired over the air. Black and white side was 'tactical speak' to identify the different aspects of a target building or structure. Black for the rear, White for the front, Red and left for side aspects.

The sniper pairs and ARVs clicked their radio transmitters twice in acknowledgement of Chief Inspector Murray from their support positions. From this point on, there would be radio and verbal silence apart from the final command to enter. In these type of high risk operations, silence was indeed golden; and vital.

"Red team 1 and 2, are you in position?"

Two clicks from PC Simpson, and two clicks from PC O'Keeffe gave the signal they were ready.

"Blue team are you in position?"

The adrenaline was pumping hard now. If Foster had had the time he would have taken off his respirator and thrown up as the nausea he was feeling bubbled up from his stomach. However, now knelt on top the Land Rover clutching his HK MP5 9mm carbine rifle, he was definitely not going to get an opportunity to do so. Next to him MacNeil was knelt holding a pole that was attached to the explosive charge that would destroy the bedroom window. Hanging off the back of his black overalls and tac vest there was also an array of entry gaining equipment that ranged from a spike and hammer, to a Benelli shotgun that could be used to blow the hinges of a locked door too. All of this extra equipment was to help MacNeil in his job as a Specialist Method Entry Officer (SMOE), whose role was to smash their way into a property using any means necessary, even tractors had been utilised before. Op Barrier would have four of these officers to make sure nothing would obstruct them.

Blue team had now made it to their FAP on the side of the house, camouflaged by darkness, trees and mud; lots and lots of mud. The crappy conditions made Sgt. Marriot fantasise about how things might have been less messy and pleasant if Mahood had waited until summer. In the front of the line of six men that made up Blue team, PC Collins stood covering the front door with his MP5 Whilst PC Lewis 'Conan The Barbarian' Durant, a huge imposing man who had previously been a semi-pro body builder, anxiously waited with his Benelli shotgun in preparation of blowing the door clean of its hinges, allowing the stick of five men behind him to rush inside. The first section of Red team were now in position too, with Simpson covering the window above them with his gun while Allen and Evans waited with the ladder and window charge. There may have been verbal and radio silence, but the sound of the officers collective heart beats inside their masks could not be suppressed, the vein bursting adrenaline making them beat loud and rapidly.

"SILVER, SILVER. TEAMS STAND FAST, STAND FAST!" Murray suddenly blasted over the radio, causing the members of Red and Blue team to look at each other with wide eyes as they tried to fathom out why the entry was being delayed.

Foster looked to O'Keeffe for answers, but his eyes returned the same confused look that Foster's had. A stand fast at an FAP was unprecedented; and for good reason. The longer an entry team waited in such close proximity to the target, the higher the risk of being compromised. It was now or never! Not wait a minute while command decided what they wanted do.

Unbeknown to the two teams, one of the ARV crews that was parked on the main road that led to Poland Lane, had detained a resident of the Lane after he had refused to wait for the road to re-open. Due to his attitude they became concerned that the male might have had links to the address, so the officers arrested him, but not without a fight, which resulted in the male being tasered. The situation had panicked Chief Inspector Murray who was now worrying about the identity of the man and whether the operation had been compromised.

"Sir they have to move now, forget the arrest they've been there for almost five minutes, it's too long to wait, call the strike now"

PC Phelps implored Murray as he continued to hold an unnecessary dialogue with the ARV officers to try and ascertain the male's identity.

"But what happens if they've been compromised??" Murray responded, the trembling tone in his voice indicated that the pressure had got to him.

"SIR, they've been there for too long already, you can't wait any bloody longer. For God's sake call the strike or I fucking will". Phelps said before picking up the radio.

Murray grabbed the radio from him and raised it up to his mouth to speak with his hands trembling under the pressure, beads of sweat beginning to roll down his face. At the side of the house the members of Blue team were growing more concerned by the second. PC Robert Jones, a Welsh man in his late thirties, turned to look at Marriot, his eyes reflecting everyone's thoughts.............. 'What the bloody hell were they waiting for?'. Marriot, confused himself, looked back at Jones and nodded with a slow calmness, signalling to him to remain sharp and to face forwards again.

"STRIKE, STRIKE, STRIKE" Murray abruptly boomed out over the radio with Phelps screaming that he should have given the team some warning after the unexplained long wait.

The members of Red and Blue team jumped to attention like racehorses reacting to a starter pistol as the instantaneous call of strike took them by surprise. The armoured Land Rover's powerful engine roared into action as the vehicle raced towards the front of the house. At the same time Blue team ran up to the front door as Simpson's second section of Red team slammed their ladder against the wall and began rapidly scaling it. Within seconds of the Land Rover arriving at its destination, O'Keeffe sent the ladder on top of the vehicle crashing against the front of the house, landing with pin point precision beneath the main bedroom window seal. Without any delay they flew up it as if the four stone of kit they were wearing was as light as a feather.

BANG, BANG, BANG. The sound of 'Conan' blowing off the front door's hinges echoed around them. The door had barely come to a rest on the floor before Collins threw a stun grenade into the hallway, the device delivered nine loud bangs and vision distorting flashes before Blue team charged in after it. As if part of a well-choreographed ballet, Evans and MacNeil, Red team's SMOE officers, simultaneously placed their charges against the double glazed windows above their heads and detonated them.

BOOM, BOOM the percussion of the explosions echoed out into the distance. The combined flash of the charges making the lane momentarily appear as though it was day, lighting up each and every one of the black clad, respirator wearing officers smashing their way inside.

Inside, Jennings fell to the floor clutching his throbbing ears that were suffering with ringing akin to an extreme bout of tinnitus from the explosions. In the front room the four middle eastern men cowered down low in fear. Collins joined by Jones and Palmer entered the room after throwing yet another stun grenade, the ear drum bursting bangs sent the four men reeling to the ground, unable to deal with the hardcore assault on their senses. With the room spinning, the men opened their eyes just in time to see two large, blurred shadowy figures flying into the room.

"POLICE, DOWN ON THE FLOOR NOW, GET DOWN,

GET DOWN!" Collins and Palmer screamed at the four men who were in no position to do anything else.

Semi-blind, with their ears still ringing, the four men laid face down on the floor with their hands on their heads. Any remaining fight they may have had (if there had been any in the first place) was now completely gone. Jones stood in the door way, covering the hall whilst being ready to move in and assist them should they have required it.

Above their heads, the two sections of Red team barrelled into the house through the destroyed windows, guns raised up as each and every one of them jumped off their ladders and into the rooms, preceded by more stun grenades. Once inside they progressively began smashing their way through their respective pre-determined 'limits of exploitation', a term used by firearms officers to describe a designated area where a team would work within, and not beyond, preventing them from running into each other.

Mahood fell against the bathroom wall, startled by the sudden explosions. He knew what was going on from the very second it had started. There was no way he was going to spend the rest of his life in a cell, so he composed himself and burst out of the bathroom into the hallway looking for a safe route to escape through. As he paused to quickly weigh up his options, he could just about hear the voices of Simpson, Allen and Evans calling out to each other from inside a bedroom to his right through his dulled hearing. This was definitely not the way he was going to go. Mahood turned on his heels and ran back towards his bedroom at the front of the house, he would jump clean through the window if he had to.

As Foster moved inside the room, the torch on his MP5 lit up the corners of the large bedroom, revealing a king sized bed, sofa and walk in wardrobe, all of which would need checking. Knowing full well that O'Keeffe and MacNeil would carry out a swift search behind him, Foster moved towards the door whilst trying to recall the floor plan in his head as to what lay beyond it. With less than ten feet to go, Foster raised his MP5 up so that it was ready to cover the door in preparation of O'Keeffe and

27

MacNeil joining him to move into the hallway.

Just before he reached it, the door abruptly and without warning burst open, startling Foster in the process. His huge, surprised eyes locked on the dark figure marauding into the room. In the split second that he caught a glimpse of the figure, Foster knew it was Mahood.

BANG, BANG the sound of the MP5 discharging two 9mm rounds reverberated around the room. Mahood who was still in full flight was sent tumbling into the dresser adjacent to the bed, sending photo frames and ornaments smashing through the air in his wake. He crashed to the floor with a thud, making no effort to break his own fall and came to a rest face down.

The first 9mm round had torn through Mahood's jugular causing the large artery to blast a large volume of blood equal to the English channel across the floor. The second had entered his chest cavity, deflating his right lung in the process and inducing a catastrophic bleed inside his chest cavity that would have been impossible to stem.

Foster instantaneously felt a deep sinking feeling as he realised what had just happened; he had shot a man, and perhaps killed him. MacNeil ran past him and covered the door as O'Keeffe started carrying out first aid on Mahood's motionless body. They could have had all the equipment necessary to carry out open heart surgery but it still wouldn't have saved Mahood. He was now nothing more than another dead terrorist.

"Where's the gun, where's the gun?" Foster desperately asked O'Keeffe who unable to see the gun, didn't answer.

"I know I saw a gun, I'm sure I saw a gun!" Foster repeated again and again.

But there wasn't a gun! As a result of the door unexpectedly flying open in the darkness, a surprised Foster had reacted to movement and instinctively fired off two shots in a panic at the emerging figure of Mahood who was dead before he hit the floor.

"I've screwed up, shit what am I going to do. He wasn't armed!!" Foster continued.

Downstairs, Marriot with PC Alex Moore, an officer in his twenties, and Conan were rapidly clearing the remaining rooms without a sign of the other suspects. Until all six men were accounted for and the building was declared a hundred percent clear, there was still a threat. The three officers reached the kitchen which was the last room to be searched, still totally oblivious to the situation unfolding upstairs only feet above their heads. Marriot checked the door.

"It's locked Conan, sort it out" Marriot commanded.

Conan moved up to the door and aimed his shot gun at the top hinge, waiting to blow it off when his two colleagues were ready in position to move in neutralise whoever was inside. However, Jennings who was on the other side of the door had other ideas and like Mahood, he was not going to come quietly. He grabbed the AK47 that he had been cleaning, loaded it and cocked it, placing a round into the chamber ready to be fired at anyone or anything that showed itself through the door. From his training with the Taliban and rebels, Jennings knew that a stun grenade would come crashing into the room first, so he trained his rifle on the doorway and closed his eyes to prevent him being blinded by the flash. He would then wait a split second before pulling the trigger, knowing for a certainty that the officers would be entering straight onto automatic gunfire. There wouldn't even be a need to aim.

BANG, BANG, BANG, Conan blew the hinges off the door and stepped to one side to allow his colleagues unobstructed access to the room. Watching the last hinge fly off, Marriot and Moore braced themselves before charging into the kitchen. As they did, Jennings pulled the trigger on his assault rifle and sprayed a wall of bullets at the doorway, timed to perfection.

The first 7.62 round went straight into Marriot's left leg and tore through his femoral artery whilst the second, third and fourth sliced through his protective ballistic vest. Stumbling for a couple of footsteps, he then fell lifelessly to the floor. Directly behind him Moore felt a searing pain as a bullet entered his right shoulder and came out of his back. A split second later he felt another huge impact as a second bullet hit him square in the chest, smashing the extra ceramic plate that was housed inside his ballistic vest. Moore's MP5 dropped to the ground as he landed on his side with 7.62 rounds peppering the walls above him, covering his face and body in plaster and brick dust. Outside the room Conan stood frozen as he hugged the wall, trying desperately to shield his huge body from the hail of bullets coming towards him. Inside the room there was a sudden silence. Jennings opened his eyes and looked down at his rifle which had ceased firing after running out of rounds.

There was no way Conan was going to let him reload to finish off him or his downed colleagues. As Jennings hurriedly to grab another full magazine clip, Conan spun on the door frame so that he and his Benelli shotgun were pointing into the room and fired one shot from it; it was all that was needed. The solid Hatton slug exploded out from the barrel of the shot gun, leaving in its wake a mixture of flame and smoke as it hurtled rapidly towards its target.

The solid metal slug slammed into Jennings right arm with a force akin to a freight train, dumping all of its kinetic energy into him and sending a huge chunk of bloodied flesh into the air. Jennings fell to the floor letting out a banshee like scream of pain. Conan charged into the room, stepping over the strewn out bodies of his colleagues towards Jennings who was prostrate behind the kitchen table crying and clutching the shredded flesh that was his right arm. Conan squeezed the handle of shotgun with his right hand at the same time ripping off his helmet and mask with his left. This little bastard had just shot his friends, and maybe killed them, he needed to pay.

Collins, after hearing the sound of automatic gunfire followed by screams, yelled at Jones to locate and support Marriot as he and Palmer continued to cover the four prostrate and terrified terrorists in the front room. Jones nodded and then moved through the downstairs as quickly as possible whilst still scanning for danger, if he missed a threat and was taken out he wouldn't be able to help anyone. He arrived outside the kitchen and was met by what looked like a hundred bullet holes in the wall opposite and screams from within.

Jones stacked up against the door frame, took a deep breath and rapidly entered the kitchen. As his eyes scanned for threats he saw the sight of Marriot and Moore covered in blood and lying perfectly still six feet into the room. Remaining as professional as he could, Jones continued to assess the rest of the room in less than two seconds before his focus fixed onto Conan who was towering over a whimpering Jennings.

Seeing that Conan had Jennings covered, he peered down at his fallen colleagues once again. Unable to deal with the shock of the sight that greeted him, he vomited inside his respirator. Struggling to breath and see, he ripped of his mask and fell to his knees as he sucked in a massive lungful of air before composing himself; it was time to man up and help them.

"Check them! Please, please check them!" Conan said with a trembling voice that soon switched to pure venom as Jones pulled Marriot onto his back and away from the horrifying pool of blood that he had been face down in. Moore started to moan as he became semi-conscious again, however he would have to wait as Marriots silence indicated a bigger problem. Jones reached forward and touched the Sergeant's pale, clammy face; it was frozen. If the amount of blood on the floor wasn't categoric enough, his pallor and lack of pulse was, Marriot was beyond help. Only feet away Moore began to open his eyes so Jones swiftly moved across to him. He could see that blood was trickling from his overalls by his right shoulder. Jones tore into the material and applied a field dressing directly over the gaping wound, feeling relieved that it had been a clean entry-exit type of wound. With the bleeding stemmed, he carried out a search of Moore's body for further injuries. Amazingly there weren't any, only the remnants of the disintegrated extra ceramic chest plate that had saved his life.

Jones looked up and told Conan that Moore and Marriot needed to be medically evacuated out of the scene as soon as possible. Conan took a moment before enquiring how bad Marriot was. Jones looked down at the floor fighting the urge to break down with emotion.

"Fuck! I think he's dead Conan" he replied in shock.

Conan started to breath heavily with anger as his finger moved towards the trigger, prompting Jennings to plead with Conan not to shoot him. Jones yelled at Jennings to shut up, knowing full well Conan was about ready to explode.

"Don't do it Conan, don't give him the easy way out" Jones said calmly, hoping and praying that Conan wouldn't do anything crazy.

"This little prick should die for what he's done. Prison's too good for this piece of terrorist shit" Conan replied through his tears.

"You're wrong mate, prison will be hell for him, he's a British terrorist, in a British prison, he'll be brutalised daily for being a traitor." Jones stated looking directly at Jennings who looked back at him with an expression of disbelief on his face at what the officer had just said.

Conan lowered his shotgun and Jones let out a sigh of relief. A solid slug from a Benelli would have blown Jennings' head clean off making it obvious that it had been an execution; hardly something that would be seen as proportionate.

Jennings realising that he was now safe, grew a pair of balls and started shouting loudly with audacity about how Conan had tried to kill him. Jones interrupted him and explained that he'd not seen anything and to keep his mouth shut, otherwise he would put the word out in the prison community that he liked spending his spare time on his knees, servicing naked men. Jennings laid back down without saying another word. Conan may have wrestled with the idea of killing him, but he had still made sure that his size twelve boot was crushing Jennings arm pit to stem the flow of blood, paradoxically saving his life whilst he weighed up whether to execute him or not.

Jones picked up his radio transmitter and requested urgent support and an immediate medical evacuation for Marriot, Moore and Jennings. Unfortunately though, Marriot's body would be left in situ for the Paramedics to officially confirm he was dead (something which police officers could not do, as obvious as it may have been) before it became part of the crime scene.

Simpson responded over the radio that the upstairs was clear and that he would be sending Allen and Evans down to assist while he supported O'Keeffe's team. Jones copied his update, followed by Murray who sheepishly called over air that he and the Gold commander required an urgent situation report.

O'Keeffe from his knelt down position next to Mahood, looked up at Foster whilst maintaining constant eye contact with him, and slowly updated Murray that Mahood had been shot and was believed to be dead. Downstairs, Jones glanced up at the ceiling and took a deep breath, before levelling his head and updating that Moore and Jennings were in a serious condition and needed urgent medical attention.

Then came the hardest update he would ever have to give.

"Sgt Marriot's................."

Snakes and Ladders
Chapter Five

DI Anaura sat behind his desk in the Vice unit office in the City's Central District Police Station. He looked down at his stylish Storm watch, and not for the first time that week he saw that it had gone past eight o'clock in the evening, three hours after the time he should have finished. Anaura rubbed his closely cropped hair while tilting his head to one side, his wife Laura was not going to be happy with him; again.

Detective Inspector Peter Anaura, warrant number A001, was an unusual sight in the City's Police Force, not to mention the UK in general because of his unique appearance. Anaura, the product of a mixed marriage between his mother a British doctor, and his father a New Zealand Maori, was very distinguishable from those around him, something that had been a positive from time to time with the opposite sex.

In nineteen sixty seven, Anuara's mother, Kate, had emigrated to New Zealand to practise as a physician after finishing university and feeling as though she had missed out on the opportunity to travel after spending seven years qualifying as a doctor in Southampton, Hampshire. Kate had seen the opportunity to kill two birds with one stone, see another country and use her hard earned Ph.D. to finance it. After arriving in the country it hadn't taken long for her to become fascinated with the Maori people and their culture after treating a number of the interesting ethnic group in her hospital in Wellington.

And on one weekend during a busy double shift in the Emergency room, she was met by the sight of a tall, good looking and colossal Maori named Mani Anaura. Mani had been playing rugby for a local team when his eyebrow had been torn by a stray boot stud from the opposition during a 'Forwards' maul. It would have been a stretch to call it love at first sight but it was certainly lust at first sight; love came later. After a year of dating the couple married in a Christian church followed by a traditional Maori ceremony called a Karakea and moved into an apartment in the centre of Wellington.

Peter Anaura was born on 13th August nineteen seventy one, a year after his parents union. And with what seemed to be a running trend in Peter's family, he was big, weighing in at over ten pounds, a fact that his mother reminded him of whenever he complained of an ache or pain. In her eyes whatever injury he had sustained, it could never have been as bad as what she had gone through giving birth to him. The approach meant that he would only ever moan if he was really hurt which was when his mother would rush to care for him. The family lived in New Zealand for a further twelve years before moving to Portsmouth, Hampshire in England when his maternal grandfather's health had deteriorated. During the years in New Zealand, Peter had taken an interest in Rugby and Maori culture whilst never forgetting his Western roots, something his father had instilled in him. In his father's words he 'wasn't Maori or British; he was both.

After his arrival in Portsmouth in nineteen eighty three, Anaura enrolled at the prestigious Portsmouth Grammar School which was not far from the city's harbour. Although he was excited at the prospect of attending school in his mother's homeland, it didn't take long before his 'differences' were noticed. Looking more Maori than white quickly drew the negative attention of the older school bullies who felt the need to terrorise the new foreign boy. However, Peter was not your average sized twelve year old and gave the misguided, older pupils a good kicking, almost getting himself expelled in the process. Luckily for him, a P.E teacher saw potential in this five foot seven twelve year old and got him involved with the school's rugby team which diverted the head teacher's wrath away. Four years later and in college, Anaura, who was now more disciplined, had decided that he wanted to follow in his maternal grandfather's footsteps by becoming a copper. The decision was welcomed by his parents who were concerned that his sole obsession with becoming an England Rugby player was a little unrealistic and at the time, not for pay!

Fast forward twenty four years, and two years shy of that in the Police Service, Anaura was now a forty two year old, six foot three man, with a smile as big as his frame. Although being in his early forties, Anaura had a fresh, youthful and lightly tanned complexion that gave the impression he was ten years younger than he really was. And after years of playing Rugby and fitness training, he had a developed powerful body to go with it. These combined attributes were not wasted on the fairer sex with women becoming dizzy in his presence. Whether it was his female colleagues or women in the street, everyone noticed him, something which made his wife of 13 years, Laura, proud but equally jealous at the same time.

Other women's desires aside, what made Laura the most jealous was his relationship with the 'job', a mistress that her and their two children, Anya and William had to battle with to get their fair share of his attention. Yet in difference to this perceived devotion to his job, Anaura's family was everything to him, and had Laura ever asked him to quit or be posted to a quieter department, he would have done it a heartbeat. Laura being who she was though, would never ask him do that.

On this night like so many others before, with most of his staff gone, Anaura sat behind his office desk in his usual tie-less, brightly coloured shirt and a black suit. This favoured tie-less look of Anaura's had managed to piss his superiors off on a number of occasions as it was seen as an unprofessional look. In spite of this he would continue to rock this look to wind up the ambitious rank ladder climbing snakes in command (as he referred to them) because it was one of his favourite hobbies. In Anaura's opinion a lot of the command ranked officers had joined the job to become political desk jockeys and not true coppers. It was an unreasonable opinion but in some people's case, it was very true.

Tie or no tie, Annaura believed that he looked smarter, stylish and more approachable than they ever could with their ties and uniforms. Although it wasn't just the lack of a tie that wound them up the most, it was the way that he would listen to their orders, and then do his own thing anyway in spite. Command may have agreed that he had some great ideas, but they would never have let him know that. The constant battle between him and 'them' was a pointless waste of time but it was far too much fun to stop.

Anaura was just finishing up reading through some statements concerning a spate of drug related robberies, when he heard the voice of DC Jennifer Valera, an extremely attractive detective of Portuguese descent, coming from the doorway of his office.

"Goodnight boss" she purred, emphasising the 'night' part of the sentence in an attempt to make Anaura's brain think of nocturnal related 'activities'.

In reply he pulled his genuine trademark smile and said bye in a warm deep voice that had a hint of his homelands accent which no one could ever place. Valera reciprocated with a cheeky smile and slowly turned around in the door way so that the shape of her pert backside could be seen through her pencil skirt prior to her leaving the Vice unit's office. Whenever she would carry out this 'ritual', Anaura would always laugh to himself, yeah she was stunning and had an amazing body but there was only one woman for him, and besides it all seemed like a big act with Valera. There was definitely more to her than she let on, a hidden vulnerability.

Anaura's phone began to ring on the desk. Engrossed in his work he attempted to grab the phone without looking at it, something he soon abandoned when he failed to retrieve it after two attempts. Turning to answer it, he saw the picture of Laura with the kids on his desk. He suddenly remembered; he hadn't called her to say he was running late.

"Peter!?" Laura said, making a statement as opposed to posing a question.

"I'm sorry gorgeous, you know........I lost track of time" he replied, his cheeks becoming flushed with the knowledge that she wasn't happy with him.

Somehow despite his large stature and toughness, Laura had always managed to reduce Peter to a mere school boy whenever she gave him a look and said his name with an authoritative tone.

It was this effect and power over him that was part of his attraction to her, he knew full well she had him wrapped around her little finger but there was no place he would have rather been. Laura was his dream girl, seven years younger than him with a stunningly beautiful face, lovely deep brunette hair and a toned but curvy figure. She was a firecracker behind closed doors but exuded an elegant and classy persona to the world that instantly drew people to her. A successful business woman, Laura had quit her high flying job in London to make sure that at least one parent was at home, making inference towards him when she suggested it. If there was one thing that was plainly obvious in their relationship, it was that she was unequivocally the boss; although in a nice way.

Laura had fallen in love very quickly after they had met but did have one reservation about him, and that was that if they ever married, her surname would rhyme with her first name, something she said would sound ridiculous. However in the name of love, she accepted it.

"Peter, I suggest you get your sexy, tanned arse home right now before I throw the lovely curry I made you in the bin!" She replied sternly to his usual feeble explanation for his lateness.

"Yesssss sir! Ha ha, yeah see you soon, Bye" Anaura replied with a smile on his face. He hadn't eaten since the afternoon and his wife's amazing cooking would help soothe the hunger pangs he had been having for the past few hours; he had to get home. After hanging up, he wasted no time in tidying his desk and then switching his computer off. Just as he was about to stand up to put his suit jacket on, a figure appeared in his doorway.

"Wife trouble Peter? Oh and I see the mystery of your disappearing ties continues!?" Peter looked up feeling a sense of repulsion welling up inside him. He knew the owner of the voice before he even looked up.

There arrogantly leaning up against the door frame stood Chief Superintendent Robert Drayson, the former head of Serious and Organised Crime Unit, aka SOCU, before he had stepped aside in preparation of a promotion to Assistant Chief. Drayson was a man in his early fifties, six foot' two tall with short sandy hair who liked to wear expensive Ozwold Boateng tailored suits most of the time, something which Anaura envied with his love of stylish suits and wondered how he afforded them. But that wasn't what made him dislike the chief superintendent.

Drayson was one of the career ladder climbing snakes that Anaura despised, but the worst type, the type that still thought he as one of the boys, one of the team despite stepping on those below him to get ahead. In Anaura's eyes he was anything but one of the team. He didn't trust Drayson and although he couldn't put his finger on it, there was something wrong about him. Anaura was rarely wrong when it came to people, it wasn't quite a sixth sense, he just seemed to be able to sense what a person was about moments after meeting them and whether they were good or bad, or more importantly liars. However although he didn't trust Drayson, he wasn't as easy to read. The thing that pissed him off most with Drayson though, was his jack the lad style character and the way that he would front up to him whenever the two were standing in front of each other, in an attempt to display how hard he was. It didn't impress or intimidate Anaura one bit and although Drayson may have been a similar height, he was of a slim build and would have been knocked silly by him. Anaura may have had the warmest personality but underneath it he was one tough bastard who just didn't feel the need, unlike Drayson, to show it. If Anaura was ever asked what his opinion of Drayson was, the answer would be short and sweet "He's an arsehole!".

"Yeah, the same as usual I guess" Anuara answered.

"Are you talking about the wife or the fucking tie Peter?" Drayson replied in an obnoxious tone.

"Both Sir. Anyway, I'm late so I better get home to the old 'trouble and strife'. Always a pleasure to see you Sir" quipped Anaura with a sarcastic tone, making fun of Drayson's fake cockney affectations before pushing past him to make good his escape. For someone who was from Eastings, the chief superintendent sounded affected and more like someone born is the east end of London. Just as Anaura was reaching the exit, he heard Drayson call out to him.

"Oh by the way Anaura, if you want to get promoted any time

soon, you best start getting those shitty little drugs dealers of yours locked up" he said with a belligerent tone and a smug expression.

Anaura just nodded back with smile that was far from being a genuine one. Anaura had no interest in being promoted, especially if it meant chasing petty criminals to bulk out his detection rate to look good. And besides, contrary to what he had just said, Drayson never chased the small fish as he seemed to have a talent for hooking the big boys, almost if the evidence had fallen in his lap. In Anaura's mind his success rate didn't add up but then again, some people were just born lucky.

He turned his back on Drayson and walked away, quietly muttering the word "prick" in his British, New Zealand accent, with a part of him hoping that he would hear him; he hadn't. Without delay he rushed to his car, hoping that Laura hadn't thrown his curry in the bin.

A Very Public Hearing
Chapter Six

"This is Janet Hill reporting for the BBC from outside The Old
Bailey Court House in London, where five men are standing trial
for terrorist related offences. One of the men, Adam Jennings of
Poland Lane, is also to stand trial for the murder of police officer,
Sergeant Kevin Marriot and the attempt murder of Constable
Alex Moore during what is being described as, a bungled police
operation!"

"I'm pretty sure there must be something more entertaining on
the TV other than the BBC news" said Liam Balham, the
Firearms Unit's Inspector before he switched off the LCD screen
that was on the wall of the court's police room. He knew full well
that the sensationalist style of reporting that the media loved was
not what the team needed to hear at that time.

The team of eleven SFO's from the operation sat in a
horseshoe shape formation around the room, all deep in thought.
The hearing should have been straight forward, a group of
terrorists were about to commit serious atrocities but apprehended
and stopped; end of. Well that's how every officer on the unit and
probably everyone else in the country saw it. However it wasn't
going to be simple, nor could it ever have been. A police sergeant
had been murdered, an unarmed suspect had been shot dead and
another police officer had been seriously injured during what, as
the reporter on the TV had said, was a bungled operation.
Questions had to be asked, and answered concerning why there
was very little planning, what the available intelligence was, why
one of the terrorist had been shot dead and another sustained
appendage deforming injuries, and of course the officers
favourite, defending the statement made by the defence barrister
"My clients were not terrorists but victims of an over the top
police operation!". You could always count on a defence lawyer

to try and turn the story back on the 'corrupt' police officers, a tactic that the media tended to adopt too. It came across as though someone in power had received one too many speeding tickets and was now hell bent on destroying the police.

Balham looked around the room. The media onslaught had really enraged him but at least the public had been supportive of them with a very different opinion from that of the media; they were scum bag terrorists who deserved to die and even mutterings of bringing back hanging! The country had spoken, they were unreservedly fed up with the terrorist threat and wanted an end to it, even if it meant using aggressive measures to achieve it. Unfortunately the public support for the police and their hatred for treasonous scum had done little to prevent the media and legal attack on the officers, namely Foster and Conan, from happening.

Conan being the tough guy who didn't care about people's opinion of him, sought counselling within weeks of the operation finishing, as he saw it, he needed help prior to facing the court as Op Barrier had been 'relatively' traumatic. He did however, always remind his colleagues that he felt no remorse for permanently disfiguring Jennings and maintained that he would have happily slotted him if the ramifications were not there. His only true regret was that he wished he had been able to get to his MP5 instead of the shotgun, the accuracy of the rifle would have meant that he wasn't just disfigured; he would be rotting in hell. After a few months he was back to his normal self, although he was beginning to become less enthused with risky work and fancied a move to the Traffic Unit, something which drew huge amounts of piss taking from the others, but Conan didn't care, it was a good role that didn't have all the constant bravado crap that went with the Firearms Unit. Once the hearing was over and done with, he would request an immediate transfer; and get it. One thing wasn't wasted on him, he was going to have to answer some difficult questions regarding his actions on that night although it would be made easier by Jones developing amnesia about the way Conan had acted towards Jennings. It was not his word against Conan's, it was obvious who the jury would believe.

For Jones there had been one comical moment when he gave

evidence in the box (although it should have sent shivers up his spine) when he was asked whether he had threatened to have Jennings raped in prison. The question causing one of the jury to burst out laughing, almost having him punished for being in contempt of court. Jones response to the barrister was perfectly executed "As a copper, how would I know, or find a prisoner that would rape Jennings on my say so?" And the truth is, he wouldn't but it had made Jennings shut his pathetic weasel mouth that night. Looking back though, he kind of wished that Conan would have taken his foot out of Jennings armpit and let the little bastard bleed to death; that would never have been proved. For their involvement, Simpson, Allen, Evans, Collins and Palmer got off pretty lightly in the witness box as their line of questioning mainly revolved around the intelligence they had received and their individual involvement. And although the operation was called by the Gold Commander Superintendent and Chief Inspector Murray, their questioning seemed a little tame considering that the team would not have been there without their say so. It wasn't wasted on the unit that there was a political agenda and some scapegoats were needed; and they were not going to be command level officers. In fact, even Phelps got more of grilling for just advising Murray. It was clear that only the constables were going to be at fault that day.

Moore, still suffering from his injuries, was given the easiest time as the defence were astute enough to know that their case wouldn't be helped by trying to pin a hero's 'bloody carcass' to the witness box through. The term 'bloody carcass' was used by top flight barristers, denoting their enjoyment of destroying a witness and reducing them to a proverbial carcass in order to win their case. Even though the term was in regular use with the highly paid lawyers, the irony of it all was that it was the officers who were seen as suffering with psychopathy. And of course Jennings who was still yet to fully heal from his horrific injuries, gave his version of events which although followed the same time line as the officer's accounts, managed to paint him as the victim of the state and police brutality. It was clear from the Jury's faces that they were not buying his story, especially when a wealth of extremist propaganda, assault rifles and other assorted weapon and explosives had been found at the house. Jennings was seriously deluded if he ever believed that he would be seen as the victim and have the public's support (who wanted to hang him in Leicester square). The court case had so far run into weeks. It was mid-March, barely four months since the job, and the weather was uncharacteristically warm and humid making the airless court room unbearable.

Apart from the stress of the court case, Op Barrier had left another legacy with the unit and the wider police family. The serious nature of it and the death of a police officer meant that it was shrouded in darkness and profoundly affected a lot of people. Marriot's funeral had been and gone, a grand ceremony befitting his great personality and bravery, and although Conan and Jones had been distraught when they saw Marriot's family and the pain they were going through, they needed to move on and get back to work to shake off the grief as soon as they could. However, there was one person who hadn't been able to adjust since that night and that was Foster who had begun to struggle with his state of mind almost immediately after shooting Mahood. And when the team had attended a secret location to be debriefed straight after the operation, he went missing for forty minutes.

After a while of searching the large secret location, O'Keeffe found Foster in one of the upstairs toilets with a ghost like complexion, gazing into the mirror at himself as if trying to work out who it was staring back at him. O'Keeffe asked whether he was alright but Foster didn't answer and continued to stare. On the third time of asking, combined with a little shake of his shoulder, Foster spun around and faced him with a distant expression on his face that O'Keeffe put down to being the result of shock at first, however it wasn't just that and he knew deep down that something else was going on behind Foster's cold fixated eyes.

All of a sudden Foster grabbed him, breathing heavily with a severe frown and huge dilated pupils. His grip was so tight that O'Keeffe didn't know whether to punch him or yell at him. However there was something scary going on inside Foster that he knew had to be dealt with cautiously.

"Ease up mate!" O'Keeffe said.

Foster began to push him backwards until he paused and then dropped to his knees, sobbing into his hands. Shocked, O'Keeffe put his hand onto Fosters shoulder which suddenly made him spring up with a face devoid of emotion. Apart from the redness of his eyes, it was like he had never been crying.

"You OK mate, what the fuck is going on?" O'Keeffe asked in confusion.

Foster shook his head and with a shrug of his shoulders answered "Nothing!" prompting O'Keeffe to tell him that he had been missing for over forty minutes. He pondered what he had said to him with confusion before replying that he had felt sick after the command team had congratulated them on a good job done and left to get some air. He then explained how his thoughts had started to race to a degree where he felt as though the only way to stop them was to bounce his head off a wall. O'Keeffe looked back at him with a sense of profound concern whilst trying to figure out how he could have gone from a cold stare, to crying, to being back to his old self again within a space of a couple of minutes and not been aware of it; it didn't make sense.

"Why were you gone for so long though? You could have asked me to come with you." O'Keeffe enquired.

"I guess I just wanted to get away, although I can't really remember what I was doing in here! It's strange but I don't even recall you coming in!" Foster said with an element of bafflement.

O'Keeffe, realising that his friend wasn't himself or fully aware of his surroundings, took the sensible way out "Ha ha, well you were so intent on sorting out your hair in the mirror, I guess you didn't notice me coming in!"

"What? When was I looking into the mirror? Why can't I remember any of this!" asked Foster with concern

"Ah don't worry about it mate, you've just been subjected to an inordinate amount of stress! You just need a bloody good rest and you'll be fine! Come on let's get back to the others before they send out a search party" O'Keeffe replied as the two men began to walk out of the toilets. Foster looked back at the mirror, desperately trying to remember what he had been doing in the toilets. He couldn't remember, but knew one thing for certain; he didn't feel himself.

"Bloody hell, that's me down with firearms work, I'll not go through that again" a severely perspiring Conan said as he walked back into the police room. Inspector Balham asked him why and how it had gone in the box, despite knowing that there was an obvious answer to his question from Conan's appearance. Conan recalled how he'd been questioned for over two and a half hours on what he had said to Jennings and whether he had pointed a gun to his head after shooting him. The shooting itself was barely mentioned, a perfect example of how the legal system worked in the country with the human rights of violent deranged criminals being more important than anything else; even their victims. It had not been a pleasant experience for him and his sweat soaked white police shirt was indicative of that. Conan was dead serious about being finished with the unit, over the years he'd grown weary of the politics of it all and how you could be criticised by others for a split second decision when you were under the highest level of pressure, he'd had enough. The traumatic nature of Op Barrier and the repeated nightmares that followed were something that would stay with him forever so he didn't fancy risking it happening again, Conan needed a fresh start and would leave the unit within a few weeks. Another thing that hadn't helped Conan was when he and Foster had been involved in a stand up row in the firearms unit's office after he had taken umbrage to Fosters new antagonistic and aggressive personality. Since the shooting Foster had been a changed man and although this was plain to see for everyone, no one had stepped in to talk to him, fearing that he may flare up at them. As the months rolled on, the womanising and drinking went up a few levels, he had even started to be aggressive towards his friends, including O'Keeffe. But no matter what he did, the others just saw it as him letting off steam and something that would get better with time, although underneath they knew he wasn't right. MacNeil on the other hand, who was one of the most level headed guys on the unit quietly approached him away from hearing shot of the others and asked him to open up. However Foster replied that he couldn't work out what everyone's problem was with him and that he hadn't changed, and cited that everyone else had. MacNeil had become even more concerned during the conversation when Foster had begun stating that he believed the organisation was plotting against him and how he had been considering joining the Intelligence services to become a spy. None of it made any sense.

Now sat in the police room at the court house, Foster was waiting to give his evidence, the last to do so. O'Keeffe and MacNeil had already been asked about their involvement within the bedroom where Mahood had been shot. The cross examination the pair received was mainly concerned with their own actions in the room and whether they had perceived Mahood to be an immediate threat, something which they both confirmed, citing that with the intelligence of automatic weapons and way in which Mahood burst into the room, they had honestly feared for their life.

Despite the understandable nature of why Foster had fired, Foster himself could not get it right in his head, not because he was concerned about Mahood dying, it was the flashbacks and fear that he may have been found guilty of an unlawful killing if the jury went against him. This was of course an unlikely proposition, but after most of the media attacks had been directed at him and his name had been released in the papers, Foster had begun to crack up even more from the pressure. He had by now, lost the ability to control his own mind. And despite once being a very popular member of the team, Foster was now sat alone in the corner of the room sporadically muttering to himself quietly, his extreme behaviour and aggressiveness towards his friends and colleagues had meant that even O'Keeffe had started to distance himself after Foster accused him of being a traitor and 'one of them'.

"PC Foster, they're ready for you" the female court clerk declared.

Foster acknowledged her as the others members of the team looked at him silently, trying to figure out whether he was going to crack under the pressure or not.

"I put it to you officer, that you shot Mr Mahood because you wanted the glory of killing an alleged terrorist, whether he was armed or not, and that you wanted to be famous, a national hero. And your attitude when giving evidence today has clearly shown that you have the total inability to display any sign of remorse or regret" the defence barrister protested from across the court room.

Foster with his lack of a valid or relevant answer during examination had portrayed a sense of arrogance and that his actions were cold and calculated that night. And after he was accused of trying to be a hero and the words 'alleged terrorist' being used, Foster had stared at the barrister with an intimidating expression with his blue eyes almost turning black due to his pupils excessively dilating. As a result the once overly confident barrister seemed to back down in fear as he looked at the judge for support. That, combined with Foster's persistent mutterings during questioning (that required the Judge asking him to speak up and repeat what he'd been saying under his breath) had well and truly painted a very bad picture of him.

"Listen, Mahood was a deranged piece of terrorist scum who was shot because I believed at the time that he posed an immediate threat to my colleagues and me! Haven't I answered that sufficiently already?" Foster snarled which caused the judge to step in and ordered him to answer the question firmly.

After three days of being in the witness box giving evidence, Foster was well and truly done. He had spent the longest time in the box in comparison to his colleagues, which was quite an achievement considering that none of them had been quick. Foster's demeanour during the hearing had also meant that the Prosecution barrister had dragged Inspector Balham to one side to discuss his poor attitude and the problems it was creating for the case. However Balham spoke to him, his words ultimately fell on extremely deaf ears. If there could have ever been a situation where the jury would be anti-police, Foster had tried his damned hardest to create it, without quite being fully aware he was doing so.

The Prosecution laid down their case, the defence theirs, the terror suspects had been examined and examined again and the officers had been publicly torn apart in an attempt by the defence to create compassion for their clients. The Judge had heard enough and adjourned for the day in preparation of a verdict the following day.

"Right, well we can't go back to the hotel and just mope, let tomorrow take care of itself. It's been a rough couple of weeks so let's go for something to eat and drink. Anthony that means you too mate!" O'Keeffe said trying to make light of the situation and hoping that Foster would get back to being himself now that the stress that lead up to giving evidence had gone. Foster, although looking less than enthused, shrugged his shoulders and agreed to go. Despite some of the hostilities, Conan and the others welcomed his agreement with a round of back slapping and grunts. Foster beamed a slightly forced smile, momentarily appearing like his old self to the others as they left in search of a nearby pub. Inspector Balham jovially told them to behave as they walked to which they all replied "Yes mum!".

The eleven officers arrived at an old spit and sawdust style Victorian pub which was just a miles walk from the court, and not far away from the City of London's police station which would provide a safe haven if the press learned of their chosen drinking establishment. Simpson, always the most pragmatic of the group had suggested that they get on the tube to travel somewhere far away from the court which would make them less obvious to the locals and at a reduced the risk of being photographed boozing by the lurking paparazzi before the verdict.

"Mate, the paparazzi didn't even see us enter the court so it's highly unlikely they would recognise us, especially now we've changed, and anyway I seriously doubt they'd even bother looking for us. Right! Onto more important business; Harvey's ale all round?!" Allen said in his usual laid back manner.

Two pints into what was meant to be a quiet drink after an uncomfortable day in the stifling court house was now becoming a little louder. Consequently Simpson and MacNeil had started to become concerned that drinking that much before the big day would only lead to bad news; literally. The others had different ideas though, especially Foster who MacNeil believed had already had his fair share of drinks and was hardly someone who should have been allowed to drink so much given his recent behaviour.

"John, do you not think it's time to call it quits? Anthony's getting a little loud and he's hardly well, right!" MacNeil said

"I know.........but it's great to see him enjoying himself with the team again. Even Conan and him are getting on! One more and we'll go for something to eat, I promise!" O'Keeffe replied, interrupting MacNeil before he finished stating that Foster shouldn't be drinking.

Simpson and Arthur finished their drinks and got up from the table to be joined by Evans, Collins, Moore and Palmer, who all said they'd had enough, with Moore stating that his pain killers didn't mix well with beer too. This left Allen, Jones, Conan, Foster and O'Keeffe, who had always been the team's hell raisers, to carry on. All the nagging in the world wouldn't have made them leave.

Forty minutes later, the combination of an empty stomach and ale meant that the five of them were starting to get more than a little drunk; like Simpson and Arthur had feared. Allen feeling nauseous from dehydration and ale made his excuses and left, causing the others to rib him about being a light weight which was not just a poke at his inability to hold his drink. It wasn't long after his departure that the conversation soon turned from being about the fit scattered female arse inside the pub to reminiscing about the good old days with Marriot. The topic should have been avoided, especially with alcohol involved. Emotions and booze were a highly combustible cocktail and after less than ten minutes of talking about the Sergeant, Foster snapped that the subject should be changed to something less morose.

Conan, who was more than a little drunk and reaching the end of his tether with Foster's attitude, suddenly confronted him about his conduct in the court, stating that he could have ruined them all with his crappy demeanour. He barely finished his tongue lashing before Foster shot up as quick as a lightning bolt and told him to fuck off, knocking a couple of empty pint glasses onto the floor in the process. O'Keeffe looked at Conan in shock and then told him that now was the not the time or place to discuss this stuff. Conan nonchalantly raised his hands up with his head tilted as if to say 'whatever' and looked at Foster with a relaxed expression and said "Let's leave it Foster, no harm done eh?".

"Come on then big man, you want to sort this out now do you? Come outside, it's time you learnt how to shut that big mouth of yours! I'm not Adam Jennings, you don't scare me!" Foster snarled at Conan who looked taken aback at how Foster was still being combative after he had backed off. A few heads quickly pirouetted from the bar behind on hearing the names Adam Jennings and Foster. Their fellow drinkers linking the two names with the story that had been dominating the news. Jones noticing the unwanted attention told Foster to sit down and Conan to shut up. Despite Conan being willing to settle it, Foster with his alcohol clouded thought processes, was not.

O'Keeffe sensing something bad was about to happen, suggested they leave the pub and go for dinner somewhere to soak up the misguided amount of alcohol they had consumed. Foster's face began to display the same vacant, aggressive expression he had witnessed in the toilets of the secret debrief location, and numerous occasions since the operation. O'Keeffe recognised it and knew that whatever was going on in Foster's head, it was only going to lead to one thing, and that was trouble.

"What's happened to you anyway Foster, you're a bloody mess? It's about time you started getting your shit together! Do you think you're the only one who's struggling since the operation?!" Conan asked, pissed off at Fosters inability to back off and how he had been acting over the recent months.

"Screw it down Conan you idiot, people can hear you!" O'Keeffe implored him, realising that they were being watched and knowing that Foster was just about to explode.

"Bollocks, I want to know why this little prat has been playing the post-traumatic stress card since that night. Looking for compensation are you?" Conan slurred in drunken defiance of O'Keeffe.

"Just leave it Conan!" Jones said, trying to defuse the situation.

Foster put his palms flat in the middle of the table and leant

51

towards Conan with pupils like they had been in the court room, dilated and fixated. His breathing started to become heavier with a more purposeful, slow rhythm as if he was preparing to do something terrible.

"Do you want to be the next person I kill?" Foster quietly whispered to Conan without a shred of humanity in his voice.

Sensing that Foster was going to go for Conan, O'Keeffe moved between the two men and pleaded with Foster to calm down and leave it. Foster averted his cold gaze from Conan to O'Keeffe before he relaxed and stood up from his chair. Both Conan and Jones let out thankful sighs.

"Aren't you that copper who slotted that unarmed terrorist?" said an overly confident man in his early thirties and wearing a suit with an Essex boy style hair and stubble, naively believing that his question would be well received.

Foster quickly spun around on his heels and grabbed the man by the throat before he rapidly pushed him backwards up against the bar, holding him by the throat and screaming into his face with his fist raised. The man's eyes grew as large as planets as he looked upon the enraged, flushed face of Foster, whose veins looked as big as garden hoses because of the angry adrenaline filled blood pumping around them.

"ANTHONY RELAX! Come on mate, let him go, he's not worth it" O'Keeffe pleaded with Foster who was still gripping the man by his throat and almost forcing him in half over the edge of the bar. The landlord who was standing less than six feet away didn't move an inch; no one did.

O'Keeffe desperately attempted to reason with Foster again, who after a few more seconds of holding him, let go. Foster turned around and began asking O'Keeffe where they were going for something to eat before he noticed that everyone was staring at him with worried expressions on their faces.

"Why are they all looking at me? What's your fucking problem?" asked a puzzled Foster which prompted most of the people within the pub to hastily avert their gaze and look down at the floor. Foster shook his head with confusion and muttered "Pricks!" before he walked out of the main doors in an agitated state.

O'Keeffe raised his palm up at Jones and Conan and told them to leave it before he transferred his attention to the man who Foster had grabbed and apologised profusely for his friend's behaviour. The landlord behind the bar suddenly piped up, expressing his support for them and remarking how the loss of their colleague must have been very hard on them before he 'eloquently' said in his cockney accent "You're bloody heroes for sorting those bastards out! Scum, they should all be deported!" He then leant forward and put his hand on the man's left shoulder and said "I suggest you keep your mouth shut about this boy! You don't know you're fucking born sunshine!" The stubbly man acknowledging what he said with a nervous nod before repeatedly apologising to the three officers. O'Keeffe thanked the Landlord and they hurriedly left.

Outside Conan turned to O'Keeffe and asked him what the hell was going on and that as Fosters friend, he must have known what was going on with him.

"I don't know! He had a moment like this after the shooting; I thought it was just shock and stress affecting him!" He replied.

"I can't believe this, I thought he was just playing up! I shouldn't have doubted him!" Conan reflected.

"Look, we all should have done something about him earlier, but right now, we just need to find him!" Jones interrupted. The three men looked at each other with concern before they rushed off to search for Foster.

The following morning, after failing to locate Foster, the trio discussed the night before with the others, drawing annoyed responses from Simpson and MacNeil who both stated that it had been obvious that something bad was going to happen. O'Keeffe informed Inspector Balham of what had happened, who shook his head and exclaimed "I knew he wasn't right! That's why I placed him on non-operational duties and removed his firearms permit, maybe I should have done more too. OK we'll sort this out when we get back!".

Just as the team were about to walk into the court for the verdict, Foster appeared smiling and apologising for his lateness as if everything was normal. Jones was just about to ask him where he had been since the pub but Balham tapped him on the shoulder and shook his head implying that he should leave it for now.

Twenty minutes later, the Judge asked the Jury for their verdict, causing the butterflies to flutter around each of the firearms officers stomachs. As the Jury returned a guilty verdict against the five defendants, Jennings screamed out "They're are the murderers. They're the ones who killed an unarmed man!" before he was restrained by one of the court's bailiffs. The other four defendants remained silent and forlorn as they had done throughout the hearing.

After the Judge had finished shouting for order to be restored, he finally gave his verdict, "I find the defendants guilty of planning and making preparations to commit mass murder, and hereby sentence them to fifteen years imprisonment!", the five men's faces dropped. "And as for you Mr Jennings, I also find you guilty of the murder of City police officer Sergeant Kevin Marriot and the attempt murder of PC Alex Moore, in addition I therefore also sentence you to life in prison" The Judge finished with a look of disdain for Jennings in particular which did nothing to quell the temper tantrum he'd had just moments before."

"MURDERERS! I HOPE YOU ALL ROT IN HELL!" Jennings yelled out at the top of voice prompting the Judge to order the bailiffs to "TAKE HIM DOWN!!!!!" and declare order.

He didn't go without a fight though and it took a total of four bailiffs to remove the incensed man, despite his disabled arm. Jones looked over at Conan and rolled his eyes.

"I guess it's just what happens when someone weak and vulnerable is influenced by someone evil and deranged!" Conan remarked.

Foster, who was sat in front of them, did not say a word, and just watched Jennings with an indifferent and cold stare as he was dragged from the court room kicking and screaming.

A Serious Bunch of Names
Chapter Seven

"Peter, they're waiting for you!" said DS Ian Richards, Anaura's best friend and the Vice unit's Sergeant.

Richards was a man in his early forties and the polar opposite of Anaura; he liked wearing ties for a start. He and Anaura had both joined The City Police Force at the same time and had formed a strong friendship from the outset which meant that their wives and children were very close too. Although Anaura may have been the boss, Richards was his right hand man whose opinion meant a great deal. More often than not, Richards was the angel on Anaura's right shoulder who kept him safe from the devil on his left who influenced him to rush into things without thinking.

"Ah bloody hell! Can't they wait? I'm trying to get this Billy Vine case signed off!" Anaura protested whilst leaning back in his chair and pulling an exasperated expression. He knew that the Six Nations final between England and Wales would be starting imminently and he was running out of time to get things wrapped up before kick-off.

"No Peter, they won't wait, they've been expecting you for the past ten minutes." Richards replied.

"Bloody hell Ian, I knew this was coming. RIGHT, let's get it over with"

"Are you going to take your tie off Peter? I mean it's what they would expect" Richards asked Anaura who was wearing a tie for once.

"No I'd better leave it on, don't want to get into more trouble if someone else comes in!" he stated.

Anaura stood up from his desk and walked with Richards into the main office. On his emergence the whole room stopped watching TV and looked up at him with apprehension; they knew what he was going to have to do.

"Sorry sir, they wouldn't have taken no for an answer, we had no choice" DC Carl Langford said with a sympathetic look as Valera and DC Naomi Usher looked on with expectant expressions. Anaura shook his head in frustration, the national anthems had already started and kick off was imminent, yet he had to get this rigmarole out of the way first. Why couldn't they have requested him at half time he thought to himself.

"Right then, I suppose I'm going to have to wait a bit longer before I can sit down and relax. OK, let's get it over with!" Anaura said, hoping that he would be finished in time to see the match. He nodded at Richards and Langford before he walked towards the centre of the office, and on to a large open archway that provided access to the CID office. Just before he walked through the large archway, he paused and turned around so that he was just shy of it and facing his team. The Vice detectives smiled at him.

"WAEWAE TAKAHIA KIA KINO" Anaura yelled out at them before forcefully bending his legs into a squatted horse riding stance, both fists clenched hard above one another. His eyes became sharp and angry with his face reflecting the powerful aggression that was boiling up inside him. Anaura's posture was as solid as a statue, he did not look like he was in the mood for taking prisoners

"Ooooooooo, AH KA MA TE! KA MA TE! KA ORA! KA ORA! HOOO HOOO" he chanted, yelling at the top of his voice and smacking his big hands down repeatedly on his thighs and then demonstrating an intimidating array of hand movements. The whole team gazed at him in awe.

The intoxicating mix of fear and fascination caused Valera to grab Usher's arm and squeeze it hard. Anaura had suddenly become incredibly intimidating and not her usual laid back and caring boss.

"WHITI TE RA! EEEEEEEE" he yelled as he jumped into the air with his tongue thrust out.

All of the detectives burst into applause as he landed back on the ground. Anuara walked back over to them and took a seat prior to Richards rubbing and patting his head from behind him.

"Best one yet mate" Richards said to him whilst laughing.

The uncharacteristic display of aggression had been down to a team tradition where Anaura had been duty bound to perform the Maori war dance, the Haka. The same dance that the New Zealand All blacks rugby team demonstrated before every game. It didn't matter that New Zealand were not playing, the Vice detectives just wanted to see him do it whenever there was a game on. It was moments like this that made it obvious how close and fond the team were of him. On top of this his fun loving personality, Anaura was also a copper's copper and made sure that his team did the job they loved and joined to do, which was catch criminals and not chase politically set figures.

"His wife is so lucky, why can't I find someone like him!" DC Valera said to Usher who agreed with her.

"Peter?" Detective Chief Inspector Steiner said to Anaura in a manner that wasn't so much a question but more of an order, as in, I want to speak to you now!

Anaura escorted Steiner into his office and asked him how he could help, lamenting how he had missed the start of the game anyway. As far as higher ranked officers went, Chief Inspector Jason Steiner was one of a few decent ones who Anaura got on very well with. Steiner wasn't one of those ladder snakes and had spent most of his career on the streets, and was now a thirty year plus copper. Some people just didn't want to draw their pensions!

"Peter, did you hear about Jennings and friends getting sentenced to life? The firearms officers won't be facing any further enquiry either. The fact that it was suggested after what they went through makes me bloody angry with the system. It's a bloody insult to Marriot's memory, he was a great bloke; did you know him?" Steiner said.

"It is great news. No I didn't know Marriot or the others. I've only really come across the firearms lot in passing, I guess we're at different ends of the spectrum. You're right though they should never have been subjected to a court hearing like that, especially since Op Barrier was only three months ago!" Anaura remarked.

Steiner nodded in agreement before he dumped a large file on

Anaura's desk which he picked up to have look at.

"Bradford, Pearson, Sykes, Cooper...........this is a pretty serious bunch of names Jason" Anaura declared as he flicked through the file. Steiner nodded back with his eyebrows raised.

Ryan Bradford, Larry Pearson, Nick Sykes and Paul Cooper were indeed a serious bunch of names. Born in Eastings, a rundown fishing town to the east of the City, the four men had all grown up together, and after a troubled childhood of petty crime they had developed into proper villains. The 'Gang', as they imaginatively referred to themselves, were not a bunch of small time thugs, they were the real deal. The type of criminals that could make you disappear in a heartbeat if you put a foot wrong with them. Yet not one of them had been convicted of a violent offence or pulled the trigger. Now this wasn't down to them being of a sensitive disposition, it was just that they had plenty of people to carry out their many dirty deeds for them. Now aged in their fifties, the Gang were keen to start putting things in place for a happy retirement in the south of France or anywhere where the weather was nice and the red wine was flowing.

The Gang's business that would finance this enjoyable retirement was drugs-cocaine to be exact. Bradford, who was seen as the unofficial boss of the outfit, had started selling Cannabis at the age of eighteen. When the others saw how much money could be made they jumped on board too, never looking back. From then on, they stopped getting involved in fights, rows and anything in general that would attract police attention, they even got regular jobs. The change of lifestyle wasn't to help them become more legit, it was to help them become more illegal.

If they wanted to make more money from products more illegal, they needed to be above suspicion, or at least in a position where they looked like straight shooters incapable of such dealings. And some thirty years later they had made a lot of money! However the addictive rush of crime was not an easy habit to quit and although they had enough cash to retire three times over, a few last shipments of the good stuff wouldn't have hurt.

Without any real criminal history and with an army of

employees doing their dirty work, the Gang had only been suspected of drug supply through intelligence work. There had certainly never been anything solid enough though to warrant storming in there and nicking them. And besides, being the switched on cookies they were, they had made their ill-gotten cash clean by buying up loads of property around the City and its coastline. With the protection of top flight lawyers and City council men too, the Gang were definitely not the type of criminals you wanted to nick without any evidence. As much as Anaura wanted to bring down these so called 'business men', he knew it would never happen, barring an act of God. Every time the police got close or started building a case against them, the Gang would be one step ahead and change their plans.

"What am I looking at here Jason?" Anaura enquired with confusion.

"I want these guys Peter!" Steiner replied.

"Everyone does Jason but it ain't going to happen any time soon, they look clean, they smell clean and every investigation into them has revealed them to be clean! It doesn't matter whether that's true or not" Anaura declared.

Steiner sat silently for a moment before leaning forward and quietly telling Anaura that he was setting up an operation to finally take them down. There would be no messing around anymore, if they needed evidence, they would get it; one way or another! Anaura sat there reminiscing how he had heard that said before until Steiner stated that it was going to be an operation with a blank cheque budget and all the necessary resources. Anaura liked the sound of it but reminded Steiner that this type of stuff was the Serious and Organised Crime Unit's territory and that his remit was generally restricted to low to mid-level drug dealers, pimps and prostitution, so why was he telling him about it. Steiner agreed that it wasn't in Anaura's usual remit before declaring that he wanted Anaura to head up the operation because of his knowledge of the Gang and the City's drug scene. Anaura sat there stunned as it was unusual for a Vice Inspector to head up such an operation. Steiner continued by saying that in order to catch the big fish, you needed to use decent bait, and what better to use than the City 's mid-level drug dealers who were probably linked to the Gang! Drug dealers, that Anaura would know.

"The op will be starting within four weeks. I'll let you know when we're are going to get started, I've just some political stuff to sort out first! Get you and your team ready." Steiner said with a smile and a wink before he got up and left the office.

Anaura put the lower part of his face into his hands so that the fingers joined above the bridge of his nose. Pondering what had just been said to him, he sat tapping his fingers together and letting out huffs into the space between his hands. The sound of cheers could be heard coming from the main office, by now he had missed most of the match, but for once it didn't bother him.

"You alright Peter?" Richards enquired as he popped his head around Anaura's office door.

"Did any pigs just fly past the window? Because if they didn't, I think we may have just been given our dream job. Take a seat Ian, I'll fill you in" He replied to Richards, trying to contain a smug smile.

Misguided Loyalty
Chapter Eight

Chief Superintendent Drayson pulled up to a set of locked gates that were on Basin Road, City harbour, in his expensive new blue Mercedes A45 AMG, and removed a set of keys from his trouser pocket. As a result of the rain and howling wind he dropped the keys onto the ground. Worried that someone might see him, he frantically searched around the gravel to find them, finally locating them after a number of minutes. With the gate now unlocked he drove the A class into the car park of the warehouse and parked it discreetly behind a large steel shipping crate. The sheer size of the warehouse meant that it created a massive sinister shadow in the dark, rain filled road and car park.

"It's the bloody April showers alright" he muttered to himself as he used yet another key to open the reinforced glass and wood door to the disused building. In a cautious manner, Drayson gave one last look behind him to make sure that there was no one around before he pushed the door open and entered. Inside the damp lobby he paused and pulled out a torch to illuminate the pitch black staircase in front of him. He had tried walking up them in darkness once before but the precarious undertaking had resulted in an embarrassing and painful fall. It was a silly mistake that he would not be repeating.

At the top of the short staircase his torch lit up yet another door that then led down a short concrete set of steps and into a huge expanse of dark empty space, filled with bird droppings and puddles of rain water. It was clear that whatever the warehouse might have been in its previous life, it had clearly been a busy centre for dock related industry. Drayson continued his journey through the darkness to the corner of the work floor where there was a steel stair case that led up to a bright blanket of light that penetrated through the windows of an office.

"Ello Robbie, haven't seen you in a while. Bit wet out is it?!"

Ryan Bradford said, greeting Drayson in a contemptuous manner as he walked, soaked through, into the office.

"Yeah it is! Anyway, why do we still have to meet up in this shitty old warehouse, it's damp, it's cold........." Drayson replied.

"Because it's the last place in the world that your mates in blue would think to look. And besides its got character, don't you think?" Remarked Nick Sykes, a tall, well-built and dark haired man with a stubbly face.

Drayson sat down at the table where Bradford, Pearson, Sykes and Cooper were sat around a table playing a game of poker and joking with each other. After a round of piss taking regarding Drayson's up and coming promotion and how many days he had left until his big pension, Bradford looked up from his hand of cards and asked him whether there was any new boys on the block that they needed to be concerned about. Drayson answered that he hadn't heard anything but reminded him that since his recent departure from the Serious and Organised Crime Unit, he hadn't been privy to everything that was going on. Bradford didn't acknowledge Drayson's reply, appearing as though he was more than a little frustrated with him.

"I do have some serious news though" Drayson said, this time catching the full attention of Bradford who looked up from his cards. "I overheard one of my command colleagues talking about a big drugs operation in the pipe line that was going to target the biggest drug suppliers in the city. In other words, you!" he continued to explain with a hint of nervousness in his voice.

"Well, you'd best get this so called operation called off then hadn't you?" Bradford replied with annoyance. Across the table the other three looked very concerned.

"How am I going to do that? I can't just call off an operation, definitely not one on this scale. I'm sorry you're going to have to lay low, or, I don't know, maybe call it quits before you all get locked up" Drayson remarked.

Bradford dropped his cards onto the table, folded his arms and shot a look at the other men before maintaining cold steely eye contact with Drayson.

"YOU ALL? What do you mean, you all?? What, you're not part of the Gang any more Robbie?" Bradford snapped back at Drayson who began to squirm in his seat with discomfort and perspiration developing under his arms.

"Fine, we, will have to lay low then! Seriously though, we need to consider calling off the shipment" Drayson stated.

"No, the shipment still goes ahead! If I'm honest Robbie, I expected more from you, especially after everything we've done for you over the years. We made you wealthy, we protected you and we helped get you promoted by giving you some of our associates. Get the operation cancelled!" He commented in an angry tone.

"I've told you, I can't do it! No one has the power to do that without a bloody good reason. Even the Chief Constable would implicate himself by cancelling an op like this for no good reason. Are you mad?" He replied.

"OK Robbie, it's like this, call off the operation or suffer the consequences. If we get caught, you get caught. I'm sure your colleagues would love to hear about your moonlighting activities!? Call it off tomorrow morning or there will be trouble. Who knows, in week or so, you may no longer be a copper to call anything off if I decide it". Bradford warned him.

Drayson started to feel sick to his core, and with good reason. His relationship with Bradford and the Gang had gone back as far as his school days, something his colleagues from his day job obviously were not aware of. Growing up in the same area of Eastings the five men had become acquainted after Bradford and Cooper had intervened when Drayson was being beaten up by some fellow pupils. Where the others had come from rough backgrounds, Drayson had not. Although his family weren't the richest out there, they certainly were not the poorest by any stretch of the imagination either. With the help of these new friends Drayson soon became a bully himself after gaining confidence with the help of Bradford.

As the five of them developed into teenagers, Drayson started to go his separate way as a result of his parents demanding that he stopped hanging around with such losers. At first he rebelled against them, but it was just a matter of time before they would eventually win the day. Little Robbie Drayson was not quite the rebel he had others believe, and as his mother put it "You're so gullible, these boys are using you, especially that Bradford boy. It's time to start thinking for yourself and not being so easily influenced by others. You're not a tough guy, so stop pretending to be one!"

After the dressing down from his mother, he parted ways with the other four and went to college to study psychology while the others started to get themselves arrested for fighting amongst other things. Drayson on the other hand made a full u-turn in life, and after finishing his A levels, he decided that he wanted to join the Police Force. As he began his career, Bradford and the others began theirs; drugs. A few years later when Drayson was drinking in a local pub, Bradford and the others walked in. At first he considered leaving but when he saw that they were all wearing suits and looking smart and respectable he asked them to join him believing that they had grown up. Just as it had been before, Drayson couldn't resist their charms, especially Bradford's, who almost fell off his chair when he learnt of his new career. Never one to miss an opportunity, Bradford purposefully renewed his friendship (and control) with Drayson. For the first year or two the Gang kept their business affairs hidden from Drayson until they knew for sure that he was trustworthy.

One night, many months later, Bradford took Drayson to one side and informed him what they were in to. To begin with, Drayson said that he couldn't see them again, but as usual Bradford would find a way to influence him into hanging around. As he became deeper entwined with the Gang, Bradford soon revealed how much money they were making from cocaine and informed Drayson that if he helped them to eradicate the competition through his job, he would be rewarded handsomely and made a junior partner in the syndicate. Drayson couldn't refuse and in time he would make more dirty money than he knew what to do with, hence he developed a taste for new cars and tailored suits. He may have enjoyed this easy money but as it mounted up, it soon became a problem as there was nowhere to hide it all. After a number of years, Drayson began to wonder if the risk had all been worth it. And now more than ever he wished that he had never set eyes on Bradford, realising that he had used him from the start.

Drayson got up to leave, as the realisation of what he would be facing started to sink in. He was a long serving police officer who had been moonlighting as criminal, part of a serious and organised crime syndicate for over twenty five years and made tens of thousands as a result. If his employers found out he would be well and truly fucked. There wouldn't be a chance in hell that he would be able defend the amount of evidence that Bradford and the others could spill on him. With the abuse of a position of trust, proceeds of crime, tax avoidance; and all the other crimes he had committed, he would be going away for life. There wasn't an easy solution to the conundrum that he had been presented with, he couldn't call off the operation and he couldn't grass the Gang up without implicating himself in the process. However if he just sat back and did nothing, they would grass him up first; or worse they would have him killed. Everything was going to come to an end, his job, his pension, his respectability but what was much worse, was the knowledge of what awaited him in prison, a police superintendent in with the police hating general prison population; he would be brutalised daily for his whole sentence.

As Drayson left the office, he could feel the blood and warmth draining from his face and his hands and body were drenched in sweat. He felt a severe sense of dread and anxiety, to the extent where he was considering driving his car into the harbour, after all he was going to be dead anyway, one way or another.

"Remember Robbie; screw this up and you'll be picking up the soap for the boys in prison for the rest of your life. I look forward to hearing that the operation's been cancelled soon, very soon" Bradford said in a cold hearted manner that befitted his intimidating villain persona. The other three laughed out loud, they all knew Drayson was over a barrel and would do anything he could to hang onto his police career and reputation. One thing that was becoming crystal clear to him was that he was only a friend of theirs if he served a purpose and did as he was told, if he didn't they would drop him like a bad habit.

Drayson sullenly nodded back at Bradford before he left the room and headed down the steel staircase. As he stepped off the last step and switched on his torch to light up the dark path ahead of him, he had an epiphany. Like the torch, he was faced with darkness ahead of him unless he found a light, an idea, to illuminate his path and guide him out of the darkness. He knew what needed to happen, he had to get to the Gang first before they could get to him; he just needed to work out how!

Foster sat in the waiting room of the Force's Occupational Health Department feeling a sense of apprehension and betrayal. Within days of the team's return from the court hearing, Inspector Balham had called Foster into his office and stated that he wanted him to see the force doctor prior to being given the all clear to return to full operational duties. The conversation had taken Foster by complete surprise and he had a meltdown in Balham's office, throwing a glass across the room and smashing it. Balham being the calm man he was, didn't react to it and gently told Foster that he had not been himself since the shooting and that it would be beneficial for him to see a professional who specialised in stress related issues. Foster shouted at Balham, accusing him of trying to send him to a shrink. Pissed off and upset, Foster left his office knowing that he would have to play ball or lose his hard earned place on the unit. At the behest of the Inspector he went on a short period of sick leave to await his appointment with a psychiatrist.

The following week Foster attended a private mental health assessment at The Abbey Clinic in the expensive end of town that was funded by the Police Federation. There was no way Foster would suffer the long waiting list to see an NHS Psychiatrist, especially when all he wanted to do was to return to operational duties so he approached the Federation for help. Despite knowing that he had no choice in the matter, he still found it unbelievable that Balham requested it. Foster knew deep down that he had not been himself at times but it did not stop him from feeling as though everyone had it in for him, a belief that had slowly been building in his mind over the previous months.

Foster was called in from the waiting area of the large former Victorian house that had been converted into the Abbey clinic, by a young and friendly Psychiatrist by the name of Dr Tom Banks. As Foster stood up he smiled at the pleasant red haired receptionist who he had considered asking out but changed his mind when he suddenly began to worry that she would think he was there because he was mad.

"Hello Anthony, I'm Dr Banks. What we're going to be doing here today is discussing how you have been feeling recently. I'm not here to make a diagnosis of any kind today, I just want to establish how you've been coping," he said in an empathetic tone.

"Look, I'm here because I have no choice. There's nothing wrong with me, so let's get this bollocks over with". Foster snapped. The appointment had barely started but he was already growing tired of it.

After that appointment, Foster had been required to attend a number of follow up appointments, something he put down to the clinic trying to pinch more of the federation's money. However as the appointments progressed, Dr Banks began to slowly establish a detailed family history of mental illness, childhood trauma and a degree of delusional and paranoid thinking that was exacerbated by alcohol consumption.

Now he was sat in the Occupational Health Department waiting to be seen by the Force Medical Examiner (the force's dedicated doctor) who would examine and assess his suitability to remain as an operational police officer. Foster was in a depressed state and felt as though he was awaiting his execution. In the two months since he had been assessed, Foster had lost his firearms permit and been placed on sick leave with nothing to do except climb the walls of his flat.

Foster was finally called into the doctor's office and asked to sit down. He reflected on how the doctor appeared a little distant and preoccupied that day. He had seen him a few times over the course of his mental health assessments and had taken a dislike to him as a result of his negative attitude towards him returning back to duty. Foster was convinced that he had it in for him, especially when he repeatedly heard the doctor make underhand comments underneath his breath.

"What did you just say? If you have something to say, just

come out and say it rather than whispering it!" Foster enquired angrily after he believed that the doctor had said something under his breath again.

"Anthony I didn't say anything, we've spoken about this before, I wouldn't say anything derogatory to you, it's just the auditory hallucinations. It will get better with the right treatment and care, I promise. OK, we've received Dr Bank's diagnosis and prognosis letter and I'm here today to discuss your options" the doctor commented in an empathetic tone. Foster shook his head at him with contempt.

The doctor asked him if he had read it, Foster rolled his eyes and nodded back at him, he knew full well the bullshit that was in it. The moment he laid eyes on it, he knew that everyone was conspiring against him, including the federation, to have him removed from the Force and blamed for the Mahood shooting. Ever since the shooting he had heard them whispering in dark corners and plotting against him. There was no one left he could trust.

The doctor discussed Foster's treatment with him and asked whether the medication had been helping, to which Foster replied that they had; even though he had only taken them for a couple of days after deciding that he didn't need them. He then asked Foster if he'd had any visual hallucinations which caused Foster to ask with annoyance why the doctor kept mentioning hallucinations. After numerous questions about his family and friends that he did not see any more, the doctor finished up by explaining to Foster that he would be placed on permanent restricted duties and that he would only be allowed to carry out office work in the future. In addition he would be advising the Force that Foster was eligible for medical retirement and that the option should be explored due to Fosters aversion to being stuck in an office environment.

Foster sat there stunned and asked the doctor why he was going to write that when it wasn't the truth. The doctor softened his expression and explained that Dr Bank's report and Fosters refusal to accept his condition and unwillingness to fully participate in his treatment meant that he would struggle to hold down a busy job within the Police Service. He also reminded Foster that he himself had remarked that he would rather die than work in an office for the rest of his career. Foster did not comment and just sat there staring into space which prompted the doctor to explain it in more compassionate terms.

"Anthony I know it's very difficult for you and I know that you believe everyone's against you, but it's not the case. You are suffering from a nasty illness that without medication will make things very difficult for you. You need to fully involve yourself in your treatment to help improve your quality of life. Look I know you wanted to stay operational, but it just can't happen, this is the best option. It's now up to the organisation as to whether they retain you as a permanently restricted duties disabled officer, and they might if you want them to." The doctor explained.

"I knew you all wanted me out. The second I pulled the trigger I knew what was going to happen. They told me you'd do this, try to tarnish me and have me booted out. Well bollocks to the lot of you, I'll have the last laugh!" snarled Foster.

"Who told you Anthony? If you're hearing voices you need to speak to Dr Banks, and please keep taking your medication, it really is the best thing for you. Things will get better, I promise, just try to reflect on your thoughts and emotions, don't them get out of control. Look after yourself."

"Whatever, I think you need to look after yourself first." he responded before quickly standing up to leave. As he reached the door, he paused and then asked the doctor whether he could have the copy of Dr Banks' letter as he had lost his, the doctor nodded and handed him it before repeating for Foster to look after himself.

Foster pulled an insincere smile and picked up the report before he walked out of the room without saying goodbye. He walked out into the car park and towards his car, a Lotus Elise, something that had added to his financial woes when he had bought it. Foster stared at his pride and joy before he suddenly kicked the driver's door as hard as he could in a rage, denting it in the process. Foster looked down at Dr. Banks report, feeling disgusted at how everyone was trying to ruin him. He finished reading the report and tore it up into tiny pieces in anger. The scattered pieces of paper fell at his feet and were then blown around the carp park by the brisk breeze. Foster hadn't really needed to read it again, what was on the paper would be burnt into his memory forever..........

The Abbey Clinic
Specialists in Mental Health Services

Occupational Health Department
City Police HQ

Patient number: AF:1000230

Dear Insp Balham and the Force Medical Examiner.

I am PC Anthony Foster's primary care psychiatrist who was appointed by the Police Federation. Over the past seven weeks I have been carrying out a range of psychological assessments to establish Anthony's mental condition and wellbeing. He was not always forthcoming with answering questions during these sessions, however I believe I was able to make certain important observations.

During the appointments I established the following facts, Anthony has a history of mental illness on his maternal side, and although he could not be sure of the diagnosis he did allude to the possibility that it may have been Schizophrenia. He was subjected to trauma and drug abuse as a teenager, and of course most recently the incident on duty as a firearms officer.

From the outcome of the tests, it is my observation that there is strong evidence to support the assumption that Anthony is suffering from a mental health disorder namely Schizophrenia (paranoid sub type with a degree of disorganised sub type). He also displays the clinical presentation of Dissociative Identity Disorder, formerly Multiple Personality Disorder. Both of these disorders can be highly debilitating in nature if left untreated. Anthony's main symptom presentation ranges from delusional and disorganised thinking, audio hallucinations, anxiety and severe mood swings, through to dissociative amnesia.

As part of his treatment plan Anthony is being prescribed a 400mg daily dose of Chlorpromazine to help control his symptoms. However this will need to be reviewed at regular intervals in order to ascertain its effectiveness. Although patients with these two disorders can live productive lives with the correct balance of medication, therapy and effective lifestyle parameters, thus far Anthony is struggling with the diagnosis and is therefore somewhat removed and unwilling to accept it. This is not uncommon and can improve with the right help and time.

Overall, his prognosis is to be closely guarded until we have pursued all of the available treatment methods. However I think it is safe to say that it would be highly unlikely that he would be able to function as a police officer in the future. The main obstacle to an improvement in Anthony's condition is his developing alcohol abuse. At this stage there is no evidence to suggest drug abuse, but I feel that this is something that will have to be monitored in the future.

If there is any further clarification required on this matter, please do not hesitate to contact me.

Yours sincerely,

Signed electronically to avoid delay.

Dr Tom Banks
Consultant Psychiatrist
The Abbey Group.

Operation Spear
Chapter Ten

Anaura made his way through the corridors that led to the station's Command Officers Suite. It was mid-July and four months since DCI Steiner had attended his office and informed him of the Gang operation, and yet there was no movement or word on when everything would start. It was time for him to ask what was going on.

"Bloody hell, come in." Steiner said from within his office in the command suite after Anaura had knocked on it hard and repeatedly.

"How's it going Jason?" Anaura enquired.

"Ah Peter, I know what you're here for! Take a seat." He said with a smile.

He sat down and waited to be advised on whether the delay meant the operation had been cancelled. Steiner began reassuring him that everything was still on and that the long delay had been down to a few political and financial issues. Anaura probed Steiner to learn more about the nature of the issues. Steiner shook his head before he told Anaura how certain members in command, namely Drayson, had raised some questions about whether the expensive operation was appropriate given the previous failures and when the force was currently going through harsh financial cuts. Steiner smiled and said that in the end the Chief had signed it off and Drayson had to go along with it, something he allegedly was not happy about.

Anaura wasn't surprised as to the identity of the saboteur. He knew that the moment Drayson discovered that he would be heading the investigation up, he would want it postponed or cancelled. There was no way that Drayson would want Anaura claiming all the glory, especially when it was busting the county's biggest organised crime syndicate; something he had failed to do

74

or get close to during his tenure as head of the Serious and Organised Crime Unit.

"Monday 22nd July, that's when we'll begin! Are you ready for it Peter?"

Anaura replied that he had been ready for months since the day the Job had been mentioned to him.

"Christ that's not long away! So what's the op name Jason?" he enquired.

"Operation Spear, do you like it?"

"Ha ha, who wouldn't, it's a good name. Let's hope that spear ends up in a few places where the sun doesn't shine" Anaura said with a pleased look on his face before leaving the command suite.

As he walked back to the Vice Office, he felt a sense of smugness that Drayson's attempts to prevent the operation had failed. If they had to be one person who would have tried to throw a spanner in the works it would have been Drayson.

On his arrival back in the Vice Office, he was greeted by Valera and Usher who were asking him for his authorisation to carry out a search in the home of a local pimp who had been arrested on suspicion of possessing marijuana with the intent to supply. Anaura signed the search form and asked the two women whether they fancied something a little more interesting to do than chasing pimps.

"Errrrrr I think you want to be telling us what it is, yeah!!" Usher said win a mock American gangster accent that reflected her fun loving personality.

"Mmmmmm, what did you have in mind sir?" Valera asked with an air of sexual innuendo.

Anaura smiled and then told the two detectives that it was a better job than the one they were currently dealing with and how Valera would really, really enjoy doing it! The comment caused her to blush deeply as she hadn't anticipated Anaura reciprocating with another innuendo. The detectives looked at each other and then replied that they were up for it.

"Settled then! The two of you and Ian will be on an operation with me from next week, pass the pimp job onto Carl Langford and clear your desks of any rubbish jobs you have left, you won't have a chance to deal with them!" Anaura said.

"Nice one.......! Who are we after sir?" Usher asked with her usual exuding enthusiasm.

He replied by telling her to be patient as all would be explained on the 22nd but insisted that they wouldn't be disappointed when they found out what it was. The funny thing was that Anaura was telling them to be patient despite being like an excited child himself inside.

"Go on then, get your work sorted. Scram!" Anaura ordered in a playful tone as he walked back into his office.

Inside his office Richards was sat waiting to hear whether the operation was still on or not. Anaura walked in without saying a word, knowing that the suspense would drive Richards mad.

"Well?" Richards asked with a desperately inquisitive tone.

"Well what Ian?" Anaura replied with a smile.

Richards crossed his legs like a pregnant woman trying to stop herself from peeing through laughter, calling Anaura a bastard and begging him to spill the beans. Anaura sat in his chair, enjoying the power that came with the knowledge afforded to him.

"22nd of July mate, that's when 'Op Spear' will officially begin!" Anaura said, leaning back in his chair with his arms behind his head.

Richards clenched his fist and shook it with excitement. After the very long wait they finally had a start date. In less a week they would finally get a chance to build a decent case against the county's biggest crime syndicate and hopefully put them away. Anaura updated Richards that he was going to have Valera and Usher seconded onto the case too, due to their investigative talent and understanding of Surveillance Ops, the result of the two detectives having spent six months attached to the unit and being his two best officers. Richards whole heartedly agreed and put forward that he thought Langford should assume the role of acting Sergeant on Vice while they were gone. Anaura nodded and cited that it was better to have an experienced detective constable in Vice running the show than an inexperienced Inspector!

Anaura rubbed his hands together, daydreaming with the

thought of finally locking up the Gang. It was time for these four arseholes to go down, and Anaura believed he was going to be the man to do it. With the solid 'copper's copper' DCI Steiner running the show at Command level, and Anaura as the grass roots boss, things were shaping up so that the 'spear' would most definitely and painfully end up where the sun didn't shine!

That night with a spring in his step, Anaura returned home on time for once. The second he walked in through the front door, the amazing smell of Laura's cooking hit him. She had cooked lamb (New Zealand Lamb to be exact) tagine; it was just the type of dish that he felt would round off such a brilliant day.

"You've spoilt dinner Peter, it's going to be hot now, how will you eat it like that, it's not cold?!" Laura said in a sarcastic but playful tone aimed at his early return from work.

Anaura gave her a flirtatious wink and walked over to sample the dinner that was waiting for him. With just a sip of the sauce he knew it was going to be perfect, and yet he couldn't help winding Laura up with a cheeky remark about it needing more salt. She reacted by picking up the closest cooking utensil to hand and smacking him across the backside with it. At first Anaura laughed until he realised that she had swiped a little too hard and that he could now feel a burning like sting radiating from his right buttock. Laura smiled smugly and told him to be a good boy or there would be more of that. Anaura replied, with a smile, that he bloody hoped not as one smack had been sufficient!

Anaura left the kitchen and went upstairs to say goodnight to his two young children, Anya and William. The moment he entered each of their rooms he knew that it had been a bad idea as they leapt out of bed with excitement. He loved the two of them more than words could describe and wished that his hectic job would allow him spend more time with them. He sat on the edge of their beds and asked them about school which was met with the usual reply of "Boring!!" from the pair of them. He could have stayed there with them for hours, talking or having fun, but he knew that it would not be long before Laura told him off for keeping them awake. If there was one thing that Anuara was set on, it was making sure that he didn't interfere with the kid's routine, at the end of the day it would not be him dealing with tired, grumpy kids the next day. There were times though when he considered the possibility of Laura returning to work and him leaving the police. Financially it would make sense due to the money she could earn, not to mention that he would get to spend a lot more time with the kids, but it would mean that Laura would be sucked into her previous hectic, London work life and the kids would then see less of her; either way they would lose one parent to a demanding job. And besides, Anuara's cooking skills were hardly Jamie Oliver standard; in fact they were diabolical. The overall end result of him becoming a stay at home dad would have meant one thing, the kids would be have been suffering from malnutrition within weeks. It was probably best that they kept things how they were, for the time being it worked and Laura felt empowered by shunning the business woman life by becoming a mum. Something which angered some of her clients and colleagues who declared that she was becoming a slave of a patriarch society by becoming a house wife. If there was one thing that would made Laura furious, it was when other women inferred that being a mother or a housewife was something to be viewed as negative and anti-feminist.

Anuara said 'night' to the kids and returned to Laura in the kitchen who had laid the aromatic dinner out onto the table. Over a glass of red wine and the Moroccan tagine they discussed the usual nonsensical and random conversational topics that as a couple they were known for. Anaura and Laura could literally talk for Britain; even if it was a load of rubbish they were spouting.

"So Peter, come on, out with it! You've been smiling like the Cheshire cat all evening. What's going on?" She enquired with a slightly raised right eyebrow. Anaura instantly felt turned on, the raised eyebrow expression she had made her look like a naughty secretary flirting with the boss.

"The operation; It's on!" Anuara said with a huge beaming smile. Generally speaking officers were not meant to discuss work related issues with anyone outside of the job, however Anaura, like most other officers, still told his partner everything unless it was something top secret.

Laura was really pleased for him and leant over to give him a kiss on the lips. She knew how long he had been waiting for the Operation, or any job like it, for quite a while. As they continued talking she told Anaura that he had her full support and if he was required to work over and above his normal hours, she and the kids would be OK with it. As always, Laura's devotion made him remember why he loved her so much and was one of the reasons that he was starting to consider a quieter role in another unit in order to be able to be at home more. However for the moment, Op Spear was calling him.

Laura gave him a huge proud smile and stood up to take the dishes over to the sink. Just as she was about to start rinsing them, she felt Anaura come up behind her and start kissing her neck softly with his large muscled chest pressing into her back. Whatever it was in his pocket that was thrusting into her toned and pert backside, it was obvious that he was very, very happy to see her. Anaura partially lifted up her top and tenderly kissed the tattoo on her lower back, sending goose bumps rapidly popping up around her whole body. He pulled the top of her jeans down slightly further and firmly kissed the crease and top of her bum before spinning her around and kissing her on the lips. Laura felt electrified as he grabbed her hips and pulled her in close to him, she could have melted right there. He then maintained eye contact with her as he pressed her up against the work top. His arousal clear to see; and feel.

"I'll do the dishes later, Laura-Anaura!" He said in a deep playful tone, making fun of her rhyming names.

Shaking hard with excitement, Laura found it hard to catch her breath as he suddenly lifted her up off the floor as though she only weighed the same as a couple of bags of sugar. His strong arms wrapped tightly around her and his right hand firmly caressed her left bum cheek through her tight jeans. It was now clear to see through Laura's top that she was happy to see him too.

"Mmmmm! I've been thinking about this all day!" She said in a jittery voice.

Anaura carried her up the stairs and over the threshold of their bedroom, like a groom would with his bride.............................and closed the door!

Drayson pulled up at the City Police Headquarter's gates and placed his warrant card over the electronic card system that read the chip within it, raising the gates when the system established he was an authorised person to enter the HQ. He drove up the drive in his 'company' Ford Focus towards the reception car park about two hundred meters from the entrance. Although Drayson liked being seen in his Mercedes, he generally kept it quiet at work that he owned one. For one he didn't want people to see it at work and then spot it in certain places where it should not have been. He applied the handbrake harshly on the Focus. In his opinion the car was a piece of crap but at the end of the day it was free to drive and abuse. Spending the public's money was never really one of his major concerns, unless he was trying to have an operation delayed or cancelled due to the implications for the tax payer; and more importantly, himself.

Drayson had tried his hardest to have Operation Spear called off by expressing his fake concerns about the Force's budget, which had been a good idea in theory and one that would not have implicated him. However despite the intuitive plan, it had ultimately failed and he was still left with the 'small' problem of the Gang either outing him or sorting him out when they found out the operation was still on.

Even though Bradford had threatened that he would only have a week to get things sorted, Drayson had somehow managed to avoid the catastrophe when the operation had been delayed for a couple of months, partly as a result of his challenge on budgets. The tactic although pointless in the end, had bought him time and allowed him to make out to Bradford that it had been called off. But it hadn't, and now he was panicking more than ever. He knew that the Gang could find out he was lying at any moment if they caught wind that they were being watched and followed, and even if they didn't, he would still be in for if they were arrested and charged.

Drayson got out of his car and walked into reception and began instantly flirting with the blonde receptionist. Despite being a little past it, and perhaps never actually having it, he would move from one female member of staff to another displacing borderline sexual harassment behaviour. And yet somehow no one had ever made a complaint or challenged his inappropriate actions.

After making a few tea stops around the different departments at HQ, Drayson decided to attend the Tactical Firearms Unit office. As usual he didn't have any real police work, or any work for that matter to do but somehow he still managed to look busy, a rare talent that only a handful of people ever masterfully pull off. He had always been relatively well received in the firearms unit because of his 'down with the lads' attitude, and although he would never see it that way, he was basically a firearms groupie, someone who wished that he had followed the same career path, if Bradford had let him.

He placed his warrant card against the card reader of the Firearms unit's back door and waited for the electronic lock to disengage. Drayson then walked through the door and along the white washed corridor, passing the locker rooms after checking there was no one inside to chat to.

Just as Drayson was about to reach the main office door he could hear a pre start of duty briefing taking place. Being the nosey and sly character he was, he stood just shy of the door and listened in for any juicy gossip about jobs or fellow officers that would not have been said in his presence. In Drayson's eyes, if he knew the current gossip, he could make out that he knew more about it – trying to assert his rank over theirs. For once though, he could hear a serious topic being discussed and listened in with an acute interest.

Around the long oval briefing table in the Firearms Unit's office, the members of Blue and Red teams were discussing Foster with a few colleagues from another firearms team.

"Have any of you heard from Foster recently?" a member of the A section armed response team asked.

"Nothing! I've tried calling him over and over again, but he's not interested. He believes it's our fault that he's been pensioned out and that somehow we're all conspiring against him. He's not a well man" PC Allen replied in an exasperated tone.

"It gets worse! I spoke to a district officer the other day, who had to detain him under the mental health act after he went banzai in the Dragon Inn in West Ording. Apparently he really lost it and was lucky not to be nicked for assault or a public order offence. When I heard I tried calling him but he wouldn't answer so I went to the Dragon and spoke with a bar maid there who Foster and I used to chat to. I asked her how he was doing and she said that he allegedly been taking cocaine in the toilets, drinking like a fish, talking to himself in the corner of the room and telling anyone that would listen that he's being watched and followed by people and can hear their voices. He doesn't sound well at all!" O'Keeffe said appearing deeply upset at what had happened to his friend.

Drayson stood there, captivated by what he was hearing. He had come across Foster many times before in the past due to his involvement with the unit a Chief Inspector Silver firearms Commander. He had heard on the grapevine that Foster had been struggling but had not been aware he had been medically retired because of a mental illness.

O'Keeffe continued by telling the other team that Foster had ended up getting himself barred from the Dragon as a result and was now drinking in the Cliffe Pub in Cliffe Road, West Ording which was a fairly rough town ten miles to the west of the City. He explained to everyone around the table that although they may have wanted to help Foster, he was best left alone until he was feeling better and approached them first. The combination of cocaine, alcohol and his mental health condition meant that he could be volatile if provoked or stressed, and especially if he saw someone from the unit that he believed had conspired against him. The consensus around the table was that he was best avoided for the moment.

The most bewildering part of the update to members of A

section was how the custody doctor who had assessed him after he was detained under the Mental Health Act, had blamed his aggravated state on drugs and alcohol and that once sober his mental health condition would be stable. He was after all supposedly on strong medication. The lack of foresight from the doctor had been ill advised at best. There was one thing that was for certain though; it wouldn't be long before Foster came to light once again.

Drayson didn't walk into the office and instead turned around and headed out of the door. He had an idea, a potentially fool proof one to rid himself of his problem with the Gang, but it wasn't going to be easy to pull off, even if he could find the bottle to go through with it. He slowly walked back up the stairs and out to the car park where after he climbed into the driver seat of his Command Focus, and took a moment to reflect on what he had just overheard. It could not have been just a coincidence that he stumbled on the conversation that the firearms officers were having, it had to have been fate; it was time to have a chat with someone who could help him with his plan.

The Briefing
Chapter Twelve

On Monday 22nd July 2013, Anaura walked into the briefing room on the fourth floor of the Central District Police Station with Richards, Valera and Usher. For the coming months at least, the Vice unit's huge work load would be well and truly at the back of their minds. They entered the large airy room that had a row on windows on the right side that provided an amazing unobstructed view across most of the City and the sea. After admiring the view for a second, something Anaura always did, he headed past the rows of officers from Surveillance, the technical support unit and the Intelligence Unit to the front of the room and took a seat next to Steiner who was looking a little excitable. He had not been exaggerating when he spoke about the budget, there was twenty plus officers in the room who would be doing nothing except chasing the Gang on a daily basis. Maybe this could be the operation that finally gets the Gang, Anaura thought to himself.

Richards, Valera and Usher sat down at the back of the room which made Anaura shake his head at them as they had fed him to the wolves by leaving him at the front of the room without their morale support. Anaura knew that to start with, a few of the SOCU surveillance officers would not be happy with a Vice Inspector running the show over one of their supervisors. At the back of the room there was no such problem as Valera and Usher were set upon by the male officers that surrounded them. In her element Valera set about using her feminine charms to sell Anaura to the officers to help his cause a little bit. As a result of the hot July weather she was wearing a light weight grey suit with a white blouse underneath; an open white blouse, which was open just enough so that when she leant forward or to the side, her lightly perspiring and tanned cleavage could be seen pushed up in her bra. Usher on the other hand, flirted but didn't go to the same lengths that Valera would to get attention. As the males officers flocked to seat nearby, Richards sat there smiling to himself as none of them had a chance, although this wouldn't stop them trying.

As the testosterone in the room reached fever pitch and was threatening to set off a sexually crazed riot in the heat, Steiner stood up and introduced himself, much to the disappointment of the male officers who were each convinced they were about to get Valera's number. Steiner directed the room's attention to the front where they was a smart board with a slide show presentation waiting to be viewed. The first slide displayed the name of the operation which each officer duly wrote in down in their pocket notebooks. As the slides continued the four faces of the Gang suddenly appeared on the screen creating a few nudges and comments from the around the room. Prior to the slide presentation they'd had no idea who they would be investigating due to operational security protocol dictating that no one should be made aware until after the briefing where the names of all the officers present would be recorded to prevent any possible leaks to the subjects. Things like that rarely happened, rarely, but not ever though, precautions had to be taken, even with police officers. With the slides passing on one by one, the operation became clearer to the officers, watch the Gang, hound them, attempt to break up their network, and lock them up for a very long and happy time.

Steiner finished the presentation and introduced Anaura who stood up to address the room, but not before Usher received his introduction with a round of applause and cheering which drew a stunned and shocked look from Steiner. Usher being Usher though, didn't care how the outburst looked to anyone else.

"How's everyone doing? Before we get down to business, I just wanted to say that I know some of you feel uncomfortable about me being in charge as opposed to one of your own, and I can understand that. But, as it stands I am running this job and I need all of us to be singing off the same hymn sheet alright? I know a lot about the drugs trade in the City from the roots up to the fruit, therefore you need me as much as I need you. So let's

86

try and get along and do a bloody good job on these dick heads!" Anaura said with a mix of warm smiles and serious expressions. If any of them weren't taken in by Anaura's presence at the front of the room, they soon would be by his personality, and failing that he would give them a few verbal slaps if necessary to enforce the matter. No matter how much someone resisted him, they would soon yield to him as a result of his friendly personality or his aversion to take shit from people. The open and honest approach that Anaura had employed during the introduction had appeared to have proven effective as he was greeted by open expressions and nods that indicated that the officers were thinking 'fair enough'.

"Ok, any questions?" Anaura asked.

"Where are we going to be working out of?" one of the surveillance officers enquired.

"We're taking over the ground floor of Shoreton Police Station. New blacked out secure doors have been fitted which only allow authorised people to enter, reception hours have also been really reduced to limit the amount members of the public coming in. Of course you guys and girls from Surveillance will be doing your usual and starting off from designated points; but if you're lucky, we might let you come pop in now and then for a spot of tea!"

Anaura's light hearted comment helped the SOCU officers warm up to him even more.

"Sir, will we be having firearms support?" Another officer asked.

"Not on a week to week basis, no. At this stage we will not be moving in on anyone, and generally speaking the Gang and their minions don't carry guns as standard, unless someone needs knocking off! However that being said, I have liaised with Inspector Balham of the Firearms Unit and he has agreed to providing a standby MAST team of plain clothed SFOs who will be ready to support any part of the operation if required" Anaura said. MAST firearms officers were plain clothed Specialist Firearms Officers who supported Surveillance Operations whenever there was a threat of a weapon or intelligence to suggest it. When the time came to apprehend the subject, the

MAST team would be the ones who would be steaming in on foot or in with an unmarked vehicle to take them out at gun point. Anaura waited for the next question.

"What's the overtime code sir?" An officer called out, resulting in him being verbally assailed by his colleagues. If there was one thing that would be asked at an operational briefing without fail, it would be what the overtime code was. And every time it was asked about, it always managed to piss off the command team no end. If there was overtime, the code to claim the extra pay would be provided, asking for it just made the enquirer sound like an idiot who wasn't really interested in the operation itself but was more concerned with how much money it could make them. It was hardly a valid question that would help with expanding the officers' awareness of how the operation would play out over the coming months. The question was, as it sounded, bloody unprofessional.

"I'm not even going to grace that with an answer! But for those of you who are a little more restrained with your questions about financial implications, the overtime code will be posted on a board in the operational suite." Anaura replied in an exasperated tone.

Anaura nodded at the officers and noticed Valera and Usher at the back of the room silently cheering him on by waving their arms about wildly. He gave them a pretend frown as he went to sit down again next to Steiner. He was going to have his work cut out keeping these two in check each day. Normally he only saw them a couple of times on a daily basis but now he was cringing at the thought of what these two partners in crime would get up to during the operation. Anaura inwardly laughed to himself as he realised that whatever they got up to, he would soon find out due to working closer with them on Op Spear and having a tighter leash on them. In front of them Richards repeatedly turned around to see what they were up to before spinning back around and attempting to contain his laughter at their antics. 'Oh God' Anaura thought to himself as he came to realise that Richards was in on the jokes as well. It looked like it was going to be a case of, if you can't beat them, join them.

Steiner thanked Anaura once again and retook charge of the closing stages of the briefing by directing the room's attention to a table where there was a large number of operational information packs for each of the officers which reiterated everything that had been explained during the briefing. Steiner knew full well that most coppers had the attention span of a gold fish when it came to long briefings, and by this stage of it, half of them would have to be reminded where they were and what day it was. Especially the ones who were imitating the nodding dogs you see in the back of cars, trying their damned hardest to remain awake. No matter he thought, they would get the job done when it counted; even if they were asleep. Steiner repeated a couple of vital points and told everyone in the room to get their 'house' in order in preparation of relocating to Shoreton District Police Station over the coming days.

"Oh and just in case it wasn't obvious enough, please don't bloody leave any of the Op information packs lying around. And please, please, please don't discuss this with anyone outside of this room that means other nosey command officers too. You have my permission to tell any of the superintendents or assistants chiefs; and even the Chief Constable to Fuck off if they try to find anything out about the operation! If they go mad, tell them that I ordered you to say that and that it's none of their business; that's a joke by the way before anyone considers being a smart arse at my expense. However all joking aside they shouldn't be asking, if they don't know, they don't need to know! Right, let's get moving then!" Steiner said with enthusiasm.

The newly appointed officers of Op Spear began pouring out of the room group by group with their obvious enthusiasm clear to see by everyone in the station. Whenever there was a big briefing on the fourth floor everyone that was inside the station would be desperate to learn what they were doing and who they were after. In fact Anaura himself had been in their shoes when he had been a probationer on the City's Neighbourhood Response teams, and would watch the specialist officers preparing for an operations with green envy too. From the very day he joined, Anaura wanted to be at the sharp end of policing, to catch the big boys. However after finishing his probation and enjoying getting stuck into emergency Grade 1 calls and investigations, he had lost some of the awe he possessed for the tactical specialists. When the time came to decide which route he wanted to take, Anaura had decided on being a detective as he was too noticeable for Surveillance, firearms wasn't his bag and he had been told by the Driver Trainer Unit instructors, that although he was a very quick driver, he lacked restraint and was too ragged to be an Advanced driver, so that was Traffic out of the equation as well! Investigations was the speciality where he belonged and besides the other units came with a lot of job losing risks, you only had to take a look at what had happened to the Firearms Unit the year before to understand that. Although Anaura would have loved the action and probably been good at tactical policing, he just wouldn't be able to stomach the proverbial hitting the fan when something could inevitably go wrong. No, he had seen enough firearms and traffic officers have their careers ruined or thrown out of the job for decisions that they only had milliseconds to make.

Anaura tapped Steiner on the shoulder and told him that he would catch up with him later before he joined Richards, Valera and Usher who were heading back to the Vice office to pack their stuff up.

"Awwwwww, this is a wicked job sir!" Usher blurted out the second they got back into the office.

"I know Naomi, just keep the excitement down, I don't want to make any of the team feel bad when they see that you and Jennifer were picked over them!" Anaura implored her.

"Sir, I've got a bit of a random question!" Valera said, causing the three others to look at her with shock. A serious question was hardly something you could expect from Valera on a regular basis.

"Can I take my chair with me? I sometimes get a sore bum after the gym and this one seems to be the only one that has a decent cushion." She asked with not a hint of sarcasm in her voice.

"Erm, yeah of course Jennifer! I'm sure...............we can have that arranged!?" Anaura replied with a confused expression as he tried to fathom out whether Valera was taking the mickey.

Richards and Usher looked at each other with smirks of disbelief and asked her whether she was actually suffering with piles before bursting out laughing. Valera faked a smile before replying that she didn't whilst shaking her head. It still was not clear whether she was telling the truth or winding them up or if she did actually have haemorrhoids. However for whatever reason, she wanted the seat, as strange as it may have sounded. Valera's normally cool exterior began to slip somewhat as she stood there, her olive cheeks turning crimson red with embarrassment which drew even more questions from Richards and Usher as to her real reasons.

"Leave her alone you two! Anyway, at nine am tomorrow we're shipping out to Shoreton, so spend the rest of the day finishing up here please" Anaura's defence of Valera's sore muscles; or piles, made her smile at him in a less flirtatious way for once.

Underneath it all Valera was not the man-eater she portrayed herself to be and had actually been distraught when her boyfriend of five years had dumped her for someone else a few years before. By the time she arrived on the Vice unit from CID two and half years previously, she had transformed from a conservative girl into a quasi-member of the Pussy cat dolls to hide her deep insecurities. As a result of his ability to read people like a book, Anaura knew this and empathised with her, despite playing along with her act. Valera was an incredibly attractive, intelligent and caring girl that most decent men would die for, she just needed to be herself and drop the compensatory overly confident act, or she would keep attracting the losers.

"Jennifer, can I have a moment?" Anaura requested, deciding that the embarrassment might have been a cue to have a friendly chat to clear the air before the operation started when they would be spending a lot more time together.

Valera followed Anaura into his office and he closed the door behind them as Usher and Richards joked that he had finally wilted and was going to give her one over his desk. He sat down in his chair and leant across his desk towards her. At first she tried to shake off the embarrassment of the piles comment and reignited her faux confident persona, but Anaura just tilted his head towards her with his eyebrows raised, inferring that he knew she was not as happy as she was making out. Valera sat there looking uncomfortable as she gave up on the act.

"How are things Jennifer, I mean really how? Are you ok?" Anaura enquired, his deep voice being softened to a degree.

At first Valera replied that she was fine with her normal sunny disposition, but her eyes were beginning to betray her as they started to become reddened. Anaura could see that she was trying her hardest to stop the tears from flowing. It wasn't a pleasant sight watching her grow more upset as the minutes passed, but he knew that it was something that finally needed to happen.

"Come on Jennifer, it's OK to let it out." He assured her.

In a totally uncharacteristic display of emotion, she began sobbing into her hands, prompting Anaura to get out of his chair and walk around his desk to where she was sat. He crouched down next to her so that his large stature was not casting an overbearing shadow over her and placed his arm around her shoulder. In many offices around the country this would have been seen as inappropriate, especially in today's world of sexual harassment cases, but Anaura didn't care, she was one of his and she needed a shoulder to cry on. He rubbed her shoulder as she continued to cry and asked her what was the matter and that the piles comment was just a joke and couldn't have upset her this much.

She stopped crying and composed herself as much as possible before telling Anaura that she had gone out with a guy who she really liked for a couple of drinks, it had been one of only a handful of dates she'd had over the past couple of years despite what she made out to everyone. The night before had been their third date and being the type of bloke he was, he had decided that the third date meant sex and had made strong advances towards her. When she explained that she was not going to sleep with him so soon, he reacted with anger and started yelling at her, stating that she was a tease who dressed and acted like a slag for attention. As if the insult wasn't harsh enough, he went on to

92

claim that he had only wanted her for a shag, and that no one in their right mind would be interested in having a relationship with someone like her who blatantly fancied herself.

Valera was crushed by his cruel comments, but it had made her realise how she wasn't being her true self and how she hadn't been since being hurt by her ex. Despite the realisation, it still had not stopped her from wearing yet another provocative outfit that day. Anaura remarked how the guy sounded like a complete dick and that she'd probably had a lucky escape. He then leant across his desk and grabbed a box of tissues.

"I've always known this was all an act Jennifer! The moron's wrong about you, trust me. I know this is going to sound harsh; but as long as you keep pretending to be someone else, someone cocky and flirty, the longer you're going to have to put up with dick heads like him. Come on, you're a great, lovely person and if I'm honest, if I was single I'd be chasing you all around the station; well, only if you were being yourself that is!" Anaura's warm hearted comments brought a smile to Valera through her tears.

Valera blew her nose and nodded to him with a smile of gratitude before telling him that she did require the chair due to a haemorrhoid she had and the pair of them burst into laughter. After a minute or so, she stopped laughing and apologised to Anaura for the way she could behave at times. Anaura being as laid back as he was, shook his head and brushed it off as if nothing had happened, telling her that it was just time to drop the act and start being herself. Valera articulated her concerns that everyone would think she was fake if she suddenly started acting and dressing different. Anaura replied with a wink and told her that he had it covered, his plan was that when she started wearing more conservative clothes, she would tell everyone that it was at his behest while they were attached to Op Spear and how he had finally given her a bollocking about her dress sense. Valera smiled from ear to ear as she thanked him.

"And anyway Jennifer, poor Ian's going to have a heart attack if you keep dressing like this! I assure you though, you'll get a lot more positive attention if you're just you. Right, new start from

93

tomorrow that's an order DC Valera!!" Anaura jested with her before saying that he would get her a coffee and her bag so she could sort her smeared make up out and compose herself. His kindness made Valera start crying with happiness.

"Pull yourself together you silly mare" He said in a playful tone before he left her in his office, closing the door behind him again.

As he grabbed her bag off his desk, acting DS Langford who had arrived whilst she was in the office with him, made a quip about the pair of them being in a locked office. Anaura pointed at him with a bouncing finger, which although light hearted, informed Langford it was time to shut up. A few minutes later he appeared from the kitchen with two coffees which drew jeering from the rest of the Vice team who took umbrage to him not making them one.

"You've got legs, make your own drinks" the bantering remark subsequently drawing more jeering and insults from the other detectives. Anaura shouted in response

"Is everything alright Peter?" Richards asked with concern.

"Never better mate!" Anaura replied with a wink and a raise of the coffee mugs.

"Nice bag sir, it's just your colour" DC Tom Payne, a youngish Vice detective shouted out at Anaura who was still carrying Valera's bag.

"Pipe down you! Or you'll be wearing it out on patrol for the rest of the day!" Anaura responded in a jovial manner, causing the other detectives to burst into laughter.

Anaura returned to his office and placed the coffee down in front of Valera and gave her a wink and a thumbs up. After ten minutes she sorted her makeup out, quickly downed her rapidly cooling coffee and thanked him again for his advice and understanding before taking a deep breath and leaving his office as if nothing had happened.

Anaura's phone started ringing.

"Hi Peter, how's your day going?" Laura's asked in her usual warm tone of voice.

"Hi sweetheart! Not too bad, just playing team Chaplain!

How's your day?" He replied.

"It's going well thanks. Chaplain, really, for who?" She replied in an inquisitively.

"Jennifer Valera! She's got man trouble and as a result she's finally opened up about her insecurities and said that she wants to make a fresh start."

"We knew that one was coming! Does that mean she's going to stop flirting with you now? Laura said.

"Who knows? We'll see if it lasts!" He replied

"So are you happy and all set and ready to go?"

"Hell yeah!!!! My dream investigation is about to start and most importantly; my team are all happy, it's going to be a good few months!" Commented Anaura.

"Things are really good!"

An 'Amazing' Opportunity
Chapter Thirteen

Parked in the darkness of Amelia Crescent, West Ording in his ill-gotten Mercedes, Drayson sat contemplating what he was about to do. There would be no going back if he did this; he had to be a hundred percent committed. The risks were inordinate, the result of his plan failing, unimaginable but desperate times called for desperate measures; and these were now seriously desperate times!

Drayson removed a gram of cocaine from the secret compartment he had made under his seat. He needed a 'hit' of the good white stuff before he did this, something to help focus him. He was jacked with adrenaline and fear, something which made him question whether what he was about to do was a sensible idea. The plan he had devised could go wrong from the outset, within seconds in fact, and what would happen if someone saw him there, he thought to himself, trying to think positively and he struggled battling with his doubts in his head.

SNIIIIIIFFF. Drayson snorted the gram of cocaine right up into his nostrils. Soon the drug would be working itself into his blood stream and leaving him with superior confidence and clarity of thought. After the sharpness of the powder dissipated, Drayson relaxed into his seat and turned up his Pink Floyd CD on his flash Mercedes car stereo system that was definitely not standard!

"FUCKING HAVE IT!" Drayson yelled out inside his car, slapping himself around the face a couple of times to help wake him up. He grabbed the woolly hat from the passenger seat and placed it on his head. It was hardly a disguise worthy of Peter Sellers, but it would suffice in the darkness. Drayson swung the driver's door open and let out two forced breaths before leaping out of the car, with the cocaine now beginning to work its wonderful and powerful magic. He pulled up his jacket collar to hide his face a little bit more, looking in both directions of the dark road with a sense of paranoia; cocaine had a habit of doing that! Although it could give you a huge high, the long list of negative side effects that came with using cocaine could really give you some huge lows too. It was a case of roll the dice and see what happens!

He walked out of the dark crescent and headed towards the place where his plan would either begin and save him or plummet him into darkness. As he walked up the road and past the Cobden and Jolly Brewers pubs on his left side, he gave a quick peek into the windows to see if who he needed might be in there; he wasn't. Feeling assured that his helper was where he should be, Drayson continued up Cliffe Road, past the parade of shops, looking down at the floor as he passed the queue of people outside the Fish and Chip shop.

The illuminated sign that stood proud above the entrance of a dilapidated and rough building that was located on the corner of Cliffe road and Neville road, told him he had reached his destination; The Cliffe public house. Drayson walked through the front doors and into the pub that even with the lights on, still managed to somehow appear dark and dingy, the smell of stale beer and smoke permeating the air after years of spillages and poor cleaning. It was a shit hole but it was perfect. As with every run down pub in the country, his entrance was greeted with stares from the tough regulars who were sat at the bar and playing the fruit machines in the background. He stared back at them and arrogantly walked up to the bar, totally indifferent to the local hard men who smelt like they used whiskey as cologne looking him up and down. As he pulled his nice Italian leather wallet out of his jeans pocket, he scanned the room for his target, and there he was!

Sat alone in a wooden booth in a corner of the dingy pub, was a broken, ghostly and dirty looking man staring into his pint of beer. Drayson's eyes lit up. He ordered two pints and walked over to the lone man.

"Anthony Foster! How are you son?" Drayson enquired in a

friendly tone of voice.

Foster went to jump out of his seat, his blood shot and lifeless eyes struggling to identify who was speaking to him. Although he began to feel a sense of confusion and panic that he might be seeing things, Foster slowly started to recall the stranger's face. Drayson sat down and asked him if he remembered him, after a minute of hard thinking, Foster nodded that he did. Drayson smiled at him and asked how he had been recently, not that he had the slightest interest, or that it was not blatantly obvious to him that Foster was far from OK. Whoever was sat in front of him now, it was not the Foster he had met on a number of occasions.

"Why are you here? What do you want?" Foster mumbled.

Drayson knowing full well that he was dealing with a volatile individual dived right in and told Foster that he believed his retirement had been a travesty and that he never accepted that the organisation's claims that he was mentally ill. Foster replied that it was nice someone saw it that way but reminded him that he was the only one, the doctors, the job, his friends, all believed it and it seemed as though they were the ones that mattered. Drayson saw his opportunity.

"Anthony, just because a lot of people have the same opinion, doesn't mean they're right. Sometimes when things go wrong like they did on Op Barrier, they need someone to blame for it to make themselves look better. You know how corrupt some of the bastards in command are! I tried to fight your corner, but the Chief said there was too much negative press surrounding you and that he had no choice. It's wrong, just plain wrong what they did to you son!" Drayson remarked.

Shocked, Foster nodded back at him in amazement and told Drayson that all he ever wanted was to be a copper and that they had conspired to take that away from them, he hated them for ruining his life. Drayson shook his head in sympathy and asked Foster if he was taking his medication. Foster replied that there was no way he was going to take the medication that should not have been prescribed to him anyway. Drayson whole heartedly agreed with Foster that he shouldn't be taking the medication and cited that all the medicine did was to turn people into submissive zombies, especially people like Foster, who didn't really need it. Foster smiled at Drayson who appeared as though he understood what the hell he was going through.

"Have you been taking anything else Anthony? I mean I could understand it if you had, but................." Drayson nosily enquired.

"That's really none of your business" Foster snapped.

"OK, OK Anthony. It's just that, well, I've got a proposal for you, something that could change your life but I need to know; actually forget it. I think I may have made a mistake coming here tonight, I apologise, forget I even came here, look after yourself mate" Drayson bluffed as he began to stand up to leave, something which he had no intention of doing.

"Wait a minute! I've been taking a bit of cocaine, only a little bit though. Why do you want to know and what do you mean something that can change my life?" Foster said, urging him to stay.

Drayson sat down again, trying to prevent the smug feeling he had from affecting the serious expression that he had on his face. He looked around before telling Foster that he had to know exactly what he had been taking and whether it affected his health because if it did, he may have had to reconsider his position. Foster replied that he had only taken cocaine and marijuana and that neither affected his health but they did help him think more clearly, although lately he had only been drinking because of finances.

After only a few months of being retired, Foster had spent most of the sixty thousand pound lump sum he had received, and the monthly pension that he had could only buy so many narcotics. Foster stopped talking about his personal life and asked Drayson again how he was going to change his life and why he wanted to know about his drug use, after all, he was no longer answerable as a police officer.

"OK Anthony, it's like this, I've got a job for you! However if you want it, you've got to get off the alcohol and as for the cocaine, well, I'm not sure, mmmmm, maybe it could help you, I don't know!? I suppose I can live with the cocaine for the moment but everything else has to stop. Can I trust you Anthony?" Drayson said in a serious tone. In reality he didn't give a damn about the cocaine as it would possibly help keep a leash on him, however the alcohol was a problem, it would make him slow, make him sloppy.

"Sure, sure, what's the job, what's the job? Am I going to be reinstated? I would do anything to be a copper again! Hang on, wait a minute! There's no way the Chief would ever allow me back in the Job or to be used for police work, so what's it all about?" Foster asked with suspicion.

"All in good time Anthony, all in good time. I know it sounds far-fetched but the Chief feels absolutely terrible about what happened to you and wants to make amends without anyone knowing the details! He also acknowledges that there really is no one else capable of pulling this job off. However if you have better things to do, then I'll understand!"

Foster desperately and repeatedly assured Drayson that he was very interested, his depressed mental state combined with the alcohol meant that he was unable to think with logic and question what was being said to him on a deeper level.

"OK Anthony, I can see that the Chief was right about you being the right man! In that case I want you to meet me at twelve am, in three days on the 26ᵗʰ, at the car park of West Ording forest. You'll get briefed then! This is strictly between us, and I mean strictly! This is an amazing opportunity for you Anthony, but if you can't handle it like a professional, I'll have to hand it to someone who is more capable. I need you to understand that!" Drayson said, expertly manipulating and influencing him.

Foster acknowledged that he fully understood and that he knew the secluded car park well. He also agreed to get off the alcohol and cocaine right away. Drayson responded with a wink, finished his pint and stood up to leave.

"Oh and by the way Anthony; have a bloody wash and shave, you look like crap, Constable!" Drayson ordered him. The use of Foster's former title of Constable made his face light up with happiness.

Drayson left Foster who was now rushing to gather up his

things together. As he walked out of the pub, not one person looked around at him, it was clear that his entrance had been more interesting than his departure which was a positive, as it affirmed that no one had heard, or was interested in, what he had been saying to Foster. He smiled to himself, maybe things were brightening up after all; he had found that torch he needed!

Anaura stood in the doorway of his new office in Shoreton District Police Station, nursing a cup of black coffee. The nineteen sixties style station was tucked away just a minutes' walk from Shoreton High Street, and with its discreet car park and lack of people coming and going, it was perfect location for the Op Spear headquarters. The added bonus for Anaura was that it close to his home in Bramberly, a village 6 miles out of the City. After taking a sip of his coffee, he looked at his Storm watch, it was six twenty in the morning, and as usual he was the first in and would inevitably be the last out, although he promised himself that after this job, he would be getting home on time for the remainder of his career. He continued to sip the black coffee, savouring its rich taste and waiting for the caffeine to help alleviate the tired and fuzzy head he was suffering from. Maybe it was time to reconsider his early starts too he thought to himself.

It was the first day in the office and most of his stuff was yet to be moved in, which meant that there was not a huge amount to do so he sat down to begin reading a paper he had brought with him. Within three minutes of opening the first page, he heard the main office door open. Instead of jumping up to greet whoever had arrived, he chose to finish the page he was on as he knew he wouldn't get another chance once everyone started arriving.

All of a sudden his concentration was abruptly interrupted by the loud sound of an industrial hoover being switched on. Anaura leapt up, worrying that he had left the office door open and whether there was any restricted intelligence up on the walls yet that the cleaner would see. He popped his head out of his office and said morning to the cleaner, who just smiled back and then continued with his work as if there was nothing unusual. Surprised at the cleaner's lack of explanation for being in a secure office, Anaura asked him how he had gained access to the office to which the cleaner replied that he had done it the same way he had for the past two years; he pushed the door open.

"Oh yeah, of course, sorry I'm being stupid" Anaura said, realising that the cleaner had obviously not been informed. However, what it did mean though, was that the Op Spear office security measures were about as useful as a chocolate fire-guard!

After the cleaner had finished up his work and left, Anaura walked out of the office and closed the door. He went to use his pass on the card reader but paused and decided to give it a push without it; the door opened. On his arrival at the office Anaura had placed his pass up to the door, the same way he had done at other stations around the Force and hadn't checked to see if the door was open first, and why would he have, it was meant to have been a secure unit, he had therefore been unaware that it had not been working. Anaura stormed over to his office and picked up the phone, quickly dialling Steiner's mobile number. Steiner had barely answered before he was met by an onslaught of expletives and ranting from an angry Anaura who remarked that if a bloody cleaner could get into the office, then anyone could. Struggling to deal with the sudden onslaught that boomed out of his phone, Steiner calmed him down and reminded him that they were only just moving into the office and that the locks were going to be activated that day. Anaura continued moaning that the locks should have been in place prior to their arrival and not during it. Knowing that Anaura had a keen eye for detail to the point of obsession at times, Steiner apologised and assured him that he would have it sorted without a delay despite feeling that his reaction was a bit over the top.

As Anaura finished the call with Steiner and hung up, PCs Stephen Taggart and Mark Crane from the Intelligence Unit walked in and properly introduced themselves to him. Anaura shook their hands and told them that he had seen them around the station which pleased the officers as they had said hello to him on a number of occasions and did not know whether he would remember them. This was typical of him, and a lot of coppers, he somehow managed to know everybody without knowing anyone!?

This was the result of seeing people in corridors and in refreshment rooms and exchanging pleasantries without ever stopping to talk to them properly or asking their names. It was a police thing! They were all part of the same huge family, and like huge families, distant cousins twice removed only seemed to know each other by face.

Anaura instructed Taggart and Crane to find themselves a desk to move their stuff into. Like EasyJet, he didn't like the idea of specifying or dictating where people sat, they were after all adults and who were going to be on the same team so it didn't matter where they sat. As the two officers made themselves at home, Anaura went off to the kitchen to make a coffee for them and another himself. On his return he saw that the office had become a hive of activity as a number of the other officers fought over the best desk places; the furthest away from his watchful eye. Anaura had barely crossed the threshold when they all looked up and saw the hot drinks in his hands. 'Shit', he thought to himself, he was going to have to make a lot of drinks unless he played arrogant and just walked into his office without saying a word.

"Ah fantastic Peter, you're making the drinks for everyone" Richards said with a smug look on his face, knowing full well that he had just stitched Anaura up with tea making duties.

"Bloody hell Ian!" Anaura huffed back at him, as the rest of the room looked on at him, hoping that he would save them the job of making their own morning drinks.

"Right! Where's the bloody tea trays then?" Anaura asked with playful frustration.

"In the kitchen and under the sink sir. I used to work here!" PC Sarah Williams, a twenty two year old, short and curvy brunette from the Intelligence Unit said in a sheepish voice.

Anaura glared at her, which made the young female officer shrink in her seat before he gave her one of his trademark smiles, letting her know he was just teasing her. Usher, who had arrived a few minutes beforehand, began laughing at his probationer-like tea making duties. In the Job every probationer, or a new recruit to a unit, would be tasked with making tea for everyone in the team before each briefing; and it had definitely been a while since he had been on taking making duties for the whole team.

"I'm glad you find it funny Naomi! Because you're going to bloody help me! Get a pen and paper and start taking orders!" Anaura remarked with satisfaction.

Usher stooped her shoulders and said "Ahhh man" at the same time as pulling an immature expression before setting off around the room to take orders from everyone.

"Oh and Ian; you'd better go to shop around the corner and buy a supply of tea bags, coffee and milk, I don't think there's enough left for this round. It's the least you can do for stitching me up. Go on chop, chop!" Anaura said, exacting his revenge on Richards for dropping him in it.

With everyone holding a hot drink in their hand. Anaura stood up in the centre of the room and re-introduced himself in a less formal way than at the briefing day before. The team that ranged from twelve surveillance officers in two teams being led by PS Adrian King and Simon Chalmers, to four detectives and four intelligence officers who could utilise specialist surveillance equipment, were now all present in the office awaiting Anaura's informal brief and the official start of Op Spear.

Anaura began explaining to the team that although the operation was of extremely high importance and required a high level of professionalism to be demonstrated, under no circumstances were any of them to refuse having fun as well. The last part of his sentence had clearly been unexpected and brought big smiles to all the faces in the room. He continued on, reminding them all that this was potentially a once in a life time type job and that they may never be involved in such a big case again, it was therefore imperative that they enjoyed it by working hard and playing hard. If there had been any officers left who still weren't sold on Anaura, they were now. He finished up by informing them all that they would be starting the next day at a slow and measured pace as an operation like this one, had to be taken slowly and measured to begin with. It was a day to settle themselves into the office and read up on all the available information to hand.

"Let's do it!" Anaura said, clapping his hands twice with

enthusiasm as he walked off towards his office before he grabbed Richards in a headlock and dragged him along with him, rubbing his knuckles over his head in an immature manner.

"Ahhh! You bastard Peter, I've just done my hair!" Richards exclaimed as he and Anaura sat down at their joint desks that faced one another inside the supervisor's office. Anaura replied with a wink before they were soon joined by the two surveillance Sergeants, King and Chalmers who had come in to start planning for the first week of the operation whilst outside the office the newly introduced members of the team were enjoying getting properly acquainted with each other and working through the intelligence systems. Anaura and the three Sergeants discussed with each other at length what the best angle of attack to start from was. Although the end decisions rested with Anaura, he knew that the three men were highly experienced and their input was extremely important. With hours and hours of planning ahead, he would need their help.

After a total of 20 hours of planning spread over three days, they had finally finished and took a well deserved break. The tactical phase would begin the following Monday, three days later. Although there had already been a huge amount of planning carried out prior to the official briefing, the actual process of putting feet on the ground required a little bit more on top due to the number of the subjects and choosing who was the most appropriate watch first.

With the first phase of the Surveillance operation agreed on, Anaura and Richards would tap the intelligence guys for information they had on any relationships the Gang had past or present to see if the two of them along with Valera and Usher could arrest to start placing a strangle hold on their grass roots dealing activities. Strangle the roots, kill the fruit!

Anaura knew only too well that this was not going to be an easy task. For the detectives it would take a lot of cool thinking and actions to make sure that the Gang didn't become too suspicious when their dealers began getting nabbed one after the other. Therefore they would have to tread carefully and take their time whenever they chose or moved in on a mid-level dealer and questioned them about whether they had links to Bradford et al. All easier said than done! Outside of that, it was their job to compile all of the evidence and build a solid case; not all glamour and Hollywood! It was a different story for the two SOCU surveillance teams who would track down their target and then play an exciting game of cat and mouse with them using a wide range of vehicle and foot tactics to follow them covertly; hardly boring work. It was the same for the intelligence officers who would split their time between researching intelligence on the Force's computers and setting up and staffing up Observation Posts whenever the Surveillance teams could establish where a meeting was taking place. It all made the detectives work sound boring in addition to being difficult.

After a lot deliberation it was decided, their first target would be Paul Cooper. The following Monday the Surveillance teams would start 'life-styling' him. Life styling was a Surveillance term tactic that was employed to monitor a subjects daily movements to learn their routine in order to follow them effectively and learn where they frequented. It was specialist work that would firmly place them on the front foot if it was successful.

During their discussions, Chalmers and Richards had suggested that they watch the big shot, Ryan Bradford first. However Anaura disagreed, citing that although going after the snake's head first could be a very high reward quick time game, if it went wrong they would be left with nothing, the job would be literally dead in the water. It was a sensible plan as Bradford was one of the worst type of criminals, one who could sense that a surveillance team were on him. He had proven this on more than one occasion when they had followed him in the past, when all of a sudden and out of nowhere, he would do something unexpected, to allow him to see if anyone in the area reacted or paid too much attention to his actions. On one such occasion when he was driving on the motorway, he abruptly pulled off the road to head into the City, only to change course and head back onto the dual carriageway, hoping that he would see Surveillance cars struggling to catch up with him. However the Surveillance officers were a group of highly specialist professionals who wouldn't have been caught out by such a ploy. One thing was for sure though, and that was that Bradford was a very tricky customer.

Bradford may have been like a Fox, but the other three were quite the opposite. They could have been followed every day of the week and not been aware of it and apart from shooting a few paranoid glances around now and then, they weren't as switched on as Bradford to think of ingenious counter surveillance moves.

With the Surveillance Sergeants taking care of their own teams briefings, Anaura requested that Intel officers and Vice detectives join him in the briefing room that adjoined the main office. Inside the room Anaura explained what the first week would look like, and that it would start from the following Monday. He informed PC's Crane and Taggart that they would be working with Surveillance as their Intel support while PC's Williams and Streeting would be assisting the four detectives with their workload.

Anaura turned to his three detectives and told them that they were going to start sifting through all of the available drug related intelligence before establishing a low level dealer to nick and pump for information. The plan was relatively simple but would be highly effective if it was successful. Once they had identified a subject with enough dirt on them, the detectives would carry out a mini investigation to ascertain whether there was enough evidence to perform a drugs raid, or warrant, at the dealers home address utilising the specialist skills of the City's Special Support Team who were a unit of officers trained in riot policing and unarmed raids. If the raid was successful and drugs were found, which was likely, the drug dealer would be facing a prison sentence which could be potentially shortened if, say, they were to assist officers with a larger and ongoing investigation; like Op Spear for instance. Leverage in this game was everything!

Valera and Usher whispered to each other and then looked at Anauara, their disappointed expressions were hard to miss. In their minds, the two detectives had envisioned going after the mid-level dealers from the outset and not the little scum bags who they had to endure at times on Vice.

"What's up girls?" Richards enquired.

"Boss, I thought this Op was going to be exciting! This is the crap stuff that we try to get rid of back at Vice" Usher replied.

"You're right! However if we get the right scum bag who works for one of the Gang's mid-level dealers, then we'll be in there if we can make him grass! If we nick a mid-level guy without leverage, they'll keep their mouth shut and we'll be nowhere" Richards insisted.

The two detectives sheepishly nodded back at him, realising that they should have known better than to doubt Anaura's methods, even if they did seem a little boring.

"Trust me you two. All we need to do is find a Gang related little shit and bust him until he sings who his supplier is. It will be fun!" Anaura said with a smile. He then stood up and enthusiastically said "Let's have it!" to help motivate them.

As the five officers left the briefing room to return to their desks, Anaura, in the essence of team morale building, offered to play the duties tea boy by making a round of drinks again. The officers glanced back at him with a grin. Richards stood up and offered to help Anaura, he had paid for the drink makings out of his own pocket, and with Anaura's lack of decent tea making skills, he didn't want the tea bags being wasted making a crap cuppa. The two detectives and Intel officers sat down together and began working through the intelligence relating to the small time dealers as Anaura and Richards left the room. The door had barely closed behind them before Anaura paused and put his left hand up to his head as if he had done something wrong.

"Ian, have you got your pass?"

"No, I thought you would've, especially after the rants you've been having about the card reader and everyone leaving the doors open or their passes on the desks!" Richards said with a smug grin.

"Great, I'm going to get grief from Usher on this one. I told her off about leaving the door open. And when she said that she was only getting a glass of water and would have been back within seconds, I had a go at her, telling her that it was lazy to leave her pass behind and then expect someone to open it for her!" Anaura said.

Anaura knocked on the office door, moments later Valera opened it with a confused expression as to why they had returned so quickly.

"Errrr, You've forgotten your bloody pass haven't you!? I can't believe it, after all the grief you dished out to me, you've gone and done the exact same thing!" Usher called out.

"Forgetting, is not the same as not bothering to take it at all!" He replied.

Usher simply smirked at him with satisfaction. There was nothing better than seeing your boss make the same mistake he had hauled you over the coals for only a few hours earlier. Anaura picked up his pass off his desk and waved it at Usher before he left the room for the tea making duties, laughing to himself. So far he had been having a great time with his team; but the real hard work was yet to come!

A Devilish Offer
Chapter Fifteen

Foster pulled into the West Ording Forest's car park that was
located just off the East bound carriageway of the motorway
before it entered the northern district of West Ording. Due to
falling on hard times, he no longer had his pride and joy, the
Lotus Elise. That had been sold shortly after his retirement to pay
for a large amount of cocaine and prostitutes, neither of which
lasted very long. Now he was driving a clapped out Vauxhall
Vectra that somehow defied the laws of physics when it passed
its MOT test. Regardless of whether his car was road worthy or
not, Foster was most certainly not and should not have been
driving after he stopped taking his medication and started on the
drink.

Foster stopped his car at the end of the pitch black car park.
Ahead of him all he could see was a never ending darkness
through the thick forest, it was a very eerie place, even for
someone like Foster. Ording forest was infamous for alleged
Witch craft, UFO sightings, ghosts and most disturbing of all;
Devil worship. It was a perfect choice for the likes of Drayson to
carry out his devious and sinful plans.

After ten minutes of waiting, Foster began to doubt whether
Drayson was going to show and began feeling a deep sense of
anxiety as the darkness of the forest started to play tricks on his
eyes. Other than his mental illness, what made the anxiety worse
was that some kids, or devil worshippers, had hung wooden dolls,
similar to ones in the film the Blair Witch Project, from the trees.
Just as he was about to drive off, Foster suddenly saw a torch
light breaking through the darkness of the thick trees to his left
just out of the coverage of his headlights; it was Drayson. Foster
switched off his engine and climbed out of his car to approach the
silhouette of the man in front of him.

"I'm glad you turned up Anthony. Sorry I'm running a bit late. How are you doing?" Drayon said as he switched his torch off and leant on the shovel that was in his left hand.

"Fine, although I was close to leaving Sir, it's a bit spooky round here isn't it?" Foster responded.

"Yeah it is! But it's perfect for what we're going to discuss tonight. Oh, by the way mate, call me Rob." he replied in a friendly manner that was less than genuine.

"So what's the score then?" Foster enquired with excitement and impatience.

Drayson smiled, his sly features only just visible in the moonlight that was breaking through the forest canopy.

"The Chief is going to give you an opportunity, a second chance, one that some could only dream of! It's a chance to get back into the Job with a clean slate. He and I want you for an operation, an extremely dangerous one, life or death stuff!" Drayson said with a sense of suspense and mystery in his voice.

"I'm in! Whatever it is, I'm in!" Foster blurted out with sheer excitement as if the offer might be retracted if he didn't answer instantly.

"But you don't know what the job is yet?" Drayson said in a concerned tone whilst screaming inside with joy at how Foster was there for the taking. With the power of his rank and Fosters love of being a copper plus his current mental state, he was certain that he would be able to influence him into playing his little game.

"OK Anthony; this is a STRICTLY off the record job, undercover type work. Usually we would call in the Special Forces for this sort of thing, but, with your background and experience there was no one who was more suitable!"

"I'm definitely the man for the job!" Foster said trying to display his utter commitment in the hope that Drayson would not decide to choose someone else; despite the fact that there were no other candidates.

Drayson silently nodded at him, before scanning his surroundings with suspicion. He took in a deep breath, preparing himself for the most dangerous, corrupt but highly necessary words that were about to leave his lips.

"We want you to take out each and every member of the Gang! You do know who I'm talking about don't you?"

Fosters facial expression changed to one of shock, causing Drayson to panic at the prospect that Foster might refuse. With the butterflies pounding away in his stomach, Drayson started to raise the shovel in his left hand with a sense of pure fear. If Foster tried anything or declined, he would have to hit him across his skull with all his strength to prevent him from ever repeating what had just been said to him. Foster acknowledged that he knew of them before asking Drayson if he meant what he thought he meant by taking them out, as in KILL THEM! Drayson pulled a serious expression before reeling off a story that had been rehearsed a hundred times over since their meeting in the pub. He informed Foster how the Gang's behaviour and activities were getting out of control and that they had started to become involved in child molestation and exploitation, women beating and were now suspected of funding Irish republican terrorism. It was of course all fictitious, but it had the required effect. Fosters breathing became deep and forced as the hatred boiled up inside him. Drayson only needed to mention crimes against children and women for him to become angry, but when he added terrorism to the mix, Foster would be incensed.

"They need stopping Anthony! We can't get them the normal way. They're just too powerful and well connected. With your help, we can finally rid the City of these deranged bastards, no failed cases, no corrupt judges or juries, and more importantly, no future release after half a sentence served for good behaviour. We need you mate, it has to be you, you're the only who could get the job done!" He pleaded with Foster.

Foster's thoughts raced with confusion and suspicion as he battled with doubts about whether what Drayson was saying could be real. Surely this sort of thing couldn't happen within the Police Service, he thought.

"I know this is a total mine field Anthony so I would fully understand if you were NOT up to it; maybe no copper is!? It would take an incredibly brave man to undertake such an operation!" Drayson said in a manipulative way.

When Foster heard that Drayson had doubts about his suitability, it severely angered him and for a moment he felt like going for him, but instead, he just snapped at him.

"OF COURSE I'M UP FOR IT! WHY WOULDN'T I BE? I just can't believe that this sort of thing goes on, why haven't I heard anything about it before?!".

"Alright Anthony, I just had to be sure that's all, this ain't a game mate! Believe me, on a few rare occasions this shit does happen, but only when the Force has repeatedly failed to lock the target up! Think about it, if you had heard about these sort of operations before, they wouldn't have been that secret would they?! Sometimes in order to protect the public, the good people, we have to take out the bad people by committing a little evil ourselves, unfortunately it's the only way to deal with these horrible bastards!"

Sensing that Foster was almost his but still suffering with a little doubt, Drayson began telling him a few spurious stories about how similar operations had happened in the past and how they had been hidden from everyone but the highest ranks of the service and government. He continued explaining that no one liked doing it, but when certain criminals had become too powerful, the Police Service were really left with no other option. To hype Foster up even more, he remarked that if Mahood had not popped up on the radar when he did, they would have had him and Jennings neutralised to prevent mass murder! What better and more righteous reason could there be than protecting the innocent from deranged murderers! Foster slowly nodded in acknowledgement. Drayson had him, hook, line and sinker!

"What happens if I get caught, I mean, I would face murder charges wouldn't I?" Foster enquired.

"Well for starters, you're well trained and good enough not to get caught, and secondly all your DNA and fingerprints have been wiped from our records. And even if you did get caught, which you won't, this Op goes right to the top, the PM! Do you think he wants you to blab about this shit if you get sent down? Trust me you'd be looked after and out of the country quick

114

time!" Drayson insisted.

"I guess not, I still can't believe this stuff happens, it's like........."

"MI6, James Bond stuff, I know, it pretty much is! But that's why it takes a certain calibre of person to pull it off. We need an officer who has fired a shot before or even killed a man to ensure that they wouldn't clam up at the vital moment! We need them to have had experience of dealing with highly pressured situations and to be professional enough not to go around telling anyone about the job, not now, not ever. That type of officer is you Anthony! I need you, now, to wholly commit yourself to this Operation. If not you can go back to that shitty pub and drink your life away with everyone thinking you're crazy!" Drayson said with perfect execution, demonstrating why he had such a success with his influence on people.

Foster did not say a word and just stood there contemplating his opportunity, it was obvious that he had believed every single word. The sad truth was that the Anthony Foster of old, despite being super obedient to anyone of rank, would not have bought this story. But he wasn't the old Foster, he was now an extremely vulnerable and exploitable person that would do anything to get his much loved career back and prove to everyone once and for all that they had been wrong about him.

"That's my boy! I always knew you were a special sort of officer. I mean you always stood out over your colleagues on the firearms unit, even the ones with the Special Forces backgrounds, what's their names? Simpson and O'Keeffe!? Well there will be no doubt who's the best when you return after this!"

Foster felt a deep sense of pride washing over him. This Op was a blessing, a chance to show those snakes on the firearms unit that he was better than them and not a lunatic. He took a few seconds to fantasise about the moment when he would walk back into the Unit's office and tell them who he thought they really were......................back stabbing bastards who used him as a scapegoat to protect themselves!

Drayson reminded Foster again that under no circumstances was he to talk to anyone but him about the operation, even the

Chief, who would instantaneously pull the plug if Foster even looked at him. It had to be that secretive. Foster replied that he understood a hundred percent. He looked hard at Foster one more time before giving him a thumbs up and asking him to follow him. Fifty meters into the forest Drayson stopped and shone his light onto a tree where a large X had been carved into the bark. He then explained that about two foot under the mud below the X, an operational plan and all the necessary equipment to carry out the job were buried. He ordered Foster to never carry the op plan around with him and to bury it each time after he referred to it. He then handed him two small keys, one that would unlock the box and another for the padlock of a gate and stated that he would be briefed on it later. Just as Foster was about to take ownership of the keys, Drayson paused and said "Protect these with your life Anthony!".

"Right, I guess I'll see you on the other side as they say. When this is all over, you'll be a copper again Anthony!! Although I must tell you that I doubt I would be able to get you back on the Firearms unit!" Drayson said as he walked Foster back to his car.

"I don't care, I would work anywhere if I was a copper again! Will this be the last time I see you until the job's done then?" Foster enquired.

"I'm afraid so son. It has to be that way. All the information that you need is buried in that box. Do you think MI6 agents report back to HQ all the time; they don't! It's the only way to make sure the job gets done clean and no one gets suspicious, remember you're undercover. Oh, and by the way, if there are any times and dates within that pack, they must be adhered to by the second, a lot of work has been put into this plan by the Government's National Crime Agency!"

"Sure, sure. I'll see you soon then Rob. When do you want me to start?" Foster said.

Drayson patted him on the shoulder in a sickening fatherly manner and told him that he was to return the following night to read the operational pack and that the job would start in three weeks. He commented how Foster might need to invest in a shovel too. Before Drayson walked off, he told Foster that it was good to see him looking clean and shaven again and urged him to get some beauty sleep as most of the operations would be conducted at night. Foster climbed into his car and started the engine. As he reversed he was able to see Drayson's face properly for the first time that evening in the headlights, his face pulling a sneering Janus-faced expression that Foster took for him being blinded by the headlights; he wasn't! As Foster drove off Drayson retreated to the darkness of the forest with his torch.

Less than a mile down the road, Foster began to have a panic attack at the realisation of what he had just agreed to, was it real or just in his head and could Drayson really be trusted. He swung his car into a lay-by.

SLAP. Foster smashed himself across the face, shouting at himself to 'man up'. This was his only lifeline, his only chance of getting back into the City Police Force, of being someone important again; he couldn't throw it away. Foster collected himself only for the panic set in once again.

SLAP, SLAP, SLAP. Foster repeatedly hit himself across the face, chastising himself for being a coward and a loser. The torn emotions and thoughts continued raging for another five minutes until he burst into tears.

"Pull yourself together Anthony, you pathetic little cry baby! We'll never get what we want if you're always crying like a scared little bitch!!Listen, they don't want you, they despise you, but if you kill for them, they will love you!" Foster acknowledged the voice that came from the back seat, pulled himself together and drove off.

A couple of miles away on the outskirts of the forest, Drayson climbed back into his AMG Mercedes, swearing out loud in satisfaction at how he had managed to get his foot-well carpets covered in mud. Oh well, another trip to the car wash, he thought to himself. He switched the stereo on to listen to his Pink Floyd album and then adjusted his rear view mirror towards him so that he could reverse off the driveway of the old manor house that was rumoured to have been used for Devil worship and thus it attracted the nickname of 'the Devils house'. As the mirror moved into position, Drayson a caught a glimpse of himself and smiled before he looked through the smashed window of 'the Devil's house' and back into the mirror once more.

"The Devil!? The Devil ain't shit compared to me!" He said with a sinister arrogance and huff as he pulled off the driveway and onto the dirt track.

As the interior light faded and the darkness of the night crept into the cabin, Drayson put the car into first gear and drove away from the Devil's house that was shrouded in a creepy red glow from the car's bright rear lights. It could not have been a more appropriate colour!

A Link In The Chain
Chapter Sixteen

"Carl Nash, nineteen years old and rumoured to be part of a chain of dealers that ends up being linked to the Gang. He lives in Charlton Road, Molehill District, and guess what boss? A PC on response recently submitted an intelligence form stating that a drug user had seen a decent quantity of cocaine at the address" Streeting said with satisfaction.

"Yes!!" Anaura slapped the back of his hand on the file he was holding and called the other detectives and PC Sarah Williams to quickly join them.

"Ian may have found us a way in!" he said as the four officers took seats around the computer terminal.

Carl Nash was a low level drug dealer, nothing spectacular, but he was rumoured to have tenuous links to the Gang, and that was all they needed at this stage, even if it was rumours or idle gossip. In addition to being a dealer, Nash was a perpetual user himself and probably snorted and injected more than he actually sold. He was your usual petty criminal scum bag, unwashed, dirty, and malnourished. With a record as long as your arm, but that still didn't stop him from committing crime, he was far too much of a cretin for that.

Nash's address was located in a rough estate in the east of the City, a conveniently short trip from the station. Anaura's team may have known most of the mid-level dealers but there were always the baby drug dealers who slipped through the net as they had never been on their radar and had been seen more as a nuisance that was a regular CID problem and not Vice's. The difficult thing with the mid-level players was that they were too clever to let slip who they worked for, hence hardly any of them could be linked to the Gang. However the low-level ones were, fortunately, not as smart!

Anaura smiled at the others, who reciprocated. They had found a potential source, someone weak enough to influence and exploit to help them get what they wanted; a mid to high level dealer that was possibly employed by the Gang. He jumped up and ran to his office, it was time to put a call into Steiner who would help get them a drugs warrant authorised by a Magistrate. As he picked up the phone he shouted over to Valera to contact the Special Support Team governor as he wanted them to be ready for when the Warrant was signed off. Valera quickly picked up the phone and dialled the Central District extension number for the unit.

Steiner answered his phone after less than three rings and asked Anaura what he was up to which he replied that may have found their man and needed a Warrant asap. Steiner's excitement was easily audible from the other end of the line as he assured Anaura that he would arrange one as fast as he possibly could and finished by thanking him for the team's good work. Anaura put down the phone and clenched his fist with satisfaction, the detective's involvement was finally about to commence after a week and a half of listening (with jealousy) to Surveillance life styling Cooper on the radio.

Brimming with enthusiasm, Anaura poked his head out of the supervisor's office and winked at Richards before asking Valera how she had got on with the SST. Valera replied that the units Inspector had said that team 3 were available, apart from regular duties, for the following two weeks. Anaura continued to raise his clenched fist, the wait had been killing him and although it was still only the start of things, it was a far better position than they had been a week ago.

That evening Anaura got home on time. Until the warrant was signed off there wouldn't be any point in spending hours researching everything about Nash in case the Warrant was refused. For once he had managed to get back early enough to play with the kids and put them to bed. Over a curry, he told Laura about his day and how after a boring week or so, which she knew about only too well because of his moaning, the team had made a breakthrough. Laura was pleased and asked him what they would be doing now things had got moving. He replied that

120

they just needed a Warrant sorting before they could carry out an early morning raid on his address with SST.

Laura's face dropped with an expression of worry. Anuara asked her why she looked so concerned, to which she replied that she didn't like the idea of him being involved in a raid, especially after what had happened to Marriot and the other firearms officers at the end of the year before. He quickly interrupted her and began to explain that there was nothing to worry about, for starters he wouldn't be going in with the SST and secondly that their raid would not involve gun wielding terrorists. Although Laura appeared to acknowledge what he had said, she was still showing signs of being worried, and stated that there was always a risk in those sort of operations. He wished he could lie to her, to stop her from worrying, but she was right, all police work had an element of danger, and operations like this one were even more of a threat! Anaura himself had become a cropper when he was stabbed in the arm during a raid before the creation of SST. However he wouldn't be going in on this occasion and things had become a lot more professional and tactical since those days. It definitely wasn't the old Sweeney-like times when detectives would kick doors in with their size nines and storm in with little or no protective equipment; times had changed!

Laura smiled. She had been a copper's wife long enough to know the dangers! Although she accepted the risks, when Anaura had explained to her a number of years before that firearms was not his bag, she was unable to hide her delight. That was one danger she was not as willing to accept. They finished the curry, and with a bloated stomach, Anaura asked her if she fancied a lazy DVD night. Laura responded by laughing, she knew full well why he had suggested it, he had eaten too much and was now worried that he might break wind during the 'act'. Laura agreed so they went through into the lounge to watch a film. If she had been honest, she was worried about the same happening to her too. Romance for that night at least, was unequivocally dead!

A Decent Find
Chapter Seventeen

Two days later at the ungodly time of five o'clock on the Friday morning, Anaura walked into the SST office where he was met by two officers from the unit wrestling on the floor as the others watched and cheered. He took a sip of his usual morning coffee before asking them if he was interrupting something. The officer's heads swung around and he gave them a disappointed and officious look, before suddenly grinning and asking who he should put his money on. The six officers looked relieved when they saw it was Anaura as it could have been worse, it could have been Steiner. Anuara took a seat and shared a session of bantering with the officers until Sergeant John Averton, team 3's supervisor walked into the office. Averton was a well-respected and tough officer in his early fifties, with a great personality and an even greater sense of humour to go with it. He sat down and asked Anaura how he was doing before enquiring whether the prats on his team had still been screwing about when he arrived. Anaura replied in a sarcastic tone that they had been sat down like a group of angels. SST officers were hardly angelic! A minute or so later, Richards walked in with Valera and Usher, followed by Steiner a short time later.

Steiner indicated that they should get started right away in order for the job to be carried out at six am sharp. He asked Anaura to start the informal briefing that would inform the team who and what they were dealing with. Anaura stood up and handed out a few slim operational packs. For a job of this threat level, there was really no need to labour the point with tonnes and tonnes of information and intelligence. After asking them to turn onto the first page, he began reading out the purpose of the operation and explained that they were in possession a Drugs Warrant that would be served on Nash after the SST had secured the premises.

The SST knew Carl Nash only too well, he was one of their regulars who really should have been in prison already. However with the weak legal system and Human Rights Act, he was generally released from court with few weeks community service and a slapped wrist. The threat of a holiday in prison had never been a deterrent for him so when an opportunity arose for the support team to go in heavy handed, they relished it!

As the briefing progressed, Anaura explained to the officers that he wanted them fully kitted in their level two riot equipment with each officer being armed with a round perspex shield for good measure. Although Nash was far from being the strongest man going, there was still a chance that he could have a knife close by. Anaura didn't want to take any chances, and apart from that he knew that the SST lads loved getting fully kitted up and he didn't want to spoil their fun; especially when it was at the expense of the little scum bag. And he knew, all joking aside, that if Nash was really frightened it would help their cause. He also explained that he wanted a rapid forced entry into the property due to the risk of the evidence being disposed of by Nash. As with every police briefing, he wrapped it up by informing them of the legality of the operation, citing that it was a Drugs Act search warrant and that any actions they took would need to be appropriate and justifiable in the circumstances. With his usual enthusiastic trade mark after a briefing, Anaura clapped his hands together and said "Alright, let's do this!".

The officers did not need hyping up for a job of this nature and rushed out of the office to start getting their kit ready. Richards sat down next to Anaura and began reminiscing how Vice used to do all the drug raids and that he missed it. Anaura agreed and lamented at how they only left the office on a handful of occasions per week these days, missing all the fun stuff. Valera and Usher on the other hand were always present for these style raids due to their investigations requiring rapid entries and searches, and were far from being excited. In their minds this early morning raid was a necessary evil to help propel them towards the bigger fish they needed, and although they liked the guys from the team, at five o'clock in the morning their macho bravado was less than endearing.

The officers of Team 3 walked through the Response office looking extremely pleased with themselves as the probationers on duty looked at them awe struck. For some of them, the idea of less paperwork and more action that being on the teams would bring, seemed an eternity away. The more experienced officers, however, who were sat writing up their crime reports did not even glance up from their computer screens; they had seen it all before. They reached their van and started preparing all of the required kit before returning up to the unit's office to get changed into their tactical kit that consisted of blue fireproof overalls, arm and legs guards, a stab vest and a balaclava that was worn underneath a blue riot helmet fitted with a visor. It looked as impressive as it sounded and would stun the hardest of criminals when they were rudely awoken by the sight of and sound of a fully kitted SST officer.

Anaura looked at his watch, it was five forty five and time to go. With one last check of their kit, the officers hurried out of the office and down two flights of stairs to their van which was located in the rear car park of Central District Police Station, followed by the four detectives who climbed into their unmarked silver Ford Focus. In convoy they pulled out of the rear yard and headed down the hill that led towards the main road, which after negotiating an annoying one way system, would take them straight to within a stone's throw of Charlton Road that was only a matter of miles north of them. Richards turned the volume up on his police radio and completed a communications test to ensure that Team 3 and Steiner could hear him. They confirmed he was loud and clear, followed by an acknowledgement by Steiner who was sat in his office listening intently.

"Big job on?" Drayson enquired, poking his head into Steiner's office.

"Sorry sir, I'm a little bit occupied right now, I'll catch up with you later. Anyway it's nothing special!" Steiner replied.

Drayson felt frustrated as he had hoped that he might have learnt what was happening. However he knew that the moment he started asking too many questions, he would raise suspicions, as it wasn't generally the done thing with jobs like Op Spear, especially when he had already tried to make waves to prevent it taking place. It didn't matter now anyway, the Gang were unaware that the operation was still going ahead and what was even better was that he had finally found his ace in the hole with Foster. By chance he had also discovered that the surveillance teams wouldn't be working nights which meant that Foster could work unobstructed. He smiled and nodded at Steiner before walking off towards his own office down the corridor. It wouldn't be long before all of this mess was done and dusted, and he would be able look forward to his promotion.

Sat in the front seats of their Ford Focus, Anaura and Richards were like giddy school boys which prompted Usher and Valera to poke fun at them and state that perhaps the two supervisors needed to get out more often. Richards told them to stop being bores and reminded them that he and Anaura spent most of their time having to write off their investigations, and mistakes.

Up ahead, the SST van was building up steam to get to the address in good time without the use of 'blues and twos' due to the surprise element of the job. And although Anaura knew this, he kept telling the others how he would have loved to have had the opportunity to have a rapid drive, as it had been years since the last time he had switched on the blue lights. The two detective constables looked at each other and then shook their heads as Richards whole heartedly agreed with him.

As the two vehicles pulled up into Charlton road, the van abruptly stopped and Sergeant Averton and his team jumped out and ran towards the house with shields in hand. The detectives pulled up opposite to the run down grey pebble dash house that had everything from rubbish and washing machines to a dirty sofa in the front garden. Anaura and Richards swiftly spun their heads around to make sure that they didn't miss a beat while Valera and Usher continued looking at something on Valera's smart phone; there was no need to watch.

Less than fifty feet away, Sergeant Averton and four of his officers lined up just shy of the garden gate as another two ran up to the front door and placed a hydraulic ram into it that would apply well over a thousand pounds worth of pressure through the wooden frame, before one of them would hit the door with a hand held battering ram (the Enforcer), smashing it open within milliseconds.

BOOM. The door burst open as the two Method Of Entry officers yelled out "BREACH", signalling to the rest of the team that they could steam roll their way in. All of a sudden, Averton and the four officers who were lined up with him, stormed into the address at full tilt, followed by the MOE officers. Screams of "POLICE, POLICE, STAY WHERE YOU ARE!" could be heard loudly coming from within inside the house.

"Awwww yes! Get in there my sons!" Richards said with mock cockney accent as he shot a quick glance to Anaura who nodded back excitedly before they climbed out of the car.

"I'd love to be in there right now!" Anaura said roughly rubbing his hands together.

Inside the poorly lit house where the only available light was being provided by the early morning sun shining through the curtains, the SST officers flew into each room looking for Nash and making sure they were clear of other occupants. As the downstairs was cleared with rapid precision, the officers charged upstairs to be met by Nash appearing from his bedroom, looking paler than usual and holding a baseball bat. Seeing the bat as a serious threat, Nash was sent flying backwards by one of the officers, who ran and cracked him with his round perspex shield, sending him reeling backwards into the bedroom. As team 3 piled into the room to secure him, his fully naked girlfriend jumped out of the bed and tried to grab one of the officers while kicking and screaming at him. She was quickly restrained and placed in handcuffs at the same time as Nash. With her nice curvy and naked arse now pointing into the air, one of the offices looked at the rest of the team and raised his eyebrows with a smug smile.

Once the rest of the upstairs had been checked for suspects, Averton called Anaura and the other detectives forward into the house. Anaura reflected how it was the usual scum bags home, one that smelt like stale sweat and dirt, and looked like it had never been cleaned before. The type of house where you would wipe your feet on the way out! As the detectives walked upstairs they could hear Nash and the female screaming out in protest.

"Happy customers then!" Richards said as he followed Anaura up.

As they walked into the room they were met with the sight of Nash face down on the floor in his stinky and dirty boxer shorts as his naked girlfriend was kicking out and trying to get up but being prevented from doing so by two large officers.

Valera and Usher told the two male officers that they would deal with her and found a nearby jacket to cover her up with before dragging her out of the room to be spoken to downstairs. It was a lot more dignified and negated the possibility of a sexual assault claim, despite this, all of the male officers appeared disappointed. Anaura served the Warrant on Nash and told him that his house was going to be searched under the Misuse of Drugs Act and to tell them if he had any drugs at the address. Nash told him where to go in no uncertain terms. Anaura shrugged his shoulders and warned Nash that if there was anything to find, they would, with or without his help. Nash didn't reply, so he silently signalled for him to be taken away and he was duly dragged downstairs by two of the officers whilst the rest of the team stood commenting about how fit his girlfriend was, and what an amazing arse and body she had, even for a scummy lowlife. One of them was just about to mention her pert and ample chest before Anaura interrupted him and asked for a little bit of professionalism to be displayed. Richards winked at his hypocrisy, knowing for a certainty that Anaura was thinking the same thing as every man in there, despite being a little more discreet about it. Although Richards may have been right, the horrible smell in the room combined with the knowledge that she would smell little better herself, kept Anaura's mind firmly on the task of finding some narcotics. After an hour of searching the address using sweaty rubber gloves to prevent contaminating the evidence; and themselves, Valera finally found what they had been looking for.

"Boss, I've found something!" she said.

127

"Very nice! Looks like enough to get him some prison time too. Enough prison time that he would need a good character reference just to get out within a year or two!" Richards said to Valera, looking really pleased with her.

"Fantastic work Jennifer, can you get it recorded and bagged up ready to be tested. Ian, Naomi, we'll carry on for a bit longer to be sure there's nothing else here. Can someone tell the SST lads that we'll be standing down in thirty minutes and returning to Central District and that they may as well leave now to get Nash and his girlfriend booked into custody." Anaura directed.

Richards looked at the bag Valera was holding, it wasn't the biggest drug cache they had ever uncovered, but it was enough to screw Nash. Op Spear was now officially in business.

An hour later in the SST office the detectives and members of Team 3 were writing up the job while Anaura and Richards had managed to get an expedited field test of the drug. Normally the process could take a while but with their close relationship with the lab due to being on Vice they were able to get a quick turnaround.

"It's two ounces of cocaine, pretty decent stuff too." The lab technician said.

"Excellent, thank you mate" Anaura replied prior to giving Richards a 'get in there' gesture with a clenched fist.

As the two detectives left the lab and walked back to the office, Richards commented on how it never ceased to amaze him how someone like Nash could be holding over two grands worth of cocaine and still have looked and smelt like a tramp. Anaura replied that Nash would probably have been wealthier if he had stopped snorting most of his own stash, which his supplier wouldn't have liked but would have meant that they owned him, and then used him for dangerous errands and tasks to pay back his debts. Nash was a typical screw up who was in over his head with no way of getting out; he had not even made any money to make it all worth it.

On their return to the office, Usher asked Richards if she and Valera could go up to the Vice Unit office to say hello to which he replied that it was best not to while they had Nash in custody as it would be obvious that it was to do with the operation. Usher accepted it and then joked about how the Vice team would have probably forgotten who they were by now.

Anaura told Valera that he wanted her to join him at custody to interview Nash, knowing full well that she would complement him if the good cop-bad cop routine was required. And if that didn't work, the suspect would usual end up telling Valera whatever she wanted to hear because of her attractiveness. It was a win-win situation. He left Richards and Usher to finish up the paperwork before joining them in custody so that they could return to Shoreton together.

On the way up to custody in the northern end of the City, Anaura asked Valera how she had been doing since their little chat. She replied that she had felt as though a weight had been lifted off her shoulders. Anaura said that he was glad and that her new dress sense was a lot more 'neutral' and classy; his only reservation was that he was missing her ego inflating flirting with him. Valera began to blush as she laughed and told him that she still had a soft spot for him. Anaura gave her an appreciative smile.

The two detectives arrived at custody and Anaura told Valera to park up the Focus while he went to discuss Nash with the Custody Sergeant. He walked into the custody block and approached the Starship Enterprise-like Sergeants desk in the centre of the white and green room.

"Alright Guvnor, long time no see!" said Sergeant Gosden, a blonde man in his mid-forties.

"I know, I keep being told that I need to get out more, maybe they're right!" He replied with a smile.

Anaura asked Gosden if he could have a quiet word with him about Nash. Gosden agreed and escorted him to a nearby empty side room where Anaura told him that he needed a minute alone with Nash in his cell to discuss another case without anyone else around. He stopped Anaura and reminded him that under the Police and Criminal Evidence Act all unsolicited comments would have to be recorded and that he couldn't interview him about the offence he had been arrested for without being offered legal advice first. Anaura's suspicious presence in the cell before an interview could look like he was trying to coerce Nash into admitting his drug dealing. Hardly something that would go down well with the defence! He responded by grinning before declaring that he was fully aware of the Codes Of Practice, and even the Police And Criminal Evidence Act, he was, after all, a Detective Inspector. Gosden still looked a little apprehensive until Anaura continued to explain to him that it was part of a bigger covert operation and that he only needed to speak to Nash about an unrelated suspect away from a solicitor. Gosden agreed but told him that he would still have to record that he had gone to see Nash in his cell. If there was one thing you could guarantee about a Custody Sergeant, it was that they would carry out the law to the letter, and who could blame them, after all if there was a death in Custody or something fell outside of the Codes Of Practice, the Sergeant's head would be on the executioners block.

Valera joined Anaura and together they headed to Nash's cell. As they walked through the maze of corridors, the strong, lingering chemically smell of industrial cleaning products shot up their noses. The unpleasant stench was a result of the cells having to be constantly cleaned because of the detainees smearing blood, urine and faeces around their 'rooms'. The true definition of a 'dirty protest'!

"Alright Carl?" Anaura said to Nash.

"Fuck off pig!" he sneered back.

"Well we could; but we're not! Anyway it might be in your best interests to listen to what we've got to say!" Anaura replied in a cool as a cucumber manner, not reacting to Nash's rudeness.

Nash sat looking down at the cell floor in frustration as Anaura and Valera walked into the centre of the room. When he eventually looked up and saw Velera standing in front of him, Nash instantly began to make sexual comments towards her. Valera raised her eyebrows and rolled her eyes in response; it was hardly her first time. Nash asked them what they wanted to which Anaura replied to him, without beating around the bush, that he wanted to know who his main supplier was. Nash began laughing and told Anaura that he was off his rocker if he thought that he would be that stupid. Anaura didn't find it funny though and asked him again, this time reminding him that he could be facing a potential prison sentence due to what they found and with his previous criminal exploits and that it could be for a very long time. Nash stopped smiling and told the two detectives that he wanted a solicitor right away. Anaura responded by explaining that was he was offering him wasn't best said around a solicitor. Nash looked confused and as a result of knowing his rights, told Anaura and Valera to get lost. Anaura said "fine" and went to leave before commenting that if he was convicted of drug supply, a Judge would always look favourably on an offender who assisted with a larger investigation and possibly reduce their sentence. The offer caught Nash's attention and he suddenly began begging Anaura to stay, which was almost as good as an admission of guilt.

Anaura walked over and sat down on the bench next to him. He would have to use all his influencing skills to ensure Nash helped them.

"It's like this Carl. You've been nicked for drug dealing. A decent quantity of cocaine was found at your address and if you were found guilty it wouldn't be looking good, especially with your record. You could be facing a very long stretch! However if you tell me who your main supplier is, I'll try my hardest to get your sentence considerably reduced. I'm not promising anything, but then again, what do you have to lose?".

"My life! Do you know what he would do to me if he found out I was a grass or what the cons would do to me inside if they found out that I bubbled someone up?" Nash replied in a worried voice.

"Yeah I do Carl. Although what do you think would happen if your supplier found out you'd lost over two grand's worth of his gear? Do you think you'd be safe in prison either?"

Anaura knew that he almost had him. Nash was fully aware that he was screwed, he was facing at least four years and his supplier would either kill him for being a grass or get him for losing the gear. One way or another he was in deep and needed someone to help. If Anaura locked the main supplier up then he would never learn of Nash's negative equity.

"OK, but what happens if he goes to the same prison, he'll kill me himself!" Nash said.

"I can assure you that when we get him he won't be going anywhere near you, in prison or otherwise. He'll be down for a long time, however, on the other hand, so could you if things are left how they are now!".

Nash put his head in his hands and shook his head. They had him over a barrel and there was nothing he could do about it. Either way he would be bang in trouble with his supplier, but if he went along with the coppers, he could possibly protect himself and get out after a year on good behaviour which was worth the risk.

"If you nick him, you won't tell him it was me will you?" Nash asked, desperately seeking reassurance from the detectives.

"No Carl, we will tell him that we already knew about his activities and that you wouldn't talk if he asked!" Valera interjected.

Nash whacked the sides of his forehead with his lower palms in frustration. He had no choice.

"Luke Kennedy; that's my supplier!" Nash said from behind his hands.

Anaura signalled to Valera to start recording what he was saying in her investigators note book as he asked Nash more questions about Kennedy.

"Don't you know about him already?" Nash enquired with confusion, before telling Anaura and Valera that Kennedy was twenty seven years old and lived in Warrior close, Portsden District and that he was a hard bastard. Valera jotted down all of the details down in her note book.

Anaura patted Nash on the shoulder and wished him good luck with the interview and the court case. Before the two detectives left his cell, Nash made Anaura promise that he would do everything he could to help get the sentenced reduced. Anaura affirmed that he would and he meant it. In situations like this that Anaura would develop a little respect for someone like Nash. He may have been a nasty criminal but it took bravery to grass up his supplier as in some cases it could result in fatal consequences. That was the unfortunate thing about being a criminal, you were always at risk of being locked up by the Law or having your competition hurt or kill you, or both! However when it came down to it, everyone had their choices in life and the criminals picked theirs.

Anaura and Valera returned to the Custody Sergeant's desk and made a phone call to the CID supervisor who had agreed to take the job on and interview Nash on his possession and supply of cocaine. Anaura also advised her that there had been unofficial conversations pertaining to covert operation. The female DS at the other end of the phone acknowledged his comments. He finished the telephone conversation as Valera finished hers with Richards who was waiting for them two hundred meters down the road in the North Response office with Usher. On their way back to Shoreton after collecting them, Richards asked Anaura whether he was going to tell him what had happened with Nash, knowing that Anaura was playing his usual games of building up the suspense.

"Luke Kennedy! He's our boy!" Anaura informed Richards and Usher.

"Bloody hell Peter. If I'm honest, I didn't think you'd get anywhere with him" Richards said in a surprised manner.

"Funnily enough, deep down I didn't either!" Anaura joked.

"I always suspected that nob Kennedy of dealing large amounts cocaine, however he was never lax enough to end up getting nicked. Do you reckon he's linked to the Gang?" Usher said as Kennedy had been one of her past targets who she could never quite pin anything on.

"He has to be! The gang are the main drug importers in the City and the county. If he's not linked, then the next boy up the chain will be. Either way, he's our best prospect so far. WICKED!" Richards answered with enthusiasm.

Each one of the detectives sat there with a smile on their faces as they drove the twenty minute journey back to Shoreton. It even looked like they might get an early slide after the five am start. Whatever Kennedy's involvement might have been with the gang;

they were definitely starting to move in the right direction

Buried Secrets
Chapter Eighteen

The following night after his 'official' briefing in the spine tingling forest, Foster returned to the tree where Drayson had carved the letter X into its ancient bark. He scanned the darkness around him to ensure that there no one was watching. The only signs of life were the bright headlights of passing vehicles that were less than four hundred meters away on the dual carriageway. Foster slammed his shovel into the damp mud and began digging away at the soil until he heard the familiar sound of a shovel hitting something metal beneath; but unlike the tales of pirates discovering a hidden chest, what was inside the box was unequivocally not buried treasure! He reached down into the hole and removed the dirty red tin box from the earth before placing his torch between his teeth and taking the keys from his pocket to unlock it.

Foster's eyes lit up as he saw the contents of the box for the first time. Inside there was a crocodile clip clasping a thick wedge of twenty pounds notes, a Sig Sauer P226 hand gun with 15 rounds, an operational information pack, and paradoxically a bag containing at least four grammes worth of cocaine. Foster could barely contain his excitement or his jumbled thoughts. The only thing that puzzled him was why Drayson had placed cocaine into the box, it wasn't exactly the type of thing that he would have expected on a police operation, but before the suspicious doubts could set in, a voice inside his head reassured him that it was normal for an undercover officer to act the part. He dipped his fingers into the bag, pinched a small amount of the drug and snorted it before rubbing the dusty remnants around his gums, causing them to tingle within seconds. The cocaine thoroughly sharpened his focus with confidence as his heart rate began to speed up with the drug's effects. It was now obvious to Foster why Dayson had supplied him with the cocaine; he knew it would help to him focus when the time came for him to carry out the nastier sides of the operation.

"It must be a special type of cocaine, one that makes you faster and stronger!" Foster said in a manner that appeared as though the words were being said to him by someone else.

He knelt down on the ground, making the knees of his jeans dirty with mud, and pulled the Op information pack out of the box. As he opened it, he saw the word 'secret' headed on the cover followed by maps, pictures and intelligence segments on the pages that followed. There was now no doubt in his mind that this was a hundred percent the real deal, this was an official operational document, the type he had seen a thousand times before; there was no way someone would make this up. Foster skipped the intelligence segment of the first page. He didn't really need to know anything more than how to find and neutralise them. They were all pieces of shit who were hurting innocents and getting away with it, the 'who, what and where' didn't matter at the end of the day. The fact that they were hurting people and flouting the law, made Foster want to teach them a lesson, a grave lesson.

His eyes continued to rapidly digest each sentence until he reached what he was searching for, the first subject, Nick Sykes. Foster had heard of him and although their paths had never crossed, he knew that he was seen as untouchable; they all were. Foster pulled a sinister smile, Sykes' luck was about to run out. He had his subject, now he just needed to know when and where.

And there it was, half way down the second page of the booklet, the information he required........

Sunday 18th August 2013, midnight, at the Devils Valley public house car park. If subject is a no show, follow up at the same time nightly until contact is made.

Intelligence suggests that the subject, Nicholas Sykes 15/01/1961, 6'2, medium build, dark blonde hair, is believed to frequent the Devils Valley public house's rear car park for the purpose of meeting men for dogging activities.

Subject's vehicle: Dark Blue BMW X6, VRM: GU12 XNM.

Threat level: Medium. Subject has studied martial arts in the past. Is not believed to carry weapons.

Op plan: Due to location being a popular dogging area, create a discreet scene that points towards a spontaneous killing (possibly a rape scene) if it is found. No firearms are to be deployed to neutralise the subject; silent means only to prevent compromise. Approach subject in vehicle and coerce him into following you, preferably a nearby secluded woodland area and then; **Terminate with extreme prejudice**.

Use available operational funds supplied within the box to purchase a different vehicle and any other equipment that is deemed necessary.

Self-brief the second phase of operation 7 days after subject one has been eliminated.

Destroy this document by fire after reading.

Foster digested the information as the adrenaline bubbled up inside him from the apprehension. This really was a real life black op. Only the necessary information to carry out the job, working alone in the shadows with weapons supplied; it was like an assassination program straight out of Vietnam, he reflected. He removed the lighter from inside the box and set light to the two first pages of the pack that related to Sykes. Foster continued to hold it until it was fully alight before he dropped it to the ground and made sure that it was burnt entirely through, leaving not a trace. He picked up his shovel, scooped up the charred remains and then laid it flat on the floor next to him to await disposal. He took one thousand pounds from the crocodile clip and placed it into his pocket. Just as he was about to close the box he eyes locked on the Sig Sauer hand gun and he picked it up. The moment the cold steel touched his hand he began having flash backs to killing Mahood and how he had felt afterwards. In a haze of blurred thoughts, he stood there questioning whether he would be able to kill another unarmed man, let alone with a knife or his bare hands. Was getting back into the service worth this?! As his thoughts raced, Foster began to have a panic attack with the realisation of what horrors might lie ahead of him.

As quick as the anxiety attack began, it bizarrely stopped as though it had never happened with his attention rapidly shifting back to the other contents of the box. Once again he reached into the bag of the white powder and grabbed another pinch of it, snorting it up his nose with force. As the extra hit of the drug entered his blood stream, the rush took hold and he started to nod his head with purpose.

"You've done it once before; you will do it again!". A voice reassured him.

Foster poured some of the powder into a smaller empty bag that was in the box, closed the tin lid, locked it, picked up the shovel and headed towards the road. He then cast the mixture of dirt and ashes out onto the carriageway where it was dissipated into a thousand flecks of dust as a passing truck sucked in up into the night air. He carefully returned to the box and buried it after one last check for anyone loitering around, which was unlikely in such a place. He did not read any more of the pack, at this point he only needed to know what his first assignment was, any information other than that would have just clouded the issue. He took a sharp deep breath and walked back to his car feeling indebted to Drayson for the opportunity he had given him. He wouldn't let him down.

Uncontrollable Rage
Chapter Nineteen

"Ah Robbie, what can I do for you?" Sykes said at the other end of the line.

"Just wondering what you're up to mate?" Drayson enquired.

"Just having my usual quiet Sunday!"

"So what you're really saying is that you're up the Valley?!" Drayson said.

Although Sykes was a married man, he harboured a naughty little secret; he was bisexual, possibly leaning more to the same sex. The Gang and Drayson had known about it and although they found his dogging activities a little seedy, none of them questioned him on it. It was a bit of, 'don't ask, don't tell'.

"Well; OK, yes I am. The wife's doing me nut in so I need a little stress release if you know what I mean?" Sykes replied sheepishly.

The two men laughed, and after another few minutes the call was ended with Syke's location now confirmed. Drayson was sat inside his spacious front room drinking a large measure of Jack Daniels bourbon, hands trembling with the knowledge that tonight would be the night when Sykes asked the wrong person into his car. He returned the pay as you go phone into his pocket, the lack of contract meant it was easier to remain anonymous should anyone decide to look into the Gang's phone records. As Drayson sat in his chair with the nerve calming whiskey, his wife Sharon came into the room and asked him why he insisted on doing police work even when he was at home and told him to switch his phone off for once. He nodded in agreement. Sharon had no idea that the nice things she was able to buy were not as a result of his chief superintendent's wage, she didn't even know he was friends with Bradford et al.

Back in the dark car park of the Devils Valley pub, Foster

140

stood motionlessly inside a bushed area near to where Sykes was sat inside his BMW X6 with his interior light on listening to his radio, a sign that the dogging fraternity used to indicate their availability to others. Foster hadn't taken any risks in getting to the car park, he had bought a clapped out Ford Fiesta for eight hundred quid and parked it a mile away in a dark country lane so that it wouldn't be seen anywhere near the car park, a legacy left by his covert firearms training and experience. He jogged the rest.

Foster reached into his pocket and pulled the small bag of cocaine out, took a hit and psyched himself up for what would be most dangerous and dirty act he would ever undertake and walked out of the bushes towards the BMW.

Knock, Knock. Sykes jumped with fright, before lowering his car window to greet the good looking man stood peering into his window. In a flirty manner, Foster asked him how he was doing which Sykes answered and reciprocated. Foster had almost planned everything he was going to say that night and remarked to Sykes how he hadn't seen many women around. Sykes agreed before turning to Foster and explaining that he didn't mind as it was nice to just have a bit of male company. Foster, who was buzzing with adrenaline and cocaine was finding it difficult to keep himself under control, and he considered ending Sykes right there and then. After struggling with his emotions for a few moments, Foster composed himself once more.

"Do you want to go somewhere private to chat?" Foster asked Sykes, trying his hardest to prevent stuttering with nerves.

Sykes smiled and flirtatiously raised his eyebrows. He switched off his car, climbed out and took hold of Fosters hand. At first he went to pull away in disgust before remembering that he had to play along with it until they were in the right place. Foster looked around. They were alone.

"Latex gloves? Why are you wearing those, are you into that kinky stuff?" Sykes asked Foster.

"Ha, ha, a little bit. I just don't like getting bodily fluids on my hands, a bit of OCD if you know what I mean?" Foster said feeling a sense of pure frustration that Sykes had held his hand and noticed the gloves. It could have spoilt everything.

141

"Suit yourself! However I don't think you'll need to worry about getting it on your hands!" Sykes replied with a smug smile.

The two men walked hand and hand into the darkness of a small wooded area about five hundred meters away from the car. Foster took another look around which prompted Sykes to squeeze his backside and reassure him that no one else was around and that he had him all to his self. The repulsion boiled up inside Foster. How dare this piece of crap lay his dirty sordid hands on me, he thought. Although this wasn't the first time Foster had been under this kind of extreme pressure, it was the first time he had been molested by a perverted middle aged man. He struggled to remain professional.

Earlier on the drive up to the secluded Valley that was located a mile north of the City, Foster had been wrestling with his thoughts again, no matter how much he wanted to get back into the force, he had continued to find it difficult to make sense of it all, and with no one to talk to about it, the stress hormones were constantly being dumped into his blood stream from not knowing which way was up or down. But that was earlier and whatever ongoing concerns he may have had, they had now completely disappeared as a result of being repeatedly touched intimately by the scum bag.

The two men reached the wooded area and walked inside. Foster had barely reached the centre of the small space inside the trees, when he was asked to turn around. He spun around to be faced with Sykes standing there with his erect penis poking out of his boxer shorts. Foster felt sickened at the sight and began to feel panic rising up in his throat; he couldn't go through with it, not in this state. With the vomit threatening to burst its way up from his stomach and out of his mouth, he decided to pull the plug on the operation and tried to walk past Sykes who stopped him.

"Where are you going?" Sykes asked with confusion.

"Fuck off, you dirty old faggot! I'm out of here!" Foster abruptly snarled back at him.

"You ain't going anywhere you little prick tease". Sykes said with anger.

Sykes forcefully stopped him from taking another step and

told Foster to get down on his knees and perform oral sex on him or there would be trouble. Foster again attempted to push him away, however Sykes lunged at him, grabbing and kissing him as he tried to wrestle Foster to the ground. As the two men fought, Foster began to severely panic. The idea of killing Sykes had been a horrifying prospect, however if it was a choice between that and being raped by him, he knew which one he would prefer! The fear and repulsion boiled inside of him until he began to feel a demonic like fury about to erupt from the pit of his soul.

All of a sudden; there was nothing. There was no fear, no awareness of his surroundings, his once jumbled thoughts had transformed to one cold and calculated notion; to kill Sykes. With all his strength he fought him off and grabbed Sykes behind his head to gain control of his movement. Foster swiftly removed the Bowie knife from his jacket; and forcefully thrust it into Sykes's penis, the large serrated blade tore through his penis and scrotum and straight into his groin. Sykes head shot backwards as he let out a blood curdling scream as the extremely sensitive nerve endings in his genitals sent pain signals crashing through his brain.

Foster felt the blood spray across his hand and face, covering his gritted teeth and vacant enraged staring eyes with claret. Sykes continued to cry out, his brain unable to cope with the marauding distress signals cascading through his sensory fibres.

CRACK. Foster head butted Sykes as hard as he physically could with his forehead, smashing the cartilage and bone in Sykes nose and sending him unconsciously crashing to the floor, the knife slid out from his groin, enabling the arterial wound to spray an even larger volume of blood without obstruction. Sykes would be dead within minutes owing to the loss of blood, but he wasn't finished yet, or satisfied. With his unrelenting fury and disgust yet to dissipate, he climbed onto Sykes's chest and began stabbing him frantically in the throat sending even more blood over his clothing.

By the time he had finished, Foster could barely lift his arm. Below, Sykes's lifeless corpse was a bloody mess and although Foster couldn't see him clearly, he could feel the copious amounts of rapidly cooling warm blood through the latex gloves. He quickly stood up and spat on the body. Sykes had finally got what he deserved. But, as the adrenaline began to wear off, Foster began to shake as though it was a freezing winter's night. He stumbled for a moment and looked around him in bewilderment as if somehow he had disappeared off somewhere for a few minutes. As Foster's eyes cleared, he saw Sykes body strung out across the muddy ground. In shock Foster almost fell over as he tripped backwards struggling to work out what he had done. He looked into his hand and saw the knife before he burst into tears of panic as he began to recall some of what had taken place.

Foster charged out of the bushes and sprinted as fast as he could back to his car. As he neared the vehicle he threw the knife into some bushes he passed. It was a stupid idea that would later engulf him in paranoia due to the fact he recalled handling the knife without gloves like an amateur when he bought it. He had now left it for any potential search team to discover. When he finally reached the Fiesta, he jumped into the driver's seat and sped away, his only thought was getting back home as quickly as possible.

On pulling up to the block of Flats in Shakespearean Road, he charged into his ground floor apartment, ripping off the gloves, straight into the kitchen and poured half a pint of vodka in a glass before downing it and vomiting from the harshness of the strong spirit. He reached into his blood stained jacket with his shaking hands and removed the bag of cocaine and poured the entire remaining contents of it into the empty glass, he then poured more vodka over it. As he swiftly finished off the bitter concoction he became giddy and dropped to the floor with crash, knocking over a nearby coffee table as he did so.

Twelve hours later he was awoken by the sound of a door slamming in the flat above him. Feeling a mixture of being distant and removed combined with a severe hangover, Foster pulled himself to his feet and wearily stumbled into the flat's dirty and unhygienic bathroom that he would have been disgusted with less than a year before. He poured some water in a toothpaste stained glass that was next to the sink and quickly drank it.

SMASH. The glass dropped from Foster's sudden relaxed grip. Staring back at him was the reflection of his dry blood covered face. Stunned he looked down and saw that his jacket was black with blood stains too; all of his clothes were black. Foster fell back into the lime-scale covered bath tub and shook as the flash backs from the night before bounced around his skull. He placed his face into his hands and began to weep until he realised that his hands were now covered in blood from his face. Foster leapt up and switched the shower on, letting the hot water wash over his face while he was still fully clothed. He ripped his clothes off and threw them down onto the floor of the bath tub before sitting down under the red hot water without moving for thirty minutes. Had he really done what he thought he had? What would happen to him? Would he be caught? The questions repeatedly swirled around his head.

As he sat there motionless and overcome with emotions, Foster suddenly realised that it was Sykes' blood all over his clothes and that it was also all around his flat and inside his car. With sheer panic, his head cleared and he shot up, ripping the shower curtain down as he pulled himself to his feet. He rushed into the kitchen and grabbed an ancient bottle of bleach from under the sink and raced back through to the bath tub and poured the bleach all over the blood saturated clothes before running into the lounge and pouring more of it onto the carpet where he had been passed out. Foster continued to be gripped with paranoia as he cursed himself for screwing up so much and worrying about how Drayson would not be happy that he had left so much evidence around to be found; especially the knife.

After hours of scrubbing and cleaning the flat and car, Foster sat down at his kitchen table and poured another glass of vodka. He felt torn, a part of him was telling him to carry on with the assignment, the other that he was doing terrible, terrible things and that Drayson was using him. Foster sat on the seat without moving until the evening, stuck in the prison that was his mind. Although he was having flashbacks, he could not fully recall everything that had happened, just visions of stabbing, slashing and running through a pitch black field towards his car. He didn't even know how he got back to his flat and ended up on the floor.

"Maybe I am ill! Everyone's saying it!" Foster hypothesised until a booming voice inside his head.

"STOP CRYING LIKE A LITTLE BITCH! YOU'VE BETRAYED US BY BELIEVING YOU'RE ILL; YOU'RE TAKING THEIR SIDE, THEY HATE YOU, REMEMBER!" The voice said in an agitated tone.

Foster looked down at the glass of vodka in front of him, and then propelled it at the wall. "Get a grip!" he growled to himself in acknowledgement of what the voice had said, and recalling Drayson's remarks about staying away from alcohol. He began reassuring himself that he had only freaked out because of the alcohol he was drinking and that it had also made him paranoid. Foster promised himself there and then that he would quit the drink without delay. He stood up and loosened his shoulders before walking over to the cupboards and removing a Pot Noodle which he slammed down on the work top in frustration. He turned around and saw the teabag tin on the kitchen table where some of the operational funds were. He grabbed a twenty pound note and left his flat to buy some chips. If he was going to see this through he needed to eat more than a few Pot Noodles.

Foster left his flat feeling refocused after the shame of doubting himself had cleared. For some reason he started having flashbacks to when he and O'Keeffe had been in the secret de-brief location toilets and back in the pub near the Old Bailey. He could not recall either situation clearly or understand why he had been having flashbacks of them, however, Foster shrugged his shoulders and walked on with indifference. One thing he did know for sure was that he needed to get back up to West Ording forest soon for some more cocaine, and the next assignment.

The Right Decision?
Chapter Twenty

Sgt Chalmers and King walked into the supervisor's office in Shoreton where Anaura and Richards were discussing Luke Kennedy's movements. Anaura smiled and asked them how things were coming along with Cooper. Chalmers pulled an indifferent expression while King replied that it had all been quiet on the western front apart from following Cooper from his home address to his office on a daily basis over the recent weeks. Although Chalmers mentioned how Cooper had made two unexplained early evening visits to somewhere in Basin Road South in the harbour, where they lost him each time, however he went on to explain that Cooper was a keen fisherman and might have been going there for that purpose. Anaura shook his head and stated that he still believed night surveillance would be worth having, something that both Sergeants disagreed with but replied that they would explore the option when they moved on to life-styling Larry Pearson the following week. The two Sergeants finished and assured him that they would forward all the intelligence that had been acquired on Cooper to him before they returned to the SOCU offices to be updated on the unit's other ongoing operations. As the two men left the room, Anaura glanced at Richards who raised his hands up, implying exasperation. He placed his left elbow onto the desk, dropped his head and began rubbing his cropped hair.

"What do you reckon Ian? Is this Surveillance Malarkey worth having?" He asked Richards.

"I'm not so sure! We seem to have got further with Nash and the Intel guys than we have by following Cooper shopping!" he replied with frustration.

Anaura leant back into his seat deep in contemplation. He looked at the paperwork in front of him. They had a snitch,

Kennedy, who was someone worth watching and questioning, but up until that point surveillance had failed to turn up anything decent. He tilted his head back and then lazily dropped it back down again to ask Richards whether he believed that surveillance was still a worthwhile option bearing in mind the risk of the Gang becoming suspicious. Richards looked back at him and replied that the Intel officers were all trained in basic surveillance techniques and setting up observation posts too so they did not really need to have the Surveillance teams. As he put it, the Intel officers would be more than capable enough to find out what, if anything, was happening in Basin Road South. Even more so if they were willing to work nights.

"Right Ian, bollocks, I'm sold! I'm going to call Steiner now to discuss it with him. If we have not got anything of note after weeks of following them, then we are not likely to, it's just not worth the risk. I don't care if it takes an extra six months through using good old fashioned detective work!" Anaura declared.

"Yes Peter! I was hoping you were going to say that, we've got Nash, we're going to get Kennedy and we know something is going down in the harbour; let's not cock it up with overzealous covert work. And besides we've still got the technical support guys who can assist the Intel guys with fixed surveillance techniques." Richards happily responded.

Anaura tilted his head forwards and pointed at Richards in agreement. Although he respected the work Surveillance did, nicking the Gang came well before pissing off a few specialist colleagues. This operation called for good old investigative work with officers talking to informants, nicking and influencing the right people; with few stakeouts thrown in for good measure too. Anaura had made up his mind. Richards got up and went outside to speak to Valera and Usher while Anaura called up Steiner, who after listening to what Anaura was proposing with the surveillance teams, didn't sound too enthused with the idea.

"I'm not sure I'm in agreement with you on this one Peter. Have you considered that we could lose a vital source of intelligence from dropping them? I'm really not sure about this." Steiner said.

"Jason, listen, the Gang aren't doing anything out of place or blatantly illegal so apart from risking them becoming aware that we're following them, what are we getting that makes taking the chance so worthwhile!" Anaura replied.

"Ok Peter, it's your call, your show. If you think we're better off doing it old school then I'll support you but for the record I don't fully agree." He replied.

"Trust me Jason, you won't regret this!".

Anaura finished the call and walked out into the office.

"Guys listen up! This is now solely an investigative operation without surveillance! Ian, Naomi, Jennifer, we're going to continue rattling cages under the radar while you guys from Intel are going to start trying to locate where Cooper's been going in harbour and then setting up an Observational Post to keep an eye on him!" Anaura instructed.

The intelligence officers smiled at each other. With the departure of the Surveillance teams they would be getting out on the ground more often and not just stuck behind a desk. However the two female detectives seemed slightly more reserved about the decision.

Anaura walked over to Valera and Usher and asked them why they didn't look a hundred percent comfortable with the decision. The two detectives replied that they wondered whether dropping surveillance would create gaps in the operation and make it more difficult overall, to pin the Gang down to meeting places. Anaura sat down the opposite way around on a swivel chair, leant over it and then spun from side to side. He smiled and told Valera and Usher that ordinarily they would have been right; but then this was no ordinary job, and when Surveillance's results had been less fruitful than hoped for, it was time to focus on the tried and tested methods. Richard nodded his head in agreement. He continued to explain that if they got control of Kennedy, they would get more evidence and intelligence than following them ever could. And besides the Gang had been followed in the past and they had always seemed to know it was happening, instantly ceasing their business activities as a result. It was as though they mysteriously knew about the surveillance operations before the officers on the ground did. It just wasn't worth it. Had Surveillance come up with something solid then he would have kept them rolling. They had not but the detectives had. Valera and Usher indicated to Anaura they were totally with him despite the move being a little unorthodox by modern investigative methods.

"There is a reason I'm a DI you know!" he said, poking fun at their concerns about his choices.

He would never take offence to his staff speaking their minds or expressing their concerns. He may have been the boss but he wasn't above making poor decisions from time to time. And if they still didn't like something after a discussion, then it was perhaps something he needed to reconsider as well. Anaura rubbed his hands together and called everyone into the briefing room.

"Right we're stepping up our activities! Firstly I want you intelligence guys to watch Basin Road South in pairs from five o'clock in the evening until one am in the morning until you ascertain where Cooper and maybe the others are going. My lot, we're going to start moving in on Kennedy hard, it's been over two weeks since Nash grassed him up and we've hardly made any huge leaps forward! It's time for us to go to his address and wait for him or one of his associates to slip up, let's make something happen!"

The officers acknowledged him with enthusiasm and then left the room, leaving Richards and Anaura behind.

"Peter, do you ever get that sinking feeling where you not sure if something is going to work out." Richards enquired.

"What, like this Operation Ian?"

"Yeah." Richards replied.

"Every bloody day mate! That's why I've decided on being more direct, more purposeful. I know deep down this is our only shot at this, and I would rather have a good crack at it and fail, than sit around for months and months waiting and wishing for something solid to materialise. We need to clamp down on these bastards asap!" Anaura said.

"I agree Peter, I do, but just a friendly bit of advice mate.

Don't go steaming in headstrong to prove a point, we still need to tread carefully with these guys."

Anaura listened and digested what his long-time friend and colleague had just said to him, Richards was right, he was going to have to calm things down a bit to limit cock ups. Anaura winked at him and asked him if he wanted a brew to which Richards replied "Does a bear shit in the woods?"

He left the briefing room and told Richards that he would meet him back in their office. As he reached the main office door he was met by a smart suited man entering the room, "Bloody locks again!" He muttered to himself.

"DI Anaura I take it?" The suit wearing middle aged man asked in an extremely well-spoken voice.

"Yes, and you are?" He replied.

"Well I'm a Superintendent, so you can call me sir!" The man arrogantly replied.

Anaura had never seen this Superintendent before but was more concerned with how he had gained access to the office and enquired how he had got in. The Superintendent replied that he used his pass before changing the subject and asking Anaura if they could have a private word together. Still suspicious of the man, Anaura agreed and asked him to accompany him out to the kitchen where he was going to make drinks.

"So what can I do for you sir?" Anaura asked in an inquisitive tone of voice as he leant up against the kitchen worktop.

The Superintendent brushed some crumbs off of a chair and sat down before making strong eye contact with Anaura and asking, "Do you know Chief Superintendent Drayson, Detective Inspector?"

"I know him, why's that sir, and please call me Peter" Anaura responded with more confusion, it was the last thing he thought he would be discussing with the unknown command officer.

"If you don't mind, Peter, I'll ask the questions."

"Alright" Anaura replied with annoyance.

"Have you heard any rumours about him or his methods?" The Superintendent asked.

"Well, personally I'm not that big a fan, and I've always

151

wondered how he managed to lock up all the big hitters in the City in such quick time. But hey, I guess some people are just lucky sir!" Anaura said.

"Quite. Anything else? Was he ever successful in getting close to, say, the Gang during his tenure as the head of Serious and Organised crime?"

"No, no one's ever got close to the Gang, especially Drayson. He just never seemed to be able to make a case against them, probably why no one bothers anymore." Anaura replied beginning to wonder where this conversation was heading and trying to cover up that Op Spear was taking place.

"Right, I must go. I wonder whether you could do me a favour? Could you listen out for any gossip or info on Drayson without telling anyone else?" The superintendent asked.

"Yeah sure, although I don't really know what you're expecting to learn?"

The unknown superintendent stood up from the seat, smiled at Anaura and passed him a Scotland Yard business card with a mobile number and nothing else while requesting that Anaura immediately relay anything he might hear about Drayson back to him. The Superintendent started to walk out of the kitchen.

"Sorry sir, I didn't catch your name!" Anaura called out.

"That's because I didn't tell you Inspector" he responded arrogantly.

Anaura ran to the kitchen door and asked the Superintendent why he had asked him to have an ear to the ground about Drayson.

"Why not you? Who knows, maybe something will come up as you follow the same leads; or not?" The Superintendent said as he walked out of the rear entrance without even looking back at Anaura.

Anaura looked down at the card he had been given and tapped it on his palm as he walked back into the supervisor's office and sat down with Richards who asked him who the suited man was. Anaura replied that even after speaking to him for fifteen minutes, he still wasn't sure of his identity himself, other than that he was a superintendent. He asked Richards to keep what he was about to

152

say to him secret.

"That Superintendent has just asked me to keep an eye on Drayson and I haven't got a clue why!" Anaura told Richards with utter confusion.

Anaura had never liked Drayson but he was popular with the Chief and other commanding officers, so why would a Superintendent from London be interested in him he wondered. In the end, he didn't really care, even less so when the person asking him had been such an obnoxious former public school boy type, and especially when he hadn't been polite enough to tell him his name. Besides, the most likely scenario was that Drayson was being investigated by an outside agency to ensure that he was suitable enough to be promoted to such a high rank. This was not uncommon for roles or positions where a higher level of vetting was required, the investigators would literally try to learn everything about the officer's career and their personal life, even if it meant asking people who did not like them as well. Richards reflected his theory, citing that it was best to let them get on with it as they had bigger fish to fry.

AWOL
Chapter Twenty One

Drayson put his pass up to the Serious and Organised Crime Units office door in the City's North Police Station, and walked through after his card was accepted. This used to be his office, his unit and as a result he was always warmly welcomed by the SOCU staff. During his tenure as the head of the department he had always looked after the staff and with his high detection and conviction rate of some of the City's most notorious criminals, a lot of the officers of the unit were slightly in awe and saw him as a bit of a thief taker. However the new boss of the unit wasn't so keen on him and saw Drayson as someone not to be fully trusted.

As he walked into the main office his arrival was greeted by the unit's Surveillance teams and detectives, who asked him to take a seat to have a catch up. They exchanged pleasantries for about fifteen minutes until Drayson asked why they were all sat in the office and not out there on 'the big job'. One of the Surveillance constables enquired how he knew about the operation, and even though he didn't, he responded that he had his sources and asked what it had been like to work for the egotistical DI Anaura. The officers shook their heads before one of them answered that he had been a nice guy. No sooner than she had said it, one of the male officers piped up and told Drayson that he thought Anaura was an arsehole who didn't know the first thing about running a big operation. Drayson beamed a huge grin at him and whispered that he agreed but not to tell anyone that.

"He's thrown us off the Op sir, can you believe that?" PC James Farrell said before telling Drayson that now no one would be watching the Gang which in his mind was the worst tactical decision he had ever known a governor to make.

"Well guys, you said it yourself, he's not a SOCU supervisor so he's going to make poor tactical decisions! Anyway if we didn't manage to get them, why would the All Black succeed?" Drayson quipped referring to Anaura's 'foreign' heritage in a tongue and cheek manner.

Chalmers and King walked in and were greeted by Drayson asking them how they felt about being kicked off the job by Anaura. Chalmers glanced at King before facing Drayson and asking him how he knew about it. Drayson replied that he had his sources which made King survey the faces of his team and then shoot them annoyed looks for discussing it with him.

"Yes sir, however we've got another job on now. I suppose Anaura had his reasons and anyway we shouldn't really be discussing it with anyone who wasn't involved in the operation" Chalmers said.

Although a lot of the officers were in awe of Drayson, King and Chalmers were not, and despite being frustrated by Anaura's decision they were not going to start discussing it with him. If there was one thing Chalmers was known for, it was that he wasn't scared of speaking his mind to command. Drayson hid the resentment he was feeling towards the two men and nodded in acknowledgement with a smile, and then declaring how he had taught them well. King didn't say anything but Chalmers responded by telling Drayson that they had to get their team briefed up and would see him around. Drayson shot him a cold stare before smiling and standing up. He said his good byes and left the office. King and Chalmers may have stopped him learning the finer details of the operation, however he discovered a few things, Anaura was bungling the operation to a level of incompetence and SOCU Surveillance were no longer following his associates. It was perfect without anyone watching the Gang, Foster would be able to slip under the radar to get the job done. Even better was the fact that Anaura was screwing the job up just enough that when Fosters murders were discovered, he would be able to muscle his way into taking over the operation.

As he walked out of the office his pay as you go phone began to ring.

"Robbie. We've got a little problem! Nick has gone AWOL and we can't find him, it's been three days now. Do you know

155

where he could be? His wife's been on the phone giving me grief and threatening to call your lot, which is a bloody bad idea. I think he's gone on a bender with one of those little queers, however it's been three days! Can you help?" Bradford asked.

"Yeah no worries, I'll have a look for him myself, I've got a few ideas!" Drayson answered with fake concern.

"Fabulous. Oh one last thing, are we still good for our family's arrival in late September? Do you think your friends will be coming or have they found something better to do?" Bradford enquired using a simple coded message to establish whether the Gang's next large drug shipment was safe to proceed.

"I'm afraid my friends can't make it! I hope your family bring me a few gifts for all the trouble I went to though!?" Drayson said.

"Yeah, they'll see you right, don't worry about that. Let us know how you get on finding Nick the prick!" Bradford replied before hanging up the phone without so much as a bye.

Drayson put the phone into his pocket and carried on walking down the stairs towards the exit where his car was parked. The nerves he'd had three days ago about Foster getting the job done had been settled somewhat. To cover all bases though he decided that checking the serials for anything that might relate to Sykes was probably prudent. He sat down in the driver's seat of his command Focus and reflected on the developing situation, finding it hard to believe that he might actually be able pull it all off. Once the gang had been eliminated there would be no more worries about being outed and he could look forward to his promotion and ever approaching fruitful retirement. Then something Drayson hadn't considered during his planning abruptly entered his brain. He had been so desperate to plan and get everything moving as fast as possible that he had forgotten to work out how to deal with Foster after he was finished. Pissed off with himself for being lax, Drayson whacked the inside of the driver's door as he tried to quickly think of ideas, but nothing came to mind. Sure, Foster would be seen as a nutter if he claimed on arrest that he was on an undercover operation. However, be that as it may, it was still something that would cast suspicion, or perhaps worse for him.

Drayson drove out of the station's main green gates and began heading towards Headquarters. This was a problem, a big problem, and one without an obvious solution. Drayson explored a couple of different options in his head, one being that he would kill Foster himself, but discounted the idea when he considered that it could still potentially come back to him. As he joined the dual carriageway he shouted out "SHIT" to himself. As with every plan, there would always be a flaw somewhere, something unseen or forgotten. The conundrum of Foster was going to have to be solved, but for now he just hoped that Foster would finish the job as quickly as possible.

On arrival at his office within the main Headquarters building, Drayson jumped onto his computer terminal and sifted through the reported incidents that had come in over the past few days. After two pages there had not been any mention of anything happening at Devils Valley, until half way down that day's list, the words 'Devils Valley and dark blue BMW' were seen in the headline. He breathed in sharply as his eyes locked on the headline and then took a moment to prepare himself for what may have been Foster screwing up before clicking on the log to read through it. His jacked heart rate began to slow as he learnt that the landlord of the public house had called in to say that the vehicle had been suspiciously left there for three days, but he had been told by a call handler that it hadn't been reported stolen and if it was taxed and insured then there was nothing they could do about it unless anything was reported.

Drayson grinned, with Syke's wife being warned off reporting him missing and with the Gang requesting that he search for him, it was safe to say that before anyone discovered what had happened, it would be too late. He flicked the pendulum balls on his desk and watched as they collided with one another before swinging to and fro in unison. If he found a solution for Foster he could still come out of this smelling of roses!

An Eventful Evening
Chapter Twenty Two

Anaura and Usher had been sat up on Fox Way, Portsden District in their black unmarked Ford Mondeo for six hours looking out for any known subjects entering Warrior Close to attend Kennedy's house on the corner of the road, and bar the odd unavoidable toilet break, they had not left the spot they were in. It was seriously boring but absolutely necessary work.

"It's times like this that remind me why I didn't join Surveillance!" Anaura remarked.

"It's not all bad boss, it can be quite a good laugh at times, a bit like a game of cat and mouse!" Usher replied, having done her six month attachment to the unit not that long before.

Anaura looked at his Storm watch and saw that it was six thirty pm. Richards and Valera would be arriving imminently to relieve them which filled him with delight in the knowledge that he would soon be able to grab something better to eat than just crisps and chocolate bars. Over the past week the officers of Op Spear had been working overtime, sometimes pulling twenty hour shifts in one sitting. It had got to the point where Anaura had asked his staff to bring sleeping bags to the office to make sure they were available twenty four hours a day. Not long after he had been sleeping on the hard office floor he began to wonder whether dropping the Surveillance teams had been a good idea after all. However he couldn't go back on his decision, not unless he wanted to appear indecisive, or worse............incompetent.

With the hours rolling on by, Anaura started to question whether Kennedy had look outs around the area as he had barely left the house for two days and apart from his girlfriend coming and going, it had been dead quiet. A week or so after Nash had put Kennedy in the frame, Anaura had considered placing an Observation Post near to his home but had changed his mind at the last minute due to problems he was having with surveillance and gathering enough additional evidence and intelligence to convict Kennedy should they get a chance to arrest him.

Op Spear was rapidly approaching its fifth week, which in the grand history of police investigations was hardly a long time but Anaura and his team wanted things to move quicker. Boredom and moaning was a coppers trait and although they were all experienced enough to know that Rome wasn't built in a day, it wouldn't stop them praying for something juicy to happen.

Just as his stomach acid was threatening to burn a hole through his stomach lining, Richards and Valera turned up in a brand new unmarked BMW M1 sport.

"Bloody hell, where did you get the Beemer from Ian?" Anaura asked with surprise as the detectives had only been given Mondeos and Focus's to use as a result of their driving permits not allowing them to drive high powered cars for response purposes.

"A friend on traffic leant it to me. Anyway it would look a bit suspicious if there are two Fords with two passengers parked near the address all day and night!" Richards postulated.

"Good point. However, I know the real reason; you've wanted to drive that thing for months Ian!" Anaura remarked with a smile.

Richards pulled an ear to ear smile and revved the powerful engine which drew a 'quieten down' gesture from Anaura despite him finding his boy racer actions amusing. Usher leant across and signalled that she was starving so Anaura wrapped up the banter and told Richards to return to the base at three am if nothing was going on. Richards winked in response.

Anaura switched the engine of the Mondeo on and gave it a little rev in defiance to Richards' powerful appropriated toy. As the two men laughed a white Subaru Impreza drove past, pulled into the close and across Kennedy's driveway. The detectives eyes fixed on the two occupants of the vehicle and the front door of Kennedy's house. Richards asked Valera to run a check on the vehicles number plate. Within a minute or so, she came back with an answer, the vehicle was registered to a one Jamie Poultan, a little worm who the Vice unit had busted for possession and supplying of Cannabis after he had been caught in the company of one of their bigger targets. Richards said that something had to be going down, and Anaura nodded slowly in agreement.

"There he is!" Anaura said with excitement, referring to Kennedy who had just left his house and was walking towards the Subaru.

The passenger in the vehicle lowered the window and began having a conversation with Kennedy with the nearby detectives wishing they could hear what the conversation was about. Whatever the three men were discussing it was taking a long time. Anaura told Richards through their open windows to wait until he gave the nod to move in, knowing full well that this may be their only opportunity to get Kennedy and whoever was in the car. If they moved in without seeing an exchange of goods, they would blow it.

As the detective's hearts began to pound in their chests with adrenaline, Kennedy returned to the house and came back outside with something hidden under a jacket. He then discreetly passed a package to the passenger of the car. Richards glanced at Anaura who gestured to him to wait a little bit longer. A couple of seconds later the passenger handed a package back to Kennedy. Richards raised his eyebrows at Anaura who was still weighing up whether it was worth charging in there without knowing what was in the packages or if the subjects were armed with weapons.

"Bollocks to this! Ok Ian, let's do it!" Anaura shouted out.

Richards put the accelerator down and the BMW shot down the small hill that led into Warrior close followed by the slower Mondeo that Anaura was driving. The two cars came screeching behind the Subaru with the Mondeo crashing into the back of it before the detectives all leapt out of their vehicles and ran towards the three men.

The driver of the Subaru put the vehicle into first gear and pulled off at speed at the very same time that his passenger was attempting to get out, dragging him along as he was unable to let go of the door quick enough. The car stopped and the passenger clambered to his feet, dropping the package that Kennedy had handed him, on the ground, before running at full pelt towards the end of the close pursued by Usher. At almost the very same time Valera and Richards were leaping on Kennedy attempting to bring him down with a mixture of brute force and incapacitating Captor spray that Valera was trying to spray in his face. In the milliseconds that it took for him to see the ensuing chaos breaking out in the close, the driver was spinning his car around to drive out of the close. In the distance Usher had failed to catch the unknown passenger who had rapidly scaled a wall into the field behind the Close that led towards an old Neolithic burial ground. Anaura knew Usher would rush to assist with Kennedy so there was only one more person they had a chance to apprehend, the driver of the car.

Anaura tried to pull the Mondeo across the road to block it, but it wouldn't move. He smacked the steering wheel in frustration and saw what looked like steam bellowing out of the bonnet. He had killed the car when he drove into the back of the suspects' car. As the Subaru turned and began to head out of the close he caught a glimpse of the driver, it was Poultan. Anaura jumped out of the Mondeo and attempted to block the rapidly accelerating car himself, however he wasn't fast enough and the driver mounted the curb to get past the police vehicles. Just as he was about to swear out in anger, he saw that Richards' BMW was still running just to the side of the Mondeo, he looked up and saw the Subaru nearing the end of the Close. He swiftly jumped into the BMW and shot a quick glance into the rear view mirror to establish which way Poultan would be heading; he turned left. Anaura slammed the semi-automatic gearbox in reverse and put his foot down on the accelerator, the instantaneous beast-like power of the BMW caught him by surprise, but there was no way he was going to lose Poultan, so he gripped the steering wheel harder in an attempt to control the sports car as he reversed it at speed. When he reached the end of the Close, he spun the car on its axis so that it aggressively flicked around to face the right way within a matter of feet, something that Ushers brother, Matthew, from the close protection unit, had taught him. Anaura felt his body lean to the side with the centrifugal force of the spin. Within a split second, he pushed the electronic gear shift to first and wheel spun

161

out of the close. Although the adrenaline was pumping even harder and he had developed tunnel vision in catching Poultan, he still managed to reflect how the amazing piece of driving was an 'up yours' to the Driver trainer unit who had slated him. As he neared the end of the close at fifty mph, he gave a quick check to his right which was clear, so he proceeded to fly out onto the road with the BMW over-steering to the right. Anaura cursed as he was unable to locate the blues and twos switches that would help his cause. All of a sudden his finger slipped on a button located on the steering wheel, instantly putting the car into response mode with its lights and sirens. The abrupt and unexpected wailing made him jump out of his seat. As the car bounced over the bumpy road surface, he could see up ahead that Poultan's car turning right onto the A293 that headed towards the Old Shoreton Road.

For a second, his lost his concentration on driving when Richards urgently requested a police van on the double and an ambulance for injured officers. The request sent shivers down his spine as he wasn't there to help, but there was no turning back now, and he knew that help would be there imminently.

Anaura flew out onto the mini roundabout and swung right to chase Poultan who wasn't that far ahead due to being held up by cars on either side of the road. Anaura floored the accelerator out of the roundabout in second gear, forgetting that the BMW was still under cornering forces and that the powerful engine would send an incredible amount of torque through the rear wheels. The car snapped and slid sideways with him only just managing to correct it, but not without a few extra snaking slides up the road as he continued to forget to be gentle with the accelerator on the fast car.

Up ahead and in sheer desperation, Poutlan overtook a slow moving Mini Cooper in front of him and straight into the path of an oncoming vehicle. The fright of the move meant that he momentarily lost his concentration and forgot to brake as he approached the roundabout which led to a large supermarket or off towards the City centre. He went cascading straight over the top of it. He obviously had no intention for popping into the store

162

for his weekly shop! Behind, Anaura had made up ground owing to his blue lights and sirens and Poultan's inadvertent detour over the top of the roundabout. Poultan may have braked as hard as he could when he saw the roundabout, but it didn't prevent him from damaging the suspension and wheels and sending sparks flying out from underneath the Subaru. As Anaura began to catch up, his eyes quickly flitted around the dash board of the car. "Where's the bloody radio handset!" said to himself, knowing full well that he should have been running a commentary of Poultan's driving and requesting specialist Traffic unit support to help stop the vehicle.

Anaura negotiated the same roundabout at speed after the oncoming cars had pulled over to give him a clear route. This time he was gentler with the throttle and was able to control the car with ease.

"I need one of these!" Anaura shouted out as the speed of the sporty BMW filled him with excitement.

Less than two hundred meters ahead Poultan took the centre lane of the Old Shoreton Road traffic junction. As luck would have it, the lights were green, allowing him to continue without obstruction. Anaura increased the pressure on the accelerator until the BMW's engine was roaring with delight as its three hundred horses of power were allowed to gallop without restraint.

EeeeeeRRRRRRR, Poultan's tyres screeched as they lost traction due to the damaged suspension and the now misaligned wheels. The out of control Subaru slid sideways and straight into the curb at the side of the busy double lane arterial road.

CRASH. The high performance car smashed into the curb, ripping the front and rear near side wheels off.

Anaura crossed the junction and swiftly pulled up alongside the Subaru as Poultan was trying to escape. He jumped out and ran over the top of the bonnet, denting it under his weight, leapt off and rugby tackled Poultan to the ground before yanking him to his feet and throwing him up against the side of his car. Still desperate to escape he tried to push Anaura away and punched him in the chest, prompting the much stronger Anaura to grab hold of his hoody, lift him clean off the floor and then slam him onto the bonnet of the Subaru. As Poultan crashed down onto the front of his car, Anaura swiftly turned him over onto his front and forcefully handcuffed him before arresting him for dangerous driving, suspicion of being in possession of drugs with intent to supply, and assaulting a police officer.

"You absolute dickhead Jamie! Did you honestly think that you would get away? The bloody car's registered to you; you absolute prat!" Anaura shouted at him.

"Supplying drugs? Search the fucking car, there ain't nothing in there!" Poultan protested with frustration.

"Shut up!" Anaura yelled back at him.

A few members of the public stopped their cars in the centre of the road to prevent anyone crashing into the two men. Anaura quickly identified himself as a police officer to prevent anyone else from involving themselves. Everyone stood back, until a middle aged man approached and asked if he could help.

"Ha, ha, yeah you can. You wouldn't happen to have a phone on you? Can you call 999 and tell them DI Anaura has one in custody on the junction of the Old Shoreton Road and needs urgent assistance?" he asked with a sense of embarrassment as he couldn't figure out how to work the hidden covert radio in the BMW.

The rapidly growing crowd of passers-by all gathered around to watch the large police officer apprehending the criminal; it was just like TV. Anaura considered asking them to move on, but could not be bothered as he was more concerned about Richards and the others. In the near distance, Anaura saw a Traffic unit and a response unit speeding down the hill from the Old Station Road. After a moment of relief, Anaura suddenly realised that he would have some serious explaining to do-he didn't have the advanced driving permit that authorised him to drive the high performance unmarked police vehicle and that Traffic would stick him in the discipline book for it.

"This is going to be fun!" Anaura said to himself as the two police vehicles pulled up.

Worthwhile Injuries
Chapter Twenty Three

After spending a couple of hours booking Poultan into custody, writing his arrest statement and being interrogated by the Traffic Inspector on his driving, Anaura rushed to the General City Hospital. He burst through the A&E doors and ran up to the reception to ask whether he could see Richards et al. The stern and unhelpful receptionist told him to take a seat and that he would have to wait. Anaura demanded to know where they were to which the receptionist replied that she would call the police if he continued to cause a scene.

"I am the bloody Police!" Anaura snapped.

"It's alright, he's with us" Richards said as he appeared from the side of the reception.

"Ian, are you ok?!" Anaura said with concern as he bounded up to him and placed his hand on his friend's shoulder, noticing that Richards had sustained a cut eyebrow and swollen left eye.

Richards told Anaura to follow him to where Usher and Valera were being examined by a doctor. Anaura felt sick at the thought of what may have happened after he left. He asked him. Richards shook his head and began telling him what had occurred.

"Bloody hell he was a hard bastard Peter! Jennifer and I grabbed him and she tried to spray him with Captor which ended up being as useful as a condom in a nunnery. It basically made him become even more aggressive. As we began to lose our grip on him, Kennedy turned and head butted Jennifer, knocking her clean out. With his right hand free he then smashed me in the face, putting me on my arse. At this point as he began to come towards me, Naomi came out of nowhere and cracked him across the leg with her baton, and like the Captor spray, he took it and punched her in the face which sent her reeling too. I managed to climb to my feet and as he turned back around to have another go at me, I soccer kicked the prick right between the legs and gave him the hardest punch in the face I've delivered. The bastard dropped on his back and of course I had to clock him again for good measure; and a little revenge! All that said and done, there was a positive! We found five grand's worth of cash in one of the packages and in the other, wait for it; five ounces of the white stuff!". Richards said with a grin.

Anaura began shaking with anger on hearing what Kennedy had done and asked Richards whether the girls were alright.

"They're fine mate. Jennifer is a little bit shaken and concussed and Naomi has a bruised cheek bone, oh, and as you can see I didn't do too badly myself. We're all OK, and fortunately the district officers arrived pretty quickly to assist."

"I should have been there Ian! Poultan wasn't worth you guys getting hurt for!" Anaura said feeling guilty.

"Peter there was three of us and besides I think you'd have killed him if you got hold of him after all that, you punch a lot harder than I do! Anyway, I saw you fly off in the Beemer, how was it? Did you catch the little shit?" Richards said to Anaura with a big smile, trying to stop him from feeling responsible.

"Ha, ha, the M sport was bloody quick mate, I almost crashed it once or twice! And as for Poultan, well, I caught the little bastard on the Old Shoreton road but he didn't have anything on him so it's just going to be a dangerous driving job on him, annoyingly!".

Anaura walked into the double cubicle where Usher and Valera were in beds next to each other talking. The two of them happily greeted him as he gave them both hugs, and telling them how his heart sunk when he heard Richards requesting an ambulance. Valera reassured him she was fine and just had a bit of a headache, followed by Usher who said that she wished she had wrapped the baton around his fat ugly head! Anaura felt relief that they were all fine and still had a sense of humour about it. After berat\ing him for trying to apologise about what had happened, the two detectives asked him about the car chase. Anaura replied that it had barely lasted a couple of miles and had gifted him with a chewing out from the Traffic Inspector for

166

using an advanced car, but on a positive note he had got Poultan.

Anuara smiled before telling the two officers to go home once they were discharged and to take a few days off; after the week they'd had, they had most certainly earned it. He turned to Richards to tell him to do the same, however he raised an eyebrow back at Anaura and told him he was coming back to the office with him. Anaura smiled and remarked how Laura and Rachel would love them for failing to come home for yet another night. Richards laughed and replied how their wives knew who they were marrying from the start!

Foster looked at the date on his Chinese new year calender that he had been given by the overzealous owner of his local Chinese takeaway. It had been seven days since he had murdered Sykes and it was time for his next visit to the operational box. Over the past week, Foster had decided to obsessively cleanse his flat again due to the fear that traces of Sykes's DNA might be present. He had also disposed of his clothes from that night by taking them in a black bin liner to the Peverel Gap woods, near the West Ording seafront and burning them with a copious amount of petrol and a sole match. On top of that he had religiously cleaned his Fiesta for a number of hours which had drawn sarcastic remarks from his passing neighbours who hypothesised that he was trying to wash away the traces of a dirty little sexual encounter that had taken place in the car. Foster didn't even grace them with an answer.

Due to a lack of cocaine, Foster had been smoking cannabis and drinking a moderate amount of alcohol, moderate for Foster anyway. Either way the depressants had done little for his mood and intrusive thoughts. Deep down, Foster knew he wasn't thinking straight, however he was now fully committed to reclaiming his old life back and ignored the concerns. Even if he was ill, he was convinced that the operation was for real and believed that his strange thought processes at times had been more to do with his alcohol use than anything else. Although there was a link, Foster would never believe that he had a drug and alcohol problem, or a serious mental health disorder. In his mind it was just the stress and drink that had made him feel a little out of character. Although he had originally questioned the voices in his head, he was now, no longer able to resist or ignore them; no matter what they said or told him to do.

An hour later Foster was once again in the familiar darkness of West Ording forest, reading through the operational pack. As he scan read through the second phase of the operational briefing that pretty much went along the same lines as the first, 'neutralise another member of the Gang at this location'. Foster's second target was Larry Pearson. As he scrolled through the intelligence pertaining to him, he saw that his home address was a detached house, named Elm Farm cottage in Ridge Road, a country lane that ran adjacent to the City's University Campus and out to a semi-rural location. Foster knew it well. Whilst serving on the Armed Response Vehicles during a boring night shift, he and a colleague had gone exploring up the lane and had been impressed by the large detached houses and their quiet country like surroundings even though they were actually only a stone's throw away from the City's football teams stadium in the Falton District. As Foster surveyed the map closer, he established a discreet route in. The plan was that he would dump his car a couple of miles away in a lay by on Heathling Road north of the City's northern Hollingdale District, and jog across the fields that led to the target's address to prevent the car being seen near to the scene. From there he would force entry to the property and take out Pearson. Foster was pleased to learn that Pearson was a divorcee who lived alone; this ensured that there would be no one else to deal with.

Wednesday 28th August at one am, a time of night that was highly likely to ensure he was asleep. Everything was now set. Foster finished scanning the information which included instructions to return to the box the following Sunday, 1st September, and no later. Like before, he destroyed all of the pages that related to Pearson. He then removed the Sig Sauer 9mm handgun and loaded the magazine clip with five 9mm rounds, leaving the other ten available for the other two men. Five rounds a piece was plenty enough. He slid the clip into the gun's magazine housing and placed it down the front of his trousers, applying the safety catch beforehand to prevent any gender confusing type injuries that would result from an accidental discharge of the weapon. For a moment Foster paused as he looked at the cocaine that was left in the bag and pondered whether it was a good idea to take it, after all it had made him a little paranoid, and Drayson was hardly happy about him taking it. However as the temptation grew too strong to ignore, Foster grabbed the remaining powder and money, closed the tin and reburied it.

Before he got back into his car he took a small snort and then hid the bag under his car bonnet release catch. He then tore a hole in the rear of the passenger seat where the road map was kept and placed the gun into the hole to prevent it from being easily seen. It would be bad enough if the cocaine was found, let alone the pistol. Foster drove the long way back to his flat to reduce the risk of seeing a police unit. Unlike the Sykes job, Foster affirmed to himself that he wouldn't make any slip ups this time around. And this time would be different anyway, for starters he would be using a gun which seemed, although paradoxical, a less violent way to kill someone. As much as Foster had been somewhat traumatised by the events of the week before, during the ensuing days there had actually been a part of him that had enjoyed killing Sykes. His moods were now frequently shifting from good to bad within minutes and the voices were regularly talking to him without any reprieve. One moment he would feel as though he was about to have a panic attack, the next a sense of pride at how he helped finally rid the world of a dangerous scum bag, one who would try to rape someone if he didn't get his own way.

In the fleeting moments when Foster did feel some remorse, the flashbacks of Sykes trying to rape him, plus the angry voices in his head, would induce severe mood swings that would have him punching doors until he eventually calmed down. However, whenever he saw the damage he had caused there would always be the same haze of amnesia as he tried to recall why he had lost his temper in the first place. Unfortunately the loss of awareness and time was becoming a more frequent occurrence despite Foster being relatively indifferent as to why it was happening to him.

On his arrival back home at one am, Foster walked straight into the front room and switched the television on. Over the recent months since being retired he had either needed extremely little sleep, even when he wasn't taking drugs, or stayed in bed for days on end. And after sleeping constantly for the past week, he now felt energised, putting it down to finding his purpose in life once again, something he was good at................. stopping criminals who were ruining people's lives. There had even been moments when Foster felt as though he was having epiphanies and that somehow he was doing the work of a higher power, like he was an Archangel sent to destroy evil.

He leant back in his seat, wrapping himself up in the comfort of his delusions of grandeur, his unrealised psychosis, and began to wonder whether Drayson had been destined to help him turn his life around, to be his salvation. The sad but harsh truth was that the Drayson had no intention of saving anybody but himself.

Detective Games
Chapter Twenty Five

The following morning at seven am, after arresting Kennedy and Poultan, Anaura awoke on the hard floor of the office. He looked over at Richards whose black eye was now well and truly in full bloom. Richards woke up too and shook his head, exclaiming how his head felt like it was going to explode to which Anaura replied that he would get the coffee on the go and that because it was a Sunday he would treat him to a fry up at the café around the corner. The two men got up and changed into their suits that their respective wives had kept dropping off at the station with supplies. After finishing their hearty morning breakfast, Anaura and Richards got into one of their 'authorised' Fords and drove from the office to the custody block.

On their arrival, they were met by Sgt Gosden who asked them if they were OK after seeing Richards' eye. He explained how Poultan had been playing up but Kennedy had been quiet as a mouse which kind of demonstrated who was the boss. Anaura nodded in acknowledgement before requesting that Kennedy be prepared for interview. An hour later when his solicitor arrived, Anaura told Richards that he should sit out on the interview because of what had happened the day before, Richards agreed despite commenting on how he would like to have given him another whack.

Kennedy was removed from his cell and taken to meet Anaura and his solicitor. As he emerged from the cell block's secure steel door, he smiled at Anaura and asked how Usher and Valera were doing and stating that he would like to have had a 'go' on them. Anaura scowled and leant towards him before whispering to Kennedy that he was lucky that he was a copper, otherwise he would have been smashing him all over the custody block. Anaura stood off but maintained direct eye contact with him as

Kennedy's female solicitor asked what he had said knowing that whatever it had been, it wasn't on a professional level. Still staring at Kennedy, he then told the jumped up cow of a solicitor to mind her own business as it was between him and her client. If Kennedy wanted to tell her what he had said then that was up to him. Although she appeared to be infuriated by Anaura's attitude, she soon backed off when she saw that Kennedy was laughing at her for being flustered.

Inside the interview room the tapes were switched on to begin recording everything that was said. For the purpose of the tape Anaura stated where they were and reminded Kennedy of his rights and the police caution. After a further few seconds of staring, he began questioning Kennedy about the money and the drugs he was seen passing and receiving from the passenger of the Subaru. Kennedy didn't say a word. Anaura shrugged and continued to ask questions about who the males in the Subaru were and how he knew them and if the drugs were his. Kennedy didn't reply. The silence of Kennedy would have provoked some people, but Anaura had done it all before and although 'no comment', or silent interviews were an annoying hindrance, they were nothing new and rarely got the suspect anywhere anyway.

"I should remind you Luke that this is your chance to say something, if you don't say anything now that you later rely on in court, well the jury may wonder why and drew inference from that. Like that you're lying!" Anaura said without caring whether Kennedy listened or not.

Kennedy remained silent then crossed his arms and arrogantly smiled back at Anaura who reciprocated.

"OK Luke, lets tell it how it is. You're a drug dealer working for the Gang, namely Ryan Bradford, Larry Pearson, Nick Sykes and Paul Cooper and that was their dope you were handing to Poultan and his mate in the car, wasn't it? It ain't looking good for you mate, not good at all!"

Although Kennedy remained silent, the very mention of the Gang had made him shuffle in his seat. Anaura stared at him hard and could see that there was a sense of worry in his expression. Due to Anaura's ability to read people and seeing how Kennedy

173

was reacting, he didn't waste the opportunity to capitalise on his discomfort.

"Oooooohhhh. I just hit a nerve there didn't I? I guess your reaction tells me everything I need to know doesn't it?" Anaura said with a sneer, realising that he was finally starting to get to him.

"Go fuck yourself! You don't know anything you stupid fucking black Aussie twat! What can you prove?" Kennedy growled.

"New Zealand Maori actually; anyway, geography and ethnicity lesson over, I know one thing, mentioning the Gang is the only thing that's made you open your mouth. So I guess I know for sure now that you have some involvement with them. Not so clever after all are you?" Anaura replied with satisfaction.

Kennedy promptly refused to answer any more questions and requested that he be taken back to his cell. Anaura didn't need to know any more, Kennedy was definitely linked to the Gang and with Poultan in custody too, he had an opportunity to play them off against each other. Kennedy didn't need to say another word.

Anaura wrapped the interview up and escorted Kennedy and his solicitor out of the room and towards the custody bridge where Gosden requested that one of the custody assistants take Kennedy back to his cell. Anaura walked into the report writing room and gave a thumbs up to Richards who said back to him that the interview must have gone well. Anaura told him that Kennedy hadn't said a word until he made a reference to the Gang which instantly made him react.

"If he reacts to the mere mention of them, he has to be linked somehow!" Richards said.

"Oh yeah, absolutely. But, I'm not looking to try and extract anything else from Kennedy, he's too smart to say any more now. Poultan on the other hand; well he isn't going to be as hard as Kennedy to influence!" Anaura said, finishing the sentence with a satisfied raise of his eyebrows.

The two detectives approached Gosden and asked for Poultan to be brought down for questioning. Richards looked around and asked where Poultan's solicitor was. Anaura replied with a huge smile that he wasn't having one. No solicitor meant no witnesses, they could talk to him about whatever they wanted, with and without the tape on.

Fifteen minutes later Anaura was asking Poultan questions about what had been passed between his passenger and Kennedy, who the passenger was and how he knew Kennedy. Poultan answered each question with the same anecdotal answers about how he didn't know anything and had just been asked to drive a friend to Kennedy's house. When he didn't get anything out of him, Anaura moved onto why he had tried to get away and driven so dangerously to do so. In response, Poultan used the common criminal excuse of "I was scared. I didn't realise you were coppers so I tried to get away!". After forty minutes of questioning, Poultan finally admitted to dangerous driving but nothing else so Anaura concluded the interview.

"It's a shame that you didn't mention anything about Luke Kennedy, because he had plenty to say about you, eh DS Richards?" Anaura said, still looking at Poultan.

"I don't believe you, nice try though!" Poultan replied with a smart arse type of smile.

"Really? OK, fine, I won't tell you what he implied about your involvement with the Gang then!" Anaura said with an even bigger grin than Poultan's.

Poultan's face dropped into a shocked expression. Anaura went to pack away Poultan's file before he was stopped and asked what Kennedy had said about him.

"Actually wait a second; didn't I nick you for assaulting me too? I forgot to ask any questions about that. DS Richards can you get another tape please?"

"Wait, wait, wait! If you book me up for that too, I'm definitely going to prison for sure! I didn't mean to hit you, it was an accident. OK, OK, I'll help you with whatever you want, just don't interview me for that as well!"

"Are you trying to bribe me? I hope not. Well if you really want to know- when the Gang were mentioned, Kennedy provided us with all we needed to know." Anaura said without embellishing what Kennedy had actually said or not.

175

"That fucking liar! Right, I swear down what I'm about to tell you is the truth. I can't believe I'm going to tell you this!"

Anaura told him that he had already started and said enough to put himself in the frame, so he might as well finish.

"I wasn't involved with the drugs, that was the other two. And don't even think I'm going to tell you who was in the car with me. But yeah they were exchanging packages and it was definitely 'China white', you know cocaine!! You're right about Luke, he is involved with the Gang, he must be mad though for telling you that. Anyway I swear I don't deal drugs any more, I'm just a driver, most of the time I don't even know what or who I'm carrying in the car, Luke doesn't tell me anything, and I've never met anyone high up in the Gang, I swear!" Poultan declared.

"Yeah sure Jamie whatever. Tell me more about Kennedy and the work he does for the Gang." Anaura ordered, feeling as though Poultan was beginning to go off at a tangent to avoid answering his questions.

"OK it's like this, although they don't tell me anything, I do hear things you know. And I know that Luke has been slowly rising up the ranks in the Gang for a while now, he's one of their best dealers and he's getting even better. What you saw was tip of the iceberg stuff, I've heard he's looking to get involved with the Gang on a much bigger level. He definitely knows a lot of stuff about what they're up to. That's all I know, I swear!!"

"Are you sure there's nothing else? You haven't really given us much more than a little bit of crap wishy washy intelligence, it's hardly ground breaking evidence is it Jamie? Nothing that's going to help you anyway!" Anaura said as he began to place another tape into the tape recorder.

"WAIT! I've heard about a dirty copper if that's better?" Poultan suddenly blurted out.

Anaura sat down and looked at Richards with a frown before staring back at Poultan and asking him to expand on what he had just said whilst warning him that if he was lying, he would be in deep trouble. Poultan smirked at Anaura and Richards and said that he would only help them if they didn't pursue the assault on Anaura and helped him with the drug accessory charges. Anaura nodded before Richards interjected and told him to come out with it. Poultan paused for a moment before telling them that while he had been driving Kennedy around one night back in April, or May, they had stopped at a nice house in the rich part of the City. Richards raised an eyebrow at Anaura as Poultan continued explaining how Kennedy had told him to stay in the car before he went inside. About five minutes later Poultan said that Kennedy had called to tell him that he wouldn't be coming out for at least half an hour and that he should drive around to prevent anyone seeing his car outside the house. He then explained how Kennedy had hung up but must not have done it properly as he could overhear a man mentioning something about the harbour in the background of the open call. The other man told Kennedy about a dirty copper they had in their pockets. Richards interrupted him and asked if he had a name. Poultan shook his head and said that the unknown male never said a name and had only made references to the copper. Poultan remarked that whoever it was, the man clearly didn't trust Kennedy with the information.

Richards told Poultan to keep going so he continued, explaining how the man expressed to Kennedy that he and the rest of the group didn't fully trust the copper as they believed he was covering something up from them. He went on to say that Kennedy should try to keep a low profile until they were a hundred percent sure that no one was watching them.

"If that's true, then why have we got Kennedy in custody for supplying five to six grand's worth of 'China white' as you put it? It's hardly low key is it Jamie?" Anaura enquired feeling doubts about the legitimacy of Poultan's claims.

"Well, after laying low for a month or two, Luke took a phone call in another room when I was at his house. When he returned he told me and a couple of the other guys that we were back in business! Have I given you enough now?" Poultan said.

"I'm not sure I believe you Jamie. It seems to me as though you're just using this dirty cop story to divert our attention away from you!" Anaura replied.

"I swear on my life that it's true, I swear!" said Poultan in a panic.

"Well you swear on a lot Jamie, doesn't mean you're telling the truth though!" Richards said.

When it was clear that Poultan really did not have anything else left to say, Richards escorted him back to his cell. A few minutes later he returned to the interview room where Anaura was sat waiting for him.

"Jesus Christ Ian, what the hell is going on?" Anaura asked with confusion and worry.

"I don't know mate. And I don't know how we're meant to find out who it is either; bloody hell it could be anyone couldn't it?! That's even if he's telling the truth!" Richards replied.

"This is not what we needed! As if things weren't complicated enough already! Ian we can't trust anybody but ourselves with this stuff until we find out who we are dealing with!".

Richards sat down and the two detectives looked at one another across the table; they both needed a break!

Elm Farm Cottage
Chapter Twenty Six

At eleven thirty pm on Wednesday 28th August, Foster pulled up in a lay by on Heathling Road, a few miles north of the City. He switched off the engine and reached into the back of the passenger seat to remove the Sig hand gun he had hidden. He pulled the magazine out and checked that the moving parts of the gun were all still in good working order. Failing to check the condition of your weapon before a job could result in the gun having a stoppage at a vital moment if something wasn't right.

The action of the gun's slide was smooth and slick; satisfied he replaced the magazine into its housing and made the weapon ready by pulling the slide back, thus loading a 9mm round into the breach. He took a pinch of powder from the bag of rapidly disappearing cocaine and put the gun down his trousers in preparation for the jog to Pearson's house that was ahead of him. He got out of his car and clambered over the fence that led into the open country space before setting off towards his target. Foster moved swiftly through the field until he was within a quarter of a mile of the house and slowed down to walking pace to ensure he could approach without detection or being too out of breath.

Twelve minutes later he reached a set of bushes that lined the length of Ridge Road and peered through them to check his position in the lane. A hundred meters to his left, Foster could see the silhouette of a house in the moonlight, and in front of him another brightly lit house. He stealthily walked along the row of the bushes to prevent being seen by the occupants of the bright house until he was opposite the cottage up the road. It was Pearson's house! The small light over the door shone down onto a plaque that said 'ELM FARM COTTAGE' in big letters on it, confirming that it was the right address.

Foster moved out from the bushes and gained access to the rear of the cottage. There wasn't a light on inside the property; this was a good sign, it meant that Pearson was asleep and would be easier to get to. Foster crept over to the rear window and forced the old wooden frame open with a screw driver. He climbed through and onto a kitchen work top, closing the window gently behind him. As he silently climbed down from the work top, he removed the Sig from his trousers without taking his eyes of the kitchen's barn-like door. Foster raised the gun up to his eye line and disengaged the safety catch. Just as he had been trained to do, he began to move tactically and methodically through the downstairs rooms, with his gun raised up in front of him, ensuring that each one was clear before he moved onto the next. Only a fool would have gone upstairs without first making sure that Pearson hadn't fallen asleep in the lounge.

Without a sound, Foster stealthily moved towards the staircase, walking in a slightly crouched style that meant his movements were slow and precise; and more importantly silent! Just as he was about to place his foot onto the first step, he felt severe pain shoot through his head as flashbacks of killing Mahood and Sykes abruptly appeared. He stopped and wobbled on his feet as he raised his left hand up to his brow. The feeling was excruciating.

As the agony began to subside, it was replaced with anger as the self-hate for being unprofessional again welled in Foster. He clenched his fist and shook his head in an attempt to compose himself. There was no way that he was going to get this one wrong. Foster steadied himself and made his way up the stairs one by one, and like the downstairs he slowly opened the door of each room and cleared inside them until he reached the final room of the cottage. He gently cracked the door open and began to move through the gap.

Foster opened the door a little further whilst raising his gun up into the dark void ahead of him before moving swiftly and purposefully into the large room and towards the bed where he was greeted with a perfectly made, untouched bed. Pearson wasn't there! Foster kicked the bed in a rage questioning where he could be. Just as he was about to smash the room up in frustration, he saw the reflection of light gliding across the ceiling and the sound of a car engine. He ran to the window and saw Pearson climbing out of his car and walking towards the property.

Foster looked at his watch, it was just before twelve am, the Op pack had said to go to the house at one am, Foster cursed himself for the amateurish mistake. Downstairs he could hear Pearson entering the front door. Foster sat down in the chair that was in the corner of the room and waited. As Pearson walked up the stairs, Foster could hear his heavy footsteps reaching the top and heading towards the bedroom where he was. The door opened. Foster pointed the gun at Pearson's moonlit torso. Pearson flicked the light switch on and as the halogen bulbs suddenly illuminated the room, he was greeted with the sight of Foster sat in the chair looking directly at him.

"Who the fuck are.................".

Foster instantaneously leapt from the seat, firing two shots in rapid succession before he had fully got to his feet, leaving Pearson unable to finish the sentence owing to the blunt 9mm bullets slamming into his chest and bouncing off his spine and ribs before exiting his body. The blood sprayed up against the white horse hair plaster wall behind Pearson before he was thrown up against it from the impacts. As he slid down the wall still alive but severely injured, Foster charged towards the heavily breathing man who was struggling to fill his lungs with air, and pulled the trigger repeatedly. The last three remaining bullets burst from the guns barrel and hurtled towards and into Pearson's chest creating catastrophic injuries. Foster continued to pull the trigger until he realised the clip was empty a number of clicks ago. A third round would have finished Pearson off, but Foster was not satisfied with that and wanted to make a real mess of him. With only a total of fifteen rounds, Foster was lucky that he hadn't loaded them all into the magazine or he would not have had any left for the others as a result of his trigger happiness.

Pearson's body settled with an audible final exhale of breath. Foster checked him for signs of life; there were none. He gave a quick glance around to make sure he hadn't left anything, the pause almost allowed the pool of blood that was moving across the pine floor to touch his shoes. Foster swiped his foot away. There was no way he would make the same evidential screw ups he had with Sykes. To be completely sure, he checked that the chair he had been sat on was clear of anything incriminating before returning back to Pearson's body to admire his handy work on the villain.

A few minutes later, Foster suddenly realised that he had been stood there for far too long and snapped into action, jumping over the large pool of blood, racing down the stairs and out of the front door. After flying out of the cottage's garden gate and almost slipping, he turned right and headed up the lane, where after fifty meters he cut through the hedgerow. Foster broke through the bracken and ran as fast as he could across the field towards his car in the secluded lay by. In the distance, the familiar sound of an Armed Response BMW X5's fog horn and sirens signalling other road users to move out of the way could be heard. He started to run even faster. On reaching the lay-by, Foster tripped and skidded along the gravelly floor, grazing his knee in the process. He climbed to his feet and got into the car and sped away along the country lane towards Heathling Village at warp speed, using the main roads at that point would have been a bad idea.

Driving through the winding roads of Heathling, Foster reflected on how he had enjoyed killing Pearson, the rush of pulling the trigger was better than using an archaic knife. Foster smiled with the knowledge that he would be home safe and dry before his former colleagues on the firearms unit and CID would have worked out what had happened. The likelihood was that they would put the incident down to an armed burglar or fellow criminal. 'The Chief and Drayson will be really happy with this one" Foster said to himself as he entered Heathling Village and picked up the road that would eventually lead him safely home.

To congratulate himself, Foster took a hit of the cocaine and then yelled out with euphoria as he turned up the CD player and excitedly bounced his head back and forth to the hard pumping music that was booming out of the car's speakers. It had been a productive day at the 'office'!

Unwelcome News
Chapter Twenty Seven

The following morning, Anaura sat in the Supervisor's office with a splitting headache. After the less than fruitful interviews with Kennedy and Poultan, he had taken a few well-earned days off and told the rest of his team to do the same. However when he was at home with Laura, he could think of nothing but what Poultan had said to him about there being a corrupt copper within the Gang. If there was one thing that Anaura hated; it was a corrupt policeman. Seeing that he was becoming obsessive, Laura left the kids with a babysitter and the couple had gone out for a meal at a Chinese restaurant in Lymindale, a medieval village out of the City. Although the conversation was light hearted, Laura knew that he was still worrying about work.

An hour after they arrived home Laura asked him to discuss what was bothering him. At first he was hesitant but soon came out with it. He explained to Laura that during an interview with Poultan after the car chase (which hadn't gone down well with Laura) he and Richards were told that there was a dirty copper within the Gang's outfit. Laura looked shocked before she said "wait a minute Peter!" and asked him whether Poultan could be believed or trusted; he was after all, a criminal. Anaura hadn't thought of it from that angle and when Laura expressed concern that the information may have been used to take his attention away from the Gang, sending him on a wild goose chase, Anaura reflected that he may have rushed to conclusions through stress.

"Peter think about it. If you were in trouble and a copper offered you a deal, wouldn't you say anything to help yourself? It's highly possible that he was just trying to influence you to save his own skin." She said.

Anaura thought about it and realised that she may have had a point. After Laura's sensible advice and three days' rest, he was back in the office and firmly setting his sights on the Gang once again. Although the idea of a corrupt copper still troubled him, he knew that wasting time looking for what could turn out to be the bogey man, was potentially lost time. It was better to focus on the Gang because if they caught them, they would catch their alleged copper too, as there was no way that they would go down without him. And besides Laura was right, it may have been a load of rubbish that Poultan was spouting anyway.

Anaura reached into his locker and pulled out a small bottle of paracetamol and took two tablets that were washed down with a swig of coffee. He returned to the Op Spear related paper work and began to read, pushing through his headache. So far they had a low level drug dealer, a decent level one and a little bit of intelligence that could have been true or not. However one thing that hadn't been a load of rubbish was when Poultan had inadvertently mentioned Cooper's home address and then the harbour. This reminded him that he needed to reassess whether the Observation point was still worth having twenty four hours a day as Cooper, or any of the others, hadn't been seen going near the harbour since the Surveillance crew had followed him there at the beginning of the month. Anaura was beginning to wonder how much significance it really had. Poultan may have alluded to the harbour, but it was not as though he was fully privy to the conversation between Cooper and Kennedy anyway.

He leant back in his seat, squeezed his eyes and decided to take a rest. Richards had warned him about burning himself out or rushing into things head strong. Once again Anaura began to ponder whether dropping Surveillance had been a good idea. In his haste he naively thought that Kennedy would have given him something solid when he realised that he could be facing a long time inside; but he hadn't. Anaura was starting to realise that it was true what people said........'Rome wasn't built in a day'. After all the years of experience and a normally level head, he had done what he never thought he would; charged in like a bull in a china shop and in turn made some poor decisions. Anaura started to see how the Gang had always evaded Drayson. They were just too smart and their dealers were just too scared of them to say anything, even if it meant a very long prison sentence.

"PETER?!!!!!"

Anaura heard Richards' asking for him from the main office. He got up still squeezing his eyes to relieve the pressure, and walked over to the door to see what Richards wanted.

"What's up Ian?" Anaura said with a slight despondent voice brought on by feeling as though he had screwed up the investigation.

"You're not going to like this! Pearson's dead; murdered!" Richards said.

"You're joking, how, when, where?!" Anaura asked, his headache instantaneously lifting with the shock of the revelation.

Richards explained that he had just seen it on the BBC news and checked the incident logs which confirmed it.

"WHY THE FUCK WERE WE NOT TOLD EARLIER! THE BLOODY PRESS KNEW BEFORE WE DID!!!!" Anaura shouted as he booted the chair in front of him, sending it crashing into the desk.

Severely agitated, he spun on his heels and stormed back into his office and picked up the phone to Steiner. When he answered, Anaura barely gave him a chance to think before demanding to know why they had not been told about Pearson's murder straight after it had happened. Steiner, like so many times before, calmed him down and reminded him that no one knew that they were investigating the Gang and that he had only just found out at an emergency command meeting himself. Anaura, still reeling from his headache and the news, demanded to be given access to the crime scene to which Steiner replied that Major crime would be dealing with it. It was a murder after all and not a drugs related case. Anaura replied that Pearson was one of his suspects and that it should remain as part of his case.

"How do you propose to investigate a murder as well as run a huge drugs operation Peter?"

"Listen Jason, this case should be ours! There could be a link, something we could use." Anaura protested.

"NO PETER!" Steiner snapped

The line went silent for a moment before Steiner huffed.

"Peter, I know you want this operation to succeed, I really do, but you have to realise that no one is going to be comfortable with you dealing with a murder investigation at the same time as Spear, something would get missed. No; you need to focus your attention on the other members, like Bradford for example. You can't do that whilst investigating a murder can you??"

"I could, but I understand why you're saying I can't." Anaura said feeling dejected.

"I'll tell you what Peter. I'll pull some strings and get you access to the crime scene to see if there's any evidence of a link. Maybe it will set your mind at rest if you see that it was probably just a burglary that went wrong!"

"OK Jason, thanks.".

"Peter, had you thought about taking a little bit of time off? You know, get yourself in harmony again. You sound a little stressed!" Steiner suggested.

Anaura told Steiner that he already had but would consider another day after he had visited the crime scene. He put down the phone and felt the stress washing over him once again. The operation was spinning out of control and it seemed as though there was nothing he could do to stop it. He picked up his phone to call Laura to express how unhappy he was. She asked him whether it was time to 'hang up the gloves' and ask to be reassigned but he replied that he couldn't and needed to see it through. Laura feeling a deep sense of concern for her husband told him that it was high time that he sort a quieter posting once he finished the operation, or his health would seriously suffer. Anaura finished the call by telling Laura that he would be home on time that night and that he was even considering another couple of days off. Laura told him she would make something nice for dinner and how it would be nice to see him again properly after the week he had spent sleeping in the office and how he had done nothing but worry on his time off.

Feeling a little happier after speaking to Laura, he got up and went outside to join Richards and the other officers. Valera, who was now back on duty with Usher after the assaults, asked how he had got on with Steiner. Anaura replied that they would not be keeping the Pearson job but that they would have the opportunity to attend the crime scene. Richards replied that at least that was something, to which he just pulled a forced smile and a shrug of the shoulders.

Seeing that Anaura was far from his usual happy self, Valera and Usher offered to make everyone a drink while Richards said that he would get everyone a bacon sandwich from around the block. Anaura thanked him and then gave him a wink before he collapsed into a nearby chair, huffing with frustration and sheer exhaustion.

"Are you OK boss?" Enquired Williams.

"Yeah, I'm fine. I'm just not sure we're going to win this one!" Anaura replied.

"Why is that sir? We're doing alright aren't we?"

"Yeah you guys are, it's just that I'm not. Put it like this, by now the rest of the Gang will have heard that one of theirs is dead. The news will panic them into hiding or laying low as they'll be worried that someone is moving in on them. This was operation our window; a window that is now starting to shut!" Anaura said before standing up and telling the Intel officers to have a long break while he and Richards went to the scene.

Anaura smiled at the officers, attempting to hide his stress induced, depressed state. He wearily returned to his office and closed the door, something he never usually did unless he was having a meeting. The four Intel officers looked at each other and pulled concerned expressions. Over the weeks they had grown fond of Anaura helped by his friendly and approachable nature and it was disappointing to see him feeling so low.

PC Crane turned to the other three Intel officers and said that he had an idea and told them to follow him to the lounge area to discuss the plan he had come up with. He stood up whilst the others asked why he was being so mysterious and ushering them to the lounge instead of just coming out with it there and then.

"I don't want Anaura to hear what I've got to say as I don't think he would be very happy with me. But we might just be able to help him and this operation!" Crane remarked with a smile.

The very same day, Drayson was on his way to speak to the Chief Constable about a matter of urgency, when his pay as you go phone rang, and despite driving and risking a ticket, he answered it. Before he even removed his phone, he knew who it was.

"WHAT IS GOING ON ROBBIE?" Bradford screamed down the phone, prompting Drayson to takes his eyes off the road to turn the volume down on the handset.

"I was just about to call you Ryan. I know, I can't believe it either. I'm going to speak to the Chief now and then I'll get to the crime scene to start finding out who did this!" Drayson replied, feigning a distressed voice.

"THAT AINT BLOODY GOOD ENOUGH ROBBIE!" Bradford screamed back at him.

"Right Ryan, you're going to have to calm down mate! It looks like he was shot in a Burglary so it could have been anyone couldn't it?! What would you have me do? I'm trying to get on the case to find out who did this, that's all I can do!"

"Robbie, I don't like this, not one bit! Nick has gone missing, now Larry's dead, something ain't right!" Bradford said.

Drayson responded by telling him that he would establish what was going on and reassured him that Sykes may still have just disappeared for a while to get away from his wife and that it wasn't completely out of character for him. He then began telling Bradford how there was a Russian drug syndicate moving into the area and that they could have been responsible. Bradford went silent at the other end of the phone, he had bought the story, but Drayson knew that time was running out and that he would need to keep him sweet until Foster could get to him.

Before he finished the call, Bradford asked whether he should get a gun or leave the city. "NO" Drayson replied in a panic knowing that it would make it impossible to take him out. Just as Bradford was about to hang up, Drayson said to him "Remember Ryan, this is your city, it doesn't belong to a bunch of dirty Russians!". The parting words had more of a positive affect than anything else he had said as the sycophantic sucking up appealed to Bradford's grandiose nature. He finished the call less than a hundred metres away from the gates of Headquarters. He parked his car up and headed to the Chief's office. He needed to be on this murder case but not for the reasons he gave Bradford; no, he needed to be on the case to ensure that there could never be anything linking him to the murder, soon to be plural. He needed to control what was investigated and what wasn't.

Drayson walked into the Chief's office and was warmly welcomed by him and his assistant. As he took a seat, the Chief informed him that he would be looking to promote him as soon as possible as the current Assistant Chief's retirement was imminent. Drayson smiled before asking the Chief whether he would be able to do him one last favour. The Chief nodded with an open expression. Drayson subsequently told him that he wanted to have one last bit of glory under his belt and that the Pearson murder would be perfect. He explained that he still had a little while left until his promotion and that his successor as head of SOCU already had enough on his plate. The Chief sat back for a minute before asking Drayson if he really wanted the hassle. He nodded back with enthusiasm before asking if he could also have an appraisal of the operation that was already running on the Gang as it would help him find out if there was a link. He then went onto say that the two investigations ought to be combined and headed up by someone more experienced than Anaura; someone like him. The Chief agreed and told Drayson to get on it right away. He thanked him and left the office with a smug smile. With the murder investigation under his watchful eye and Anaura under his control, he would be well and truly back in business. He may have still had the issue of sorting out Foster post killings, but he would now be able to ensure that his tracks were covered.

Drayson headed back to his car with a slight spring in his step and stopped to speak to any passing officer or member of staff who crossed his path being the excellent PR man he was. As usual he was demonstrating his ability to survive, to adapt. If there was one person that had the ability to come up smelling of roses; it was Drayson, and as he smiled and gushed his way past his fellow colleagues he reached his car and climbed in feeling relief washing over him.

The first port of call was to get to the murder scene to start influencing the investigation's outcome. The second, was to finally rid himself of the rest of the Gang and that annoying thorn in his side-DI Peter Anaura. And the third was to make sure that Foster could never speak on what had been discussed between them. As he pulled away Drayson had a eureka moment................ Foster was an addict, a loser, and unfortunate accidents happened to addicts and losers every day; especially if they ended up taking a bad batch of drugs and overdosed in the process!

One problem sorted! Two to go!

Just a Burglary
Chapter Twenty Nine

"Jason?"

"Ah, alright Peter? Have you calmed down yet?" Steiner asked.

Anaura apologised to Steiner for his earlier outburst over the telephone and explained that the decision to block him from the murder case had come across like he was just being obstructed by Command. After a pause, he then told Steiner that in the cold light of day, he accepted that he couldn't deal with a murder in addition to the operation. Steiner gave him a wink and shook his head.

Accompanied by Richards and Steiner, Anaura entered Elm Farm Cottage and walked to the kitchen where a Scenes of Crime Officer, was dusting down the forced kitchen window, looking for fingerprints and traces of a suspect. Richards asked the forensic officer whether he'd had any success to which the forensic officer replied that apart from a few screwdriver marks and a footprint there was nothing of note and that he believed that the offender must have been wearing gloves.

"Well that's a good start!" Anaura said sarcastically, still feeling slightly depressed from the knowledge that Op Spear was beginning to come apart at the seams.

The forensic officer responded with a 'nothing I can do' gesture which made Anaura smile back at him as he realised that he had been unnecessarily rude to him. The three of them left the forensic officer and made their way around the rest of the downstairs of the cottage, each room providing the same lack of hard evidence that the kitchen had. They approached the stairs, then Steiner looked at Anaura and Richards with raised eyebrows and stated that it had been years since he had attended a murder scene and that he was quite excited to see what lay upstairs. Richards laughed and replied to him that most of the murders that

Vice attended, generally turned out to be drug overdoses; so this one would be a change.

"Ah gentlemen" Drayson said, instigating the three men to look up.

"Great, what's he doing here?" Anaura whispered to Richards as Steiner greeted Drayson with a handshake.

"What brings you here sir?" Steiner asked with a smile.

"This is my case, I'm running it. You know, one last bit of glory before I start the boring game of police politics!" Drayson said in a self-important tone.

"Well at least the case is in good hands then." Steiner responded.

"I suppose I better let you boys through to have a look then. Bit gruesome if you know what I mean, clearly a failed burglary?" He said without a shred of emotion or empathy for his old friend that he'd had killed.

The three men passed by him, with Anaura and Richards pulling forced smiles at him. Drayson feeling smug, waited a moment before he drooped the next bombshell.

"Oh by the way Peter, we'll be working very closely from now on, I'm going to be overseeing Op Spear!" Drayson said with an expression of satisfaction, knowing that the news would crush him.

Anaura replied "Yeah, whatever!" sarcastically as he looked over the bannister at Drayson who was now halfway down the stairs. Drayson stared back at him, but before he could say anything back to him, he had disappeared behind the wall as he headed towards Pearson's bedroom. The air of contempt that Anaura displayed towards the news, wound Drayson up no end and he gritted his teeth, hoping that he would get an opportunity to ruin Anaura's career as soon as possible.

On entering the bedroom, the three men were met by Foster's bloody handy work. By now Pearson's body had turned a pale blue and the copious amounts of blood that were on the floor were now beginning to congeal and dry. Richards was the first to say anything, remarking that he doubted that it was a failed burglary. Anaura pulled a screwed up expression and looked at

192

Steiner who appeared just as perplexed at how the murder scene was being considered a burglary.

Steiner approached one of the nearby detectives and asked for more information as Anaura and Richards discussed the scene.

"I can't believe Drayson's calling this a burglary!" Richards whispered the second Steiner had walked off.

"I know Ian, this doesn't make a shred of sense." Anaura replied.

"What are you two whispering about?" Steiner asked as he returned without Anaura or Richards noticing.

The two detectives replied that they were discussing why it was being called a burglary. Steiner smiled and explained that one of the neighbours had seen Larry Pearson pull up and then heard loud gun shots a few minutes later, and how it was indeed beginning to look like a failed burglary. Richards asked why that meant it was a burglary to which Steiner enquired what else he believed it could be. Someone had broken in and was caught in the act by Pearson who was killed as a result, there was nothing else to suggest otherwise yet, Steiner hypothesised.

"Jason, why would a burglar carry a gun, and even more importantly why would they have pretty much left everything in the house virtually untouched? Seems like a gang related execution to me." said Anuara.

"OK Peter, who was it then? The Gang have no competition here in the City or we would know, and you tell me who else would be stupid enough to do this other than a half-wit burglar who didn't know who it was they were burgling. And anyway at this stage there's no evidence to suggest it was a gang land killing." Steiner commented.

"I'm not buying it!" Anaura said as he walked around the room looking at the scene.

"Jason, we've got two spent 9mm shell casings over here by the seat, the seat itself appears to have slid backwards from the dusty marks on the floor, and there are another three casings by the body. Looks to me as though the killer was sat down when he fired the first two shots and then finished him off from close range; how many burglars do you know of that would sit down, wait for the owner and then kill them instead of trying to escape! And are you trying to tell me that it's likely that an untrained burglar could fire two accurate shots from over ten meters away?" Anaura exclaimed.

"Do we know how many holes are in him yet to start making judgements on accuracy? No! Do we know for sure that he was sat in that seat? No! Why couldn't he have fired the two shots from near the window when he was disturbed? And I would hardly say that he displayed that much marksmanship from that kind of distance." Steiner said.

"Are you an expert in firearms Jason?" Anaura remarked, regretting the sarcastic comment the moment he had said it.

"OK Peter I'm getting tired of this, I know you're very stressed. However it appears to me as though you've just got the hump that Drayson has taken over and that you're not doing as well as you'd hoped with the case. Is that why you're picking holes in this? Perhaps it was more than a burglary, but until there is something solid to confirm that, it isn't. This is Drayson's case now and we're to stay out of it. I suggest you drop the attitude before he has you thrown off Operation Spear!" Steiner said as he angrily stormed out of the room.

Anaura began to follow Steiner out of the room as if about to start a fight with him, however Richards got in his way, putting his hands up to Anaura's chest and telling him to chill out. Anaura swore to himself as Richards stated that it wasn't worth losing his job over. Anaura patted Richards on the shoulder and asked his friend to tell him if he had lost his edge and whether he had bungled the whole operation. He shook his head and replied that Steiner was probably just letting off some steam after being shouted at earlier. Anaura folded his arms and looked down at the floor before reaffirming to Richards that he definitely felt as though there was something seriously wrong with the murder. Richards agreed and then frowned at Anaura who asked him what was up.

"Peter, do you remember what Poultan said to us?" he asked.

Anaura placed his hand to his head and replied "Oh God, please tell me this crap isn't linked, please! You don't think that the coppers somehow had him killed do you?"

Richards raised his hands up in front of himself and pulled a blank expression, replying that perhaps they should be discussing it with someone like Drayson as he was running the show. Anaura huffed and shook his head and said that he didn't trust Drayson with most things, let alone that type of information. Richards implored Anaura to reconsider as Drayson was running things now, and hiding it could land them both in the shit. He nodded back in acknowledgement before saying that they should head back to the base before they had to endure him or Steiner again; enough was enough for one day.

As they walked past Pearson's body, Richards crouched down next to it to have one last look.

"I'm sure you would be saying the same thing as us if you still could!" Richards said in a tongue and cheek manner.

Anaura looked across to Richards and raised his eyebrows. The sad but obvious truth was; the dead couldn't share their secrets.

Foster pulled up to the car park in West Ording Forest. The killing of Pearson had been surprisingly easy. There were no blood stained clothes to worry about, no stupidly discarded weapon and unlike the Sykes job he had no painful flashbacks or doubts about whether what he had done was right. In fact he almost felt a sense of pride whenever he recalled how he had performed like a highly trained assassin. However Foster was now growing impatient, he wanted to be back in the force and although the past month had been both exciting and terrifying, time was ticking slowly. He may have felt more in control than he had before but the reality was that he wasn't.

He opened the box for what was to be the final time. Within seconds of peering inside, the cold realisation that he had used all the cocaine hit him. He may have believed that he would be able to resist but on seeing that it was all gone, the temptation and addiction flared back up with a vengeance. You always crave what you cannot have. Foster would never be able admit it to himself but it was a habit that would not be so easily conquered. The frustration boiled up inside him, he needed a hit fast and without thinking and being driven by addiction he dropped the box back into the hole and rushed off without remembering to rebury it.

An hour later, he banged on the heavy doors of the Cliffe pub where there was a lock-in being held. When the landlord opened the door to see who was knocking, Foster pushed past him and stormed into the pub to ask whether anyone had some cocaine he could buy. The locals were shocked to see him after his long absence, looking so clean. No one answered which prompted Foster to ask again with a little less politeness. Taking umbrage to the way Foster had spoken to them, a well-built local hard man stood up and approached him with his arms open before asking Foster to meet him outside. No one else got up from their seats or took notice. It was obvious that it wasn't the first time this type of thing had happened in the pub.

The two men arrived outside, and before the largely built man with tattoos running up his neck could say anything, Foster punched him with a powerful right cross. As the man fell against the wall, Foster charged towards him and kneed him in the testicles, causing the man to double over in pain. Foster grabbed him by the sides of his head and thrust it backwards so that it smashed into the pubs window and bent him the wrong way over the window ledge. Within a second of the glass shattering the man fell to the ground and Foster followed up with two kicks to his stomach. He lay there groaning as Foster reached into his pockets and stole his wallet, and to Foster's delight, a gram of cocaine.

As the locals came piling out of the pub after hearing the window smash, Foster was already on his toes and running away towards the railway crossing. They would never catch him. After taking the long way back home to avoid being seen by any of them, Foster walked straight into his kitchen and emptied the contents of the bag he had stolen into a dirty glass and poured half a pint of vodka over it. He downed the cocktail and immediately refilled the glass with more of the spirit. The short lived abstinence had actually made him crave the powder and alcohol even more.

Foster collapsed into a chair in his front room and downed the second glass full which had been a bad idea because of his empty stomach. As the drugs and alcohol began to take hold, helped by the lack of food inside him, Foster recalled that he had forgotten something important, something serious. However as his thoughts jumbled up, he gave up trying to work out what he had forgotten and succumbed to warm feeling washing over him. Time ticked by and just as he was about to fall asleep in a stoop, the image of the red operational box shot through his head. It didn't even register with him as fell asleep oblivious to the fact that he had not looked at the operational pack and worse, not even buried it again.

At six o'clock that evening, Foster awoke to the loud sound of his door being repeatedly banged. He fell out of his bed, struggling to recall how he had ended up in it. The knocking at the door grew louder and louder. Whoever was knocking, it was clear that they desperately wanted to talk to him. Foster quietly moved up to the front room's window and gently peered through a small opening in the curtain. Outside his front door, Foster could see the black uniforms and stab vests of a male and female police officer. Foster dropped down to a seated position in a panic and listened as the officers began shouting out his name and saying that they knew he was in there. But he knew better, it was the oldest trick in the copper's book. They couldn't break down the door unless they knew for sure he was in there and if they were not, there was no way he was going to tell them. After another few minutes the knocking stopped and he peered out of the curtains once more; the officers had gone. Foster let out a huge exhale of relief and began to breathe heavily as his panic stricken mind tried to work out why they had been there, but he could not.

Foster walked into the kitchen as the hunger pangs from not eating for over twenty four hours began to feel incredibly uncomfortable. He searched his nigh on bare cupboards for something to eat without success until he discovered the out of date Pot Noodle he had chosen not to eat a week earlier. Foster ripped off the lid and pondered eating it raw such was the hunger he was suffering with. He controlled himself, picked up the kettle, filled it with water and switched it on. It seemed like the kettle took an eternity to boil due to its lime-scale covered heating element. So with only semi-hot water available, he poured it into the pot and mixed the noodles up into a warm mush before devouring it. Feeling unsatisfied and still hungry Foster checked the china pot where he had stored the operational funds; it was empty. He stood there for a minute trying to search his memory for how he had spent the money but with no luck. He soon gave up and went on a rampage around the house looking for any loose five or ten pound notes. After searching the house high and low, he was still without money. Foster considered going to his bank to withdraw some of his monthly pension money, until he looked at the clock and saw that it was the evening. Just as he was beginning to accept that he would go without food once again, he reached into his pockets and found a wallet which confused him as he had lost his own some time ago. He removed the wallet and did not recognise it. He opened it up. And there inside, was about a hundred and fifty pounds worth of notes inside with five pound coins. Foster was ecstatic although somewhat baffled as to why he had the wallet so he began searching through the cards. He yanked each one out until he found a driver's licence. As his eyes surveyed the photographic licence he saw a man's face which induced a flashback of the owner of the licence walking towards him in the Cliffe pub, but nothing else.

The pleasant surprise of finding the wallet and the money was slightly dampened by Foster's inability to remember most of what had happened over the past twenty four hours. However with the hunger pangs getting worse and the cravings for cocaine developing, Foster grabbed his coat and left his flat, wearing the same clothes as he had done for the past thirty four hours.

An hour later with a bag of fish and chips and two grams of cocaine, he returned to his flat to settle down for the rest of the evening. Foster fought through the urge to snort both grams as he knew that it was better to spread them out due to his lack of funds. He snorted one of the grams and swiftly ate half of the large portion of cod and chips, before sitting down to watch TV. As the high from the drugs began to wear off and the low of the vodka he had drank replaced it, Foster took himself off to bed.

The following morning at nine am, Foster awoke up from a deep sleep and walked into his front room and sat down. He saw the half eaten portion of chips and ate them to distract himself from the temptation of wanting to use the second gram there and then. To help prevent him from using the last remaining gram even more, he licked the inside of the bag of the cocaine he had already taken and went into the kitchen to make a coffee with some slightly soured milk. As Foster searched around for a clean cup to use, he opened a cupboard and staring back at him was a bright red mug. He paused and stared at it for a moment, wondering why it had caught his attention, before suddenly realising that he had forgotten to read the operational brief and left the box exposed in his drug seeking crazed desperation. He slammed the cupboard door and rushed out to his car and pulled out of the car park as fast as he could.

Foster arrived at West Ording Forest an hour later in broad sunny daylight, something Drayson had ordered him never to do. He parked his car next to two unattended vehicles and ran into the forest towards the tree that was a lot easier to find in the daylight. Foster thanked God when he saw that it was still there. He quickly opened the box with the key and removed the operational info pack. As he scrolled though the remaining pages, constantly checking for company around him, he learnt that his final targets would be Cooper and Bradford at the same time, a thought that concerned Foster because of the added risk involved. The time of the assignment was between ten and eleven pm, and location was a warehouse on Basin Road South, the same one where Drayson had always met with his associates on the second and last Wednesday of the month. The page ended with Foster being ordered to return to the car park of the forest the following Sunday for an operational 'debrief'. With the information memorised he hurriedly stashed the remaining ten 9mm rounds into his pocket and checked the box was empty before wiping it down and burying it back in the ground.

He finished hiding the box and picked up the last remaining parts of the operational pack to burn them. He lit the pages with his lighter and threw them onto the dry mud to burn through; the last shred of evidence relating to his assignment. He stood there watching the last pages burn with pleasure, knowing that he would soon be back where he belonged, in the police. No matter how many times he had doubted whether he should have gone through with it or whether he could trust Drayson, he had always held onto the thought of getting his life back and how he was wrong to doubt him.

"I wouldn't burn that there son, lots of dry bracken, ha, ha, ha, you'll burn the whole bloody forest down!" An old sounding voice came from behind Foster which startled him and made him spin around. Although Foster regularly heard voices, this wasn't one he recognised.

"Oh, I apologise if I scared you son," said an old man in his seventies who appeared, wearing a farmer's style hat and socks with a walking cane and followed by his Cocker Spaniel dog.

"It's OK" Foster replied looking down at the pack to see if its contents had burned away yet.

"All joking aside though, you really shouldn't burn stuff in a dry forest like this, it could actually start a huge fire. I know it's unlikely, but it happens!" The old man said as he looked down at the burning papers.

Foster began to panic with paranoia as the barely legible remaining paragraphs were slow to burn away. The old man looked at Foster noticing that he was ill at ease and looked as though he hadn't had a wash for a while.

"You alright sonny?" He asked to which Foster just nodded back.

"Well OK then. Don't worry I didn't see what you were burning. Anyway none of my business, it might be a letter from your mistress ha, ha, ha!" The old man said in a friendly and jovial way before he called his dog and gave a wink to Foster. The man left and walked off towards the car park.

Foster sharply inhaled with relief, knowing that if he hadn't have got to the box in time, the old man and his dog may have found it. He smacked his forehead in frustration, cursing himself for making yet another mistake in what had so far been a long list of them. However, the old man hadn't found the box so it was finally time to finish this job once and for all. The following evening at ten pm, he would attend the warehouse and take out Bradford and Cooper, and anyone else that got in his way.

The flames engulfed the remaining pages of the document, destroying the evidence forever. As the pages turned ashes, Foster kicked them around the dry dirt and twigs before walking back to his car and leaving.

Back in Business
Chapter Thirty One

At ten thirty am on the Monday morning, an unmarked police silver Ford Focus pulled up outside a deserted warehouse and out climbed PC Crane and Taggart in plain clothes. They approached a security guard who was parked up outside the building in his employer's livery covered van. This building was the tenth they had visited on Basin Road South that morning and they were fast running out of places to go.

The uniformed guard wound down his window and asked in a suspicious tone how he could help them. Taggart, without identifying himself as a police officer enquired who owned the building to which the security officer asked who wanted to know. Taggart laughed and stated that is wasn't for anything dodgy, it's just that he and his business partner had been looking for a warehouse to run their business from and wanted to find out whether the building was up for rent. The guard asked what type of business they had and why they wanted to use such a run-down building. Crane interjected and replied that they had a storage box company and needed more space to expand their business and that the warehouse was a cheap option allowing higher profit margins. The guard laughed and remarked how their customers would not be happy if they found out that some of their stuff was being stored in a damp warehouse. Taggart smiled and replied "That's business".

The guard leant out of his window towards the pair of them and told them that the owners rarely used it anyway, although he also exclaimed that they did not hear about it from him.

"There's four owners but the one who does business with our firm is called Ryan Bradford. I've heard he's a bit of a property tycoon. I'm sure if you can track him down he'd be up for making a bit of money from renting it out." The guard said.

"You said the owners rarely use it, how rarely? I mean I don't want to waste my time contacting them if they still use it on a weekly basis!" Crane enquired, crouching down next to the window, trying to control his urge to smile with satisfaction.

"Rarely!! I've only seen them on a couple of Wednesday evenings a month.

And when they do turn up they tend to tell me or any of the other lads from the firm to piss off until the morning. They're arseholes, but then rich blokes like that usually are!" he replied.

Crane stood back up and gave a beaming smile at Taggart who thanked the security guard for his help and assured him they would not give away his identity as their business source. Crane winked at the guard and then he and Taggart returned to their car feeling chuffed. As they got inside Taggart told Crane to wait until they had pulled away to say anything.

"YES!!" Crane shouted out when they moved out of sight of the guard.

As they drove out of the harbour complex and past the City Lagoon, the two men were both elated inside the car. They had managed to do what Surveillance had been unable to do; place where Cooper had gone that night and learn that it was on a Wednesday evening. It was highly risky work, especially since they gone around most of the buildings asking questions, but with their clever cover story, the risk had paid off. The information that they had acquired meant that they could finally set up an observation post to watch Cooper and the Gangs activities within the Harbour and warehouse. However there was one potential downside, and that was that Crane and Taggart knew only too well that Anaura and Richards were going to hit the roof when they found out what they had done. Op Spear may have been starting to fall apart but with this new intelligence that could change in a very short space of time.

"So who's going to tell the boss and Richards what we've done?" Taggart asked Crane.

"I suppose it will have to be me, it was my idea after all!" Crane said.

"You know he's going to go mental about this, don't you?"

Taggart said.

"Yeah, but after he shouts and screams for a bit, he'll realise how important what we've done is. At the end of the day, we needed to find another way in, and we might have just done that!" Crane remarked with a smile.

"I guess we'll find out in half an hour won't we?"

The two men turned right onto Old Sea Road and headed back towards Shoreton Police Station where they would tell Anaura what they had done knowing full well that it would either go brilliantly or he would throw them both off the operation.

Back at the office Anaura was discussing with Richards how he was considering swallowing his pride and requesting Surveillance's support again without discussing the huge elephant that was in the room. They had returned from a weekend off and yet despite being in the office for a number of hours, they were yet to discuss how they would go about sorting out the corrupt officer business. The two detectives finished discussing the Op Spear tactical options and went back to typing and reading through the investigations file.

Ten minutes later, Richards stopped typing and looked at Anaura and said "We need to talk about this, it's been four days!" referring to the murder and their theory on the dirty copper. Anaura huffed, he knew that he could not bury his head in the sand any longer, Drayson would no doubt be visiting the office any day and would go ballistic if he found out that they had kept the information from him. As much as Anaura didn't like him or trust him, he was overseeing the investigation now and could have him removed at a click of his fingers if he did not play ball.

Anaura nodded at Richards and stood up to call Drayson who answered with his usual self-important tone. Anaura told him that he would like to start discussing the details of Op Spear, Drayson replied by telling him that he was only five minutes away from the Shoreton Station before hanging up. Anaura told Richards what was happening and Richards shook his head and said how they should have known that the second they got back from leave, he would be there questioning them about the operation.

Drayson walked into the office and without saying a word to

Usher, Valera or the two Intel officers, he made his way directly into the supervisor's office.

"Well, where are we at then?" Drayson enquired in a demanding way.

Anaura had not seen him arrive and swiftly turned his head to face Drayson. For a second he felt like making a sarcastic comment about his manners but thought better of it.

"Well, we're just going through the intelligence logs and past investigations to see what else could turn up, and following some leads that Poultan provided." Anaura said.

"So in other words you're nowhere! I think it was a bad decision calling off Surveillance, Anaura, a very bad decision! Let me take a look at those files!"

He pulled up a seat next to Anaura and began looking through the open file on his desk whilst belligerently stating how he could not work out how Anaura had landed the job when there were much better qualified SOCU detectives available. Richards glared at Drayson while his head was buried in the file.

Drayson paused from reading the file and abruptly asked Richards to make some coffees for them. Richards forced a smile and walked around to collect Anaura's cup. As Drayson leant across Anaura in a purposefully rude way to grab his mug for Richards, his eyes locked on the Scotland Yard business card that was pinned to the board next to the desk. Just as Anaura was about to look at what was catching his attention, Drayson spilt the dregs of the coffee left in the mug onto Anaura's shirt prompting him to pull away from the desk in an attempt to avoid the rest of the spillage.

"Sorry mate. Well, as you have to change your shirt, you may as well put a tie on too." Drayson remarked snidely.

Anaura felt like giving him a left hook but stood up and removed a spare shirt from his locker before going off to the toilets to change, leaving Drayson in the office. As he left the toilets wearing his new shirt, Anaura was met in the corridor by Richards who couldn't help but mention his newly adorned tie.

"Ian, do you still think we should be telling this prick about what Poultan said?" Anaura asked.

"I know the guy is a complete nob Peter, but if we don't we'll be bang in trouble. I mean the guy is going to be Assistant Chief soon, we don't want him as an enemy, he could shut the Vice unit down in a heartbeat!"

"You're right, but I just don't trust him, never have, never will!" Anaura remarked as the two men walked back to the office.

Before they walked back in, Drayson swiftly attempted to remove the business card that he had seen on the board but was unable to in time. As he sat down, he felt a desperate need to find out why Anaura was involved with Scotland Yard and whether it had anything to do with the Gang.

Richards passed Drayson his drink, feeling regret that he hadn't spat in it when he'd had the chance. Anaura closed the door behind him and the three men began to discuss exactly where they were with everything. A short time later Crane and Taggart walked into the office full with enthusiasm and sat down with Usher, Valera and the others. Crane told them what he and Taggart had achieved, prompting Valera to almost choke on her tuna sandwich.

"Are you mad Mark? What the hell were you thinking? If you had been found out or if the security guard knew the Gang personally you would have blown this entire investigation!!!" Valera declared.

"We know that Jennifer. However, Pearson has been murdered, the operation is going wrong and Drayson is going to take over and get rid of the boss, something had to be done! And besides we got away with it didn't we?" Taggart said defending their actions.

"I agree with what they're saying. I'm not working for that nob head Drayson, no way! And they're right, the investigation is taking a turn for the worst, desperate times call for desperate measures yeah?!" Usher remarked.

The six officers sat huddled around quietly discussing it, with Valera slowly coming around to their way of thinking but still citing that it had been stupid and risky whether it was a good idea or not. She also reminded them that they would still get them chewed out when Anaura found out. Crane shrugged his shoulders and said in a booming comical voice that fortune favoured the bold.

Inside the supervisor's office, Anaura finished updating Drayson on the state of the investigation and he didn't seem impressed. After making a few unnecessarily unfair comments, Drayson went to leave the office before Anaura asked whether he could have a quiet word with him somewhere private. Drayson checked his watch and pulled an uninterested expression before agreeing to talk to Anaura who led him down to the kitchen area. When they arrived, Anaura took a deep breath, questioning in his head whether he should be talking to Drayson, and then told him that he and Richards had been informed of a corrupt officer working for the Gang and he believed Pearson's murder could somehow be linked to this. Drayson felt a freezing shiver run up his spine with the realisation that he might have been discovered. The panic intensified further when he started to recall the Scotland Yard business card Anaura had, Scotland Yard being the home to specialist teams that looked into high level police corruption.

"Who told you? Did you get a name of the officer?" Drayson asked frantically.

"Jamie Poultan sir. No he didn't have a name, just that it was a City officer." Anaura answered.

Feeling a small measure of relief that Anauara didn't have a name, Drayson asked "Ok, what other evidence do you have to suggest what Poultan is saying is true?"

"Nothing at the moment sir.............."

"Well then it's a load of bollocks isn't it? It's absolute bullshit! You're telling me that because a little scum bag tells you there's a bent copper, you're going to believe him without evidence, and start trying to link the burglary to a dirty police officer. Don't you think that the SOCU would have heard of something like that when we were after the Gang?!" Drayson snapped.

"Sir, the crime scene at Pearson's house didn't look like any burglary I've seen! It looked like a hit! Are you going to ignore the possibility that something could be going on?" Anaura enquired in exasperation.

"Yes I am, and so are you! In fact I've just about had enough of you and your stupid ideas! The fact that you're believing this crap tells me that you're not suitable to be running this investigation any longer. I am going to speak to Steiner this afternoon, expect to find yourself back on Vice by the end of the week!" Drayson yelled as he stormed out of the office leaving Anaura shocked at how his theory had been received.

After hearing the rear door slam, Richards appeared from around the corner of the corridor. Anaura looked at him and asked if he had heard what Drayson had to say. Richards nodded and explained how Drayson had always been the type of guy to ignore anyone else's ideas and that he probably could not be bothered in making the case any more complicated than it already was. Anaura shook his head and asked why he would shun a valid line of enquiry, especially one that involved a police officer. Richards replied that Drayson would never go after an idea like that unless there was something in it for him, and the fact that there was no hard evidence to go on, he wouldn't touch it with a barge pole. Anaura tended to agree but still reiterated that it was ignorant.

Richards patted him on the shoulder and assured him that Drayson would probably not take him off the case but then joked how they were probably better off going back to Vice anyway. The operation was barely two months old and it had already had them sleeping in the office, and subjected them to huge levels of stress they had never experienced before. Anaura smiled and replied that he had a point; no operation was worth this kind of grief.

The two men were just about to walk back into the supervisor's office when they were approached by Crane and Taggart who asked for a word. Anaura escorted them inside as Valera and Usher looked on at the Intel officers, waiting for the moment when Crane would tell him what they had done.

"YOU DID WHAT?!" Anaura shouted. Valera looked at the others and whispered "I told you so".

"How could you be so stupid guys? You may have wanted to help but this was just plain moronic. If you'd been found out, the operation would be over and you'd be facing a disciplinary!" Richards said with frustration. Anaura asked Richards if the day could get any worse, at which point his phone rang.

"Great, it just did!" He said as he saw on the phone's digital display that it was Steiner calling him.

Richards told Crane and Taggart to get out and that he would deal with them later. Anaura answered his phone and was greeted with Steiner yelling at him about what he had said to Drayson. He tried to explain that it was information he needed to share and that Drayson's reaction to it was out of proportion. Steiner replied that Drayson was soon going to be an Assistant Chief and how telling him a far-fetched story about assassinations was never going to end well, let alone mentioning that there was a corrupt officer involved. Steiner then asked why Anaura hadn't told him first to make sure it was something that was worth telling Drayson. When he couldn't provide an answer, Steiner told him to start packing his things as he would be going back to vice that Friday at the behest of Drayson and to consider himself lucky that he hadn't been posted to a response team where he would be working nights for the rest of his career! He then abruptly hung up.

Anaura put the phone down, picked up his mug and launched it at the wall where it smashed to pieces. Crane and Taggart looked at each other outside worrying that they were about to get torn apart like the mug. Richards told him to calm down and that he had meant what he said about them being better off back at vice. Anaura reflected on how, as usual, Command had made him look like a fool because they were too short sighted to think outside the box. He placed his head into his left hand and whacked his desk. Richards, in a calm and collected manner, enquired when he was going to be taken off the case and what he was going to do in the meantime. Anaura looked up at Richards and said "watch me!" before storming into the main office.

"YOU TWO!" He shouted over to Crane and Taggart who looked up in fear.

"GET YOUR ARSES DOWN TO THE WAREHOUSE, SET UP AN OBSERVATION POST!!!! If your security guard is right you've got less than twenty four hours to set up it up. And count yourself lucky that I'm not sticking you on for your good work. Oh and don't tell anybody what you're up to!"

Anaura charged back into the office where Richards asked whether it was worth running it past Steiner first. He paused whilst pulling a 'really' type of expression at Richards, who replied by saying "Yeah you're right! Bollocks let's do it!" Anaura called his team into a briefing. If he was going down, he was going to try and take the Gang, and if he was lucky, the corrupt copper, down with him.

That night Crane, Taggart, Streeting and Williams arrived at the warehouse on Basin Road South and parked their unmarked Mondeo in the shadowy confines of a nearby building's alleyway, protected from the bright glow of the fluorescent street lights but still providing them with a view of their target. In front of the warehouse gate there was a security officer in a van from the same firm as before. Due to their chosen location for the Observation Post there was no way they would be able to move in until the security officer left, and if necessary they would have to wait there all night.

The hours ticked by but the security van remained. Streeting asked the others whether it was worth trying to covertly move into position. Williams swiftly replied that it wasn't even worth contemplating, if they blew this she knew Anaura would have a severe sense of humour failure. Just as the boredom was starting to seriously affect the morale in the car, the security van's lights switched on and the vehicle began to pull away with its headlights illuminating its path.

"Shit, he's going to see us Streeting! Why didn't you park further up the alley???" Crane suddenly called out.

"I didn't hear you suggesting anywhere else earlier!" Streeting angrily replied.

As the van began to come their way, Taggart and Crane rapidly ducked down in the rear of the Mondeo to hide themselves, followed seconds later by Streeting.

"That's going to be so obvious!" Williams said to Streeting as she grabbed him and started to kiss him passionately in the front seat just as the beam of the security van's headlights shone into their cabin. As the beam illuminated their faces, Williams faked a surprised jerk and began pulling her top about as if hurrying to cover herself up. The security van slowed as it approached the unmarked police vehicle, prompting Taggart in the back to say "he's seen us, hasn't he?" However as the van slowly passed by, the security guard looked at the two embarrassed faces staring back at him and then drove off in frustration when they did not start kissing again.

"What made you do that?" Streeting asked Williams with a big smile.

"It worked didn't it? Better than all of us ducking. How obvious would that have been?" She replied with an equally big smile.

Crane abruptly interrupted them and said that as much as he liked police weddings it was about time they got inside the empty building opposite to set up their Observation Post. Streeting drove the car into the car park and the three other officers jumped out and grabbed all the equipment they needed from boot of the Mondeo before running up to the door and breaking the padlock to gain entry. As they moved inside Streeting drove off at speed to park the car near the City Lagoon before making his way back to the building on foot.

Inside the other three got to work setting up the various equipment that ranged from long range cameras and microphones, through to laptops and recording devices. After years of service on the Intelligence Unit and countless attachments to the Technical Support Unit the three of them were now highly proficient in swiftly setting up effective and covert Observation Posts. Fifteen minutes later, Streeting returned and assisted his colleagues who were working in near darkness to prevent bright lights being seen from within the building. If someone saw a flurry of lights coming from inside, they would inevitably think that burglars or squatters were there and call the police or worse, the security firm who guarded the buildings.

After forty minutes the Observation Post was set up and ready to go. The four officers discussed between them who would be paired up and take the first watch. Before anyone could suggest anything Streeting blurted out that he and Williams would take the first shift which drew a huge flirtatious smile from her. Crane

212

and Taggart looked at one another, before Crane remarked that they were there to watch the warehouse and not each other! The two of them told Crane to piss off, feeling incredibly embarrassed on the inside. Taggart interjected that he was tired and was going to try and get some sleep in his lovely police issued sleeping bag with a half inch thick mat beneath it. If there was one thing about an Observation Post it was this; it was never going to be comfortable. Crane followed him after saying night to Streeting and Williams with a wink of inference. The two officers looked at each over whilst desperately trying to hide their coyness and commenting how they had better get started.

No sooner than they had switched the equipment on, they turned to each other and began to speak at the same time. As they both urged the other to go first, Taggart appeared from behind the wall and told them to keep it down and then spoke for Williams by asking Streeting whether he wanted to go out with her sometime, causing Crane to burst out laughing in the background. Streeting told him to go away before turning back to Williams to ask her whether she fancied it. She shyly nodded in response and pulled an extremely pleased expression.

"Now shut up love-birds and do some work!" Taggart joked as he returned to his sleeping bag next to Crane who was still laughing. He got into his sleeping bag and commented how it was about time Streeting and Williams shagged and got it over with, as the suppressed sexual tension was doing his head in.

The following morning Peter was sat in the office with
Richards wondering whether the Observation Post had been
successfully set up. Although he had calmed down somewhat
from the day before, Anaura still felt that it had been wrong how
he had been treated by Steiner and Drayson, to the point where he
was considering pulling Steiner to one side to discuss it a 'little
less formally'. The stress of the last couple of months had been
bad enough but finding out one of his targets had been murdered
and hearing rumours about a corrupt copper had well and truly
finished him off. When he got home the night before he explained
the situation to Laura which made her reply to him that it was
now, more than ever, time to transfer to a less stressful role.
Anaura whole heartedly agreed with her and informed Richards
the moment he got into the office that he was intending to request
a transfer from Vice to a project team at HQ. Richards laughed
and told him that he wouldn't last a month dealing with the boring
desk bound nerds and that all he needed was a little rest and
maybe even a few weeks off. Anaura replied that time would tell
but before he even considered putting the request in, he wanted to
at least leave the operation in a better position than it had been
and if luck was on his side, perhaps find out who the dirty copper
was.

Anaura's phone began ringing. He looked at it and saw that it
was Steiner calling and exclaimed to Richards how his day was
already set to start off badly. He stood up and shook himself off
before answering it.

"Jason, how's it going?" He said, waiting for the grief to begin.

"Peter, I hope you're a little less stressed? Because what I am
about to tell you is going send you off the rails if you're not!!"
Steiner remarked without answering Anaura's question or

greeting him.

"Hello to you too Jason! What's up?" Anaura replied sarcastically.

"Sykes is dead; stabbed to death!"

Anaura legs wobbled, requiring him to quickly take a seat on the edge of his desk to steady himself.

"Are you being serious? What happened???" Anaura asked Steiner as Richards looked up at him with confusion due to his reaction to the call.

"His decomposing body was found a couple of hours ago in a wooded area near to Devils Valley. His car had been left there for a couple of weeks but it hadn't been reported stolen. Well this morning a dog walker stumbled across a horrendous smell as they were walking past the wood, and well, they found him!" Steiner said.

"Does Drayson know yet? I don't believe this!" Anaura exclaimed.

"No not yet, I just tried calling him. I'm sorry Peter, I shouldn't have ignored what you were saying at Pearson's house. This can't be a coincidence can it? Two members of the Gang found murdered! Oh and wait it gets worse! A couple of weeks ago a member of the public, otherwise known as a dogger, who was parked up near the Valley called in saying that they had seen a male running through a nearby field and that he had got into a dark coloured Ford Fiesta with a number plate similar to X237 KNV. Well, we couldn't find a match for that but after conducting a ANPR camera check of the east and westbound carriageway near to the Valley, we did manage to find a dark blue Fiesta travelling towards the City's slip-road a couple of of hours before the call! We should have paid more attention to Syke's abandoned car............" Steiner said.

"Forget all that for the moment Jason, what about the Fiesta?" Anaura blurted out with impatience.

"Ok; it was registered to Anthony Foster, formally PC Anthony Foster of the City's Tactical firearms unit. The same Anthony Foster who is currently wanted for assaulting a man outside a pub in West Ording!"

"Jesus Christ Jason, are you shitting me? Has anyone located Foster yet? Do you think he's the one working for the Gang?"

"I don't know, he could be! But I know one thing, I've now got the pathologist's report and it states that Pearson had five holes in him, two of which were in his chest in a tight group and the other three likewise in his abdomen. You're right it definitely wasn't a burglar at Pearson's, it was someone trained, someone like Foster. I think he could be our man Peter. There's two murders, his number plate is similar to the one provided from the Valley, and we're now looking for someone trained in firearms for Pearson's murder. We need to find Foster fast!" Steiner urged Anaura.

"Right, I need the crime report for the assault, any witnesses and Foster's personnel file now. Does Drayson know yet?" Anaura said.

"I don't know, I'll call him. I'll email you the crime report now and see if I can get his personnel file quick time. I almost forgot to tell you; Forster was medically retired for mental health issues!" Steiner said.

"If Foster's suffering from mental health issues too it could be why he's going after the Gang! I'll call Drayson, you sort out Foster's file." Anaura replied before finishing the call.

Anaura looked towards Richards and started to explain what was happening before he was stopped mid-sentence by him. Richards interjected and asked Anaura whether he believed that Foster could really be the corrupt copper they were looking for as it did not make sense. Anaura paused and asked why to which Richards replied that as a firearms officer he wouldn't have had much to do with the Gang, plus Poultan never mentioned that the officer was retired.

"What are you saying then Ian, that we've got two corrupt coppers or we're off the mark with Foster; which?" Anaura enquired with confusion.

"Listen, I'm not disputing that Foster's the killer. However the rest of it doesn't match up does it? When would Foster have had a chance to meet the Gang? He wouldn't know about any drugs related operations unless they involved firearms or their competition, which in other words means that he would have

216

nothing to offer them!" Richards hypothesised.

"Alright, if he's not our bent copper, then explain to me why Foster would just decide to kill the most serious criminals in the City? And please don't tell me because of his mental health, you know it doesn't work like that!"

"I don't know. But Op Barrier and Marriot's death must have really screwed him up. Maybe he believes that by taking out the worst trash in the City he's doing righteous work and protecting people! Either way I can't see what value he would be to the Gang, he may know about terrorists and bank robbers but he doesn't know about unarmed drug dealers!" Richards surmised.

Anaura pondered what Richards had said, as usual he wouldn't just pass his opinion out of hand. After a few minutes of silence, Richards asked him if he was going to say anything, Anaura looked up and said that they needed to get over to West Ording to talk to the witnesses at the Cliffe pub. Richards replied that it wouldn't go down well with Drayson, it was after all his murder case. He smiled at Richards and remarked, with a pleased expression on his face, that the man Foster had assaulted outside the pub wasn't dead; an assault was not a murder case, so it was none of Drayson's business.

The two detectives stood up, grabbed their suit jackets and walked out into the main office. Anaura approached Usher and Valera and asked them to look into all the intelligence logs they could find relating to the Gang, Usher replied that they had already done so at the start of the operation and that it was all documented in the case file. Anaura shook his head and smiled at her before saying that he wanted to know where the Gang had gone to school, the roads they lived in as kids; anything other than their criminal history. He then told them to keep it to themselves and stated that he and Richards would be back within a few hours after an errand.

As the two men left the office, Richards asked Anaura whether he thought the pub would be open as it was only eleven o'clock in the morning. Anaura replied that it probably wasn't; but with a pub like that, it was bound to be open at twelve for the locals to begin their day's drinking. After getting into the car, Richards asked whether they should tell Steiner, Anaura's expression said it all; NO!

At twelve pm, the doors of the Cliffe pub opened in preparation for receiving its first patrons of the day. Anaura and Richards walked in before the landlord had time to return to the bar, prompting him to comment that the two men were a bit keen. Richards sat down at the bar and identified himself and Anaura, to which the barman jokingly remarked that they obviously weren't there for a beer but had a good idea what they were going to ask him.

"Let me guess, you're here to talk about Anthony again? I've already given a statement to some other officers about him beating up poor Tony and smashing my bloody window! I have nothing else to say about it really!" The burly landlord said.

"I'm sure you have, but we're not here to discuss the assault, we're here to discuss how long Anthony's been drinking here and who he drinks with." Richards said.

"Well that's going to be easy! Anthony's a bit of a loner, only talks to himself if you know what I mean? He's a bit of a nutter" The Landlord explained.

"So you've never seen him sitting or talking with anyone? Do you know anything else about him?" Richards asked.

"Nah that's it, I'm afraid officers. He only talks when he's asking for a pint!" He answered.

Richards looked at Anaura who responded by tilting his head to signal to him that they should leave. Richards thanked the landlord for his help and got up. As they walked out, Anaura cited that they would have to look at the crime report to see if there was anything else of note as this had been a wasted trip.

"Wait a minute officers! There was one bloke I saw Anthony chatting to a couple of months back. He was a fairly tall guy in his forties, with a bit of a sly, ratty face and short dark hair. He was a bit of a wide boy too with a slight Londoner twang. The two of them spoke for about an hour, maybe less, I can't remember. I don't know what they were talking about but Anthony seemed pretty excited after the other bloke left. Other than that I really can't tell you anything more, sorry."

The two detectives thanked him and walked out of the pub to head back to their car. As they walked Anuara asked Richards whether it sounded like anyone they knew or if it could have been the Gang's copper. Richards replied that he didn't and that there was no reason at this stage to believe it was anyone other than a friend of his. He then remarked that in the worst case scenario, it could have been a member of the Gang visiting him, the man was after all not far off their age, however he reiterated that he still did not believe Foster was with the Gang. Anaura pressed the key fob to unlock the Focus and went to climb in before he paused and leant on the roof of the car with his problem solving mind desperately searching for answers. He looked up at Richards who was asking him if everything was OK. Anaura gently and repeatedly banged the roof of the car with the bottom of his clenched fist, attempting to jolt his mind into life.

"You're right Ian, Foster's not our dodgy copper. Think about it, would the Gang use someone like Foster who's suffering from a mental illness to work for them? And think back to what Poultan said............the Gang gave the all clear for Kennedy to start dealing again; hardly what you would do with a mentally ill associate running around with all your secrets. You're right none of it makes sense!" Anaura postulated.

"Do you reckon the unknown man in the pub is our guy? If he was, how the hell are we going to find him? It was hardly a decent description; how many coppers are tall, have dark hair and are in their forties.......hundreds!" Richards commented.

"For the moment we need to concentrate on finding Foster. Let's go and see if he's home shall we?"

"Shouldn't we request firearms support first, Peter?"

"No! If we ask for firearms support then we'll have to tell the unit he's a murder suspect which would mean all hell would break loose! If we go to his place with minimal fuss, it won't spook him and might make him easier to talk to. Remember he's already had district officers banging on his door for the assault complaint so he's bound to be on his toes! I want a chance to talk before anyone else gets to him!" Anaura replied.

The two men got into the car and drove off towards

Shakespearean Road, less than quarter of a mile away from the pub. If they could arrest Foster without antagonising him like the Firearms Unit or response officers would, they might just be able to learn who the Gang's inside man was.

A Cool Exterior Now Departed
Chapter Thirty four

Drayson smirked as he scrolled through the details of Sykes' murder on the incident logs. By now he had been made fully aware of his demise and the circumstances. Sure Foster may have gone a little over the top but it had made the murder appear like a crime of hate as opposed to the professional execution of Pearson, Drayson reflected. His eyes continued to roll down the incident log and paperwork until he saw a number plate and a potential suspect; it was Foster! Drayson dropped his head into his hands as he fought off the urge to throw up over his desk. If anyone arrested Foster now, it would all be over as there would be three witnesses ready to act against him. Foster still had Bradford and Cooper left to kill but with the whole of the Force wanting to question him, it was looking highly doubtful whether he could finish the job.

Drayson sat at his desk struggling to hold back the tears that were attempting to force their way out of the ducts in his eyes. Things had taken a colossal turn for the worse because of one perverted dogger waiting in his car for a hand job that night. The chances of a witness seeing Foster's car, and a number plate too for that matter, were slim to none; and yet it had happened. He pulled himself together and snapped into action by calling Bradford who upon answering began to scream blue murder after learning about Sykes. Drayson told him that he would see him at the warehouse that night and he would bring all the information he had collated about the Russian syndicates who were moving into the area. At first Bradford told him that the only place he would meet Drayson was at his home where he was safe. Drayson refused, reminding him that it was too risky as someone could see him, implicating the both of them. The two men continued to argue about what they were going to do next until Drayson yelled at Bradford, expressing to him how he had never let him down before and to trust him. Bradford replied that he didn't trust anyone to which Drayson responded by imploring him to meet him at the warehouse with Cooper where they would get this mess sorted once and for all.

Bradford begrudgingly agreed and finished the call by stating that if Drayson didn't get the situation sorted as soon as possible, he would have him sorted out for good; one way or another. As Bradford hung up, Drayson threw his phone across the room and swiped the flowers and stationery off his table in sheer anger. As the loud smash of the vase rung out, his assistant came rushing in and asked him whether he was ok, to which Drayson bellowed at her to mind her own fucking business and to get out of his office. He fell back into his seat and loosened his tie before looking down at his desk and then opening the top drawer. Inside, a large bottle of extremely strong Tramodol painkillers that he had been previously prescribed for back pain was staring back at him. As the lump in his throat grew larger, making it hard for him to swallow, Drayson placed the bottle in his pocket. If Foster was caught before Bradford or Cooper were dead or before he had a chance to give him the spiked drugs, he would take matters into his own hands and end it all; suicide was a better option than facing the shame of being outed as a dirty copper and consequently brutalised in prison. However for now, Drayson would have to sit by and painfully wait to see whether everything would play out in his favour!

He looked out of the window in his office, sensing that the end could be nigh, before he heard a beep come from his computer that indicated an email had arrived. He opened it and read through its contents. As if things couldn't get much worse............it was a message from another Command officer reminding him that he had agreed to cover their Gold Commander shift that night. Drayson shook his head with despair, he was running out of ideas fast, and having to pull a late turn shift until one am in the morning was the very last thing he needed. Things were beginning to look gloomy!

Influence
Chapter Thirty Five

Anaura and Richards walked into the Shoreton office after their less than successful trip to West Ording. Richards asked Usher and Valera whether they'd had any luck with the Gang's personal history, both of the detectives shook their heads and Valera remarked how they could not find anything other than what was already common knowledge. Anaura sat down and looked at his watch, it was four pm. Apart from partly dispelling the myth that Foster may have been the Gang's dirty copper, they had wasted hours watching his home and banging on his doors in vain. It had not been the day he had hoped for; a common theme throughout the entire operation.

Richards looked at his weary friend and suggested that they get a team takeaway at six as it was more than likely that they would be working into the evening due to the Gang's potential meeting at the warehouse. Anaura agreed but hypothesised that it was a little unlikely that Bradford and Cooper would still go considering that another of their associates had been found murdered too. Richards agreed but joked that if they were going to get thrown off the case they might as well use a bit more of the operational funds to have a decent send off. Anaura smiled and shrugged his shoulders.

Three hours later with sufficiently bloated stomachs the four detectives sat watching the TV in the lounge and feeling sympathy for the Intel officers who were likely to be living off sandwiches and crisps. The conversation had generally been light hearted until Valera enquired whether her and Usher would be able to return to Vice with him and Richards. Anaura replied that Op Spear was likely to be shut down after Friday as two of the Gang had been killed and the investigation hadn't really uncovered any hard evidence or success over and above what had previously been achieved by SOCU. Both the female officers commented that it might not have come off, but at least they'd had some fun doing it. As the conversation began to dry up and the four of them watched the television, Valera suddenly asked Anaura for the real reason why he had been thrown off the case as the operation had not been that much of a failure. Richards glanced over at him to see whether he was going to say the real reason. Anaura took a deep breath before he asked the two detectives whether they could keep a secret. They both nodded so he proceeded to tell them how he and Richards had been tipped off that there was a bent copper working for the Gang and that he had told Drayson. The information combined with a few flawed operational decisions had incensed Drayson and lead to him being thrown of the operation for incompetence.

The two detectives pulled frustrated expressions as they heard Anaura say the word incompetent, as it was not a term that was generally synonymous with him or his work. In response, Usher remarked that she thought Drayson was a complete nobber and how he probably just wanted to prevent Anaura from getting all the glory when he eventually cracked the case. Anaura smiled and commented that he had still made some bad decisions, and that Drayson had just capitalised on them. Usher then asked whether they believed it was Foster who had been working for the Gang to which Richards replied that they didn't and although he was the murder suspect, something did not add up and that they strongly suspected someone else was involved too. Usher looked confused and enquired why Foster would kill the Gang for no reason if he wasn't linked to them. Richards just shook his head and explained that they didn't have all the answers but they would find them.

Anaura stood up and stated that they should get back to work as the Intel officers would be coming on the radio imminently to start running a commentary on any suspicious activity that might be happening at the warehouse. He then also cited that he needed time to figure out how to use the CCTV monitor that relayed what the Intel officers were seeing through their cameras. Before they left the lounge, Valera asked whether he or Richards were

going to inform PSD about what Poultan had said, both of them
nodded in response. She then asked whether they had told
Drayson about the Observation Post as he was the duty Gold
Commander and would hit the roof if it was kept from him.
Richards burst out laughing as Anuara raised his eyebrows,
neither of them had known that he was the duty Commander that
night. Being the duty Force command officer, he would have to
be informed about any such operations during his shift. In the
haze of the situation with Foster they had totally forgotten that
they still hadn't updated him or Steiner about the Observation
Post.

Anaura remarked with laughter how he had better call Drayson
or he would be kicked out the 'Job' forever.

"Sir, are you free to speak?" Anaura asked Drayson over the
phone.

"Yeah, what do you want?" was his obnoxious reply.

"I'm pretty sure you've heard about Foster by now. Well I'm
not sure he's the only one involved in this?" Anaura said.

"Not this fucking shit again!!! Look, Foster's nuts, he went
mental after killing Mahood and Op Barrier. And as I see it he's
going around killing people he considers to be 'bad men' because
he's lost touch with reality!

"Change the bloody record unless you've got some evidence to
the contrary!" He replied in an angry voice.

"Fine, maybe you're right, but I don't agree with that theory.
Anyway; the main reason I've called you is to tell you that we've
set up an Observation Post in Basin Road South after our Intel
officers managed to identify where Cooper had gone when
Surveillance lost him!"

"YOU DID WHAT?!! ON WHOSE AUTHORITY? CALL IT
OFF NOW!" Drayson yelled down the line.

"I gave the authority! They are in position now sir, how can I
call it off? Anyway, I don't see what the problem is. The Intel lot
have managed to learn more in one day than Surveillance did in
two weeks, and they're now placed right where the Gang may be
operating their business from, so what's your problem with this?"
Anaura asked with annoyance as he started to reach the end of his

225

tether with Drayson.

"MY PROBLEM IS THAT SOMEONE LIKE YOU SHOULD NEVER HAVE BEEN RUNNING THIS CASE FROM THE START. WHAT ELSE HAVE YOU BEEN UP TO ANAURA?"

"Right, I'm getting a little tired of you busting my eardrum from the other end of the line, if you want more details come down to the office. And if you want to know what else we've done, I'll tell you! Earlier today, Ian and I attended the Cliffe Pub in West Ording where we acquired some information about Foster meeting up with an unknown male prior to this operation starting and prior to the killings. It's possible that it's the dirty copper that you don't believe exists!" Anaura said growing angrier by the second.

"WHO DO YOU THINK YOU ARE STICKING YOUR NOSE INTO MY MURDER INVESTIGATION? I'M GOING TO HAVE YOU DISCIPLINED, DO YOU FUCKING HEAR THAT? I'LL RUIN YOU, YOU PRIMITIVE TRIBAL BASTARD!!!" Drayson yelled.

"AH FUCK OFF YOU ABSOLUTE DICK, I'VE HEARD ENOUGH!!!" Anaura said as he slammed down the phone with a lot of force.

Richards looked at him with shock and asked whether he had just said to Drayson what he thought he said. Anaura nodded in confirmation. Richards then began pleading with Anaura to reassure him that Drayson had already hung up when he swore at him, Anaura shook his head. Richards buried his face in his hands and asked what he had been thinking, telling a man who would be Assistant Chief to go forth and multiply. Anaura replied that in all honesty, he didn't care anymore and that he'd had just about endured as much of Drayson as he could, even more so when the arsehole had started coming out with racist jibes. Richards asked what he had said so Anaura explained. When Richards began saying that he should make a complaint, Anaura simply replied that he would probably just hit him whenever he next saw him. As Richards continued reeling from what had been said over the phone call, Anaura paused deep in thought before asking him if he found Drayson's reaction to the update a little strange and over the top. Richards replied that Drayson had always been a bit of a hot head when he didn't get his own way and enquired why he had asked. Anaura shrugged his shoulders and commented that he just thought Drayson seemed to over react to anything to do with the operation he was not fully aware of first. Anaura smiled and then said "Never mind, just thinking out loud." before asking Richards to help him set up the CCTV monitor that he was failing miserably to set up.

In his Central District Station office Drayson was going ballistic, throwing his stuff around in a rage and smashing anything that was to hand. Anaura had as good as buried him. The Observation Post would spot Foster and call for support to arrest him, possibly before he even got to kill Bradford and Cooper. He would then inevitably tell them what he was up to and who had ordered him to do it. The next monumental problem was that the Landlord had seen him speaking to Foster and that Anaura was now obsessed with discovering the identity of the man, namely him.

Drayson removed the bottle of Tramadol from his pocket, emptied the tablets out and opened them one by one, spilling the capsules contents onto his desk. From his desk, he removed a bottle of whiskey that had been bought for him by his assistant and that he had 'forgotten' to take home. Drayson poured a pint of whiskey and the put the glass below the edge of the desk, he then brushed the powdered remains of the hundred capsules into it, allowing the powder to mix with the spirit and settle at the bottom of the tumbler. He took a sip of the cocktail with tears in his eyes and switched on the operations channel he knew the Observation Post would be using. If Foster failed and was arrested he would down the concoction and drive himself the short distance to the City's Marina where he would jump into the water and inevitably drown in his intoxicated state. Drayson took another swig of the whiskey and rested his head sideways on his desk. He would soon learn what his fate was to be.

Fifteen miles to the west, Foster woke up in his car which was parked up in the Cissbury Hill car park that was at the foot of

large set of rolling hills and countryside just north of West
Ording. After incessant banging on his front door over the
previous couple of days, Foster knew he needed to be somewhere
else and especially after he had seen two detectives knocking on
his door when he had entered the road in his car. On seeing them
Foster did a three point turn in the road and drove up as quickly
as he could. Now lying flat on the back seats, Foster rubbed his
face roughly as if trying to wipe away the grogginess and looked
at his watch. It was eight thirty, less than two and a half hours
away until show time and the beginning of his fresh start and
career. The only thing that concerned him was the emerging but
still slightly vague recollection that he had assaulted the owner of
the wallet outside the Cliffe pub for reasons that still eluded him.
After putting two and two together he knew full well why the
town's police and two detectives were after him as he was now a
robbery suspect after taking the wallet. Foster just hoped that
Drayson could sort it for him and it would not cause a problem
for his career. He clambered off the back seat and out his car
before brushing himself off and walking down to a chip shop he
knew in the nearby parade of shops. He had a few hours to burn
and spending them hungry was not going to help them pass.

An hour later and what had seemed like an eternity of fiddling,
Anaura had finally managed to set up the CCTV relay in his
office despite his agitated state. The way Drayson had spoken to
him earlier in the evening had really wound him to no end but he
knew he needed to take a step back and calm down because if
Drayson walked in and started shouting the odds, it would result
in Anaura being arrested for assault.

"O.P to DI Anaura, O.P to DI Anaura?" Crane called over the
radio from the Observation Post.

Anaura and Drayson in their respective offices grabbed their
radios.

"Go ahead Mark." Anaura said.

"Boss we've just had a black Range Rover pull up with
Bradford and Cooper inside, and a red Vauxhall Corsa, but we
can't identify the two occupants of it yet. Standby."

"We need a swift identification of the occupants! The monitor isn't providing a clear feed." Anuara said.

"OK, one of the occupants of the Corsa has got out and is approaching Bradford; it's Poultan! Still can't ID the other vehicle's occupant.

Richards shook his head and said to Anaura that they should never have believed Poultan about his lack of involvement with the Gang. He huffed and replied "That's just the game we play!"

"Boss, can you hear what's being said over the microphone?" Crane asked.

Anaura slapped the side of the screen and complained to Richards, Usher and Valera how police equipment always seemed to fail when you needed it the most. Anaura responded to Crane, telling him that he couldn't and asked him to relay what was being said between the men. Crane said that Bradford was telling Poultan that he didn't trust their police friend and that it was time to have a chat with him. He then relayed that Bradford had said to Poultan that he would make him a very wealthy man if he did a big job for them. Anaura desperately enquired whether he had mentioned any names or specifics about what he wanted him to do. Crane replied "Negative" as their listening equipment was struggling to provide clear sound. Anaura sat back in frustration.

"Poultan's leaving in the Corsa with the unidentified male." Crane said.

Richards asked whether he wanted him picked up, Anaura shook his head and remarked that at that point they did not know what he had been asked to do and how it would be more prudent to get a Surveillance team on him the next day. Anaura then turned to Richards and asked him to get Inspector Balham on the line to request that a couple of firearms units be present and available at Central District should the need for them arise. Richards asked if he believed that something was going to go down to which Anaura said that he didn't know but that something just didn't feel right.

As Richards began to dial the internal extension for the Firearms unit, Crane updated that Bradford and Cooper had now gone inside the warehouse and that there was nothing else left to report at that time. Anaura acknowledged them and put his radio down on the table. Richards finished the call with Balham and said to Anaura that two Armed Response Vehicles would be relocating to Central District at eleven thirty after the current team had handed over to the night shift. Valera then stood up and said that she would get a coffee for everyone as it was beginning to appear as though they were in for a long wait. Anaura leant over his desk to get his mug from its usual resting position on the right side of it below the operational info board. As he picked it up, he remembered how Drayson had looked at something on the board and froze before he spilt coffee on his lap. He passed the mug to Valera and began scanning for what may have interested him, but there was nothing other than a couple of maps and mug shots. Richards asked what he was doing, however Anaura raised his hand up to implore him to wait a second.

There it was...................the business card that had been left by the mysterious superintendent from Scotland Yard. Anaura's mind began working in overdrive as it tried to ascertain why Scotland Yard were interested in Drayson and why he had taken an interest in the card himself; did he suspect or know that he was being looked into by them? Anuara raised his finger up to Richards, whatever the idea was, it was about to arrive. Anauara began bouncing his palm off of his forehead, desperately trying to kick-start his brain to help him piece everything together to get an answer whilst the other detectives looked on at him perplexed. Vivid images began to rush through his head in a super-fast sequence...............The superintendent asking him to keep an eye on Drayson, Drayson's reaction to him when he informed him of a corrupt officer, the way he muscled his way onto the case and operation, Drayson's failure to catch the Gang, Steiner informing him that Drayson had tried to prevent the operation from taking place, Drayson being from Eastings, Poultan, Foster; and finally the Landlords voice describing the unknown middle aged man.

"IAN, IT'S DRAYSON!!!!!!!!!!" Anaura yelled out.

"What, what are you talking about Peter?" Richards replied in utter confusion.

"Drayson's our dirty Copper! He's the one! How could I not

have seen it?" Anaura declared with his hands on his forehead.

"Whoa, whoa! Steady Peter, what makes you think that?" Richards asked imploring his friend to exercise caution.

Anaura quickly explained all the pieces of the puzzle to Richards and Usher who sat there with stunned expressions.

"Jesus Christ Peter, you could be right! However we need solid evidence mate, as much as I agree with what you're saying, we can't start making accusations without proof. We can't just storm into his office and nick him, he's a chief superintendent and PSD don't even know anything about it yet!" Richards remarked.

"I'm calling that superintendent from Scotland Yard; right now!" Anaura said as he hurriedly ripped the card from the board.

Valera walked back into the office with the coffees and asked why everyone had pale and shocked expressions. Richards updated her about what was going on which caused her to drop the four mugs of coffee she was holding in surprise. Anaura, who was waiting for the superintendent to answer, nodded to her to signify it was true. Richards suggested to Anaura that they should go back to the pub with a picture of Drayson to see if the Landlord recognised him. He replied by saying "Definitely! I want that bastard tonight!"

"Hello?"

"Sir it's DI Anaura. It's Drayson, Drayson's working for the Gang!" Anaura declared in an overzealous and impatient manner.

"DI Anaura what are you trying to tell me? How do you know, what proof do you have? I would urge you to tread carefully!" The Superintendent said.

Anaura began running through his theory and the obvious indications to his involvement.

"That's why you came to me isn't it? Isn't it?" Anaura enquired.

"DI Anaura, you must have proof, without proof nothing can be done! Do you think this is the only time Drayson has been in the spotlight and hidden in the shadows; WE NEED EVIDENCE!!!!"

Anaura continued pleading with the Superintendent to help him while the other three detectives looked on with apprehension.

"O.P TO DI ANAURA, O.P TO DI ANAURA?! BOSS

ANSWER, QUICKLY!" Crane yelled in a panic over the air. Richards picked up the radio as Anaura continued his conversation with the Superintendent.

"IT'S FOSTER! IT'S ANTHONY FOSTER! HE'S JUST PULLED UP IN THE CAR PARK!!!!" Crane yelled out in a trembling voice.

Anaura dropped the phone as he spun around to see the cars headlights piercing the darkness of the warehouse's carpark on the blurry CCTV feed.

"FUCKING HELL!!! IAN GET THE CAR STARTED, NAOMI, JENNIFER GO WITH HIM, I'LL BE OUT IN A SECOND, TELL THE INTEL LOT NOT TO APPROACH HIM OR MOVE UNTIL FIREARMS SUPPORT ARRIVES!!!!!!" Anaura rapidly shouted out.

He picked up his phone with the Superintendent still calling his name at the other end of the line and hung up without answering him. He grabbed four stab vests from the lockers and ran out to meet the others in the rear yard. Anuara jumped into the front passenger seat and Richards subsequently put his foot down hard on the accelerator. The Mondeo wheel spun out of the station's car park.

Drayson, who was now feeling light headed from the drug spiked whiskey and long wait, shot up in his seat as though he'd had a bucket of freezing water thrown on him. The update over the radio sobered him up almost instantaneously.

A couple of miles away, parked up in Westway Street , O'Keeffe, MacNeil and Allen were sat in a plain Audi watching the pubs fill up with students who were drinking their grants away on a Wednesday night, despite the English summer rain that was suddenly beginning to pour from the heavens. O'Keeffe, now a Sergeant, commented on how he wished that he was younger so that he could have a crack at the eighteen year old girls without them seeing him as an old pervert and that he wondered whether they were wearing knickers under their short skirts. Although there was always humorous conversations between them, on this particular night they were worse than usual as a result of being informed at their earlier briefing that Foster was now a murder suspect. The news had not been received well by any of the officers who all cited that just because Foster had mental health issues and his car had been seen on the motorway, did not mean he was the killer.

"OPS Command to team leader!" The Force Control room Inspector called over the firearms command radio channel.

"Team leader, go ahead sir" O'Keeffe replied.

The control room Inspector stated that he was declaring a Spontaneous Firearms Incident at Basin Road South and that the subject was Anthony Foster and he was believed to be armed. The three officers looked at each other with horror before Allen in the back seat hurried to remove the standard ARV guns-the Heckler and Koch G36 5.56 calibre rifles. O'Keeffe looked at Arthur and said "GET THERE AS QUICK AS YOU CAN MATE!" with a severe stutter brought on by the abrupt adrenaline dump from hearing his former friend's name. Arthur switched the Audi's lights and sirens on, causing the nearby students to jump with fright as they had not known that the parked car was a police vehicle. As O'Keeffe and the two other SFO's hurried towards the scene, PC Potter and his colleague PC Lewis who were patrolling West Ording in a marked BMW X5 ARV, informed their team mates that they would meet them as soon as possible at the City's Lagoon so that they could move forward together in case there was a need to perform an emergency hostage rescue. With the two advanced firearms drivers negotiating the roads at high speeds, the passenger from each vehicle read out the incident log to their colleagues to appraise them of the full circumstances, including that Foster was to be treated as a high threat suspect because of his previous training.

In his office, Drayson was trying to suppress the panic attack that was threatening to engulf him. As the Gold Commander he wrote on the serial that the safety of the public and the firearms officers were of the utmost importance; he left out Foster, as if somehow ignoring his presence on the log would make things turn out better.

Anaura and the other detectives were almost on scene as the Intel officers at the Observation Post gave a running commentary of what was happening, including that Foster was now inside. Richards looked at Anaura with wide eyes as he began to wonder whether they might already have been too late. As they drew closer to the scene, they heard that the ARVs were only a matter of minutes behind due to their faster cars and higher level of driving skills. Suddenly the voice of the OPS Command was heard over the radio ordering Anaura to hold off and that O'Keeffe as the ARV team leader had full authority and control over the scene. As much as he wanted to get to the warehouse as fast as possible, Anaura knew that it was one order that he couldn't break. If they steamed in there without guns or protection they would not being going home that night. The Mondeo flew into the complex and came to a begrudging halt well shy of the warehouse.

Inside the warehouse, Foster stealthily walked up the stair case flashing his torch through his T-shirt at short intervals to gain a view of where the stair case led. The minimal use of the torch through the t-shirt, helped prevent it from being easily seen by others. As he negotiated each step he walked on the outside edges of his shoes to help suppress the sound of his footsteps. He approached two doors and moved through them slowly with his Sig Sauer P226 handgun pulled in tight to his body and in front of his chest, ready to be punched out and fired if he was to meet the two remaining members of the Gang unexpectedly. Foster entered the huge expanse of darkness of the empty warehouse's main work floor where he could hear the loud sound of the rain bouncing off the corrugated roof above him. He inhaled sharply as he scanned the darkness, suddenly as he moved further into the room, he saw a light coming from an elevated position to his right. Knowing that there was nowhere else the pair would be lurking, Foster moved quickly but stealthily towards the source of the lights. Upon reaching the old steel staircase, he slowed down to a snail's pace, taking each step at five second intervals to prevent the metal giving off vibrations that would alert his prey. Although the operational pack had not alluded to the Gang using firearms, Foster knew from his training that you never assumed anything, especially whether a suspect was armed or not; that type of mistake could cost you your life.

"Guys where are you? We need to get in there!" O'Keeffe enquired from the City's Lagoon road that led into the Harbour's industrial site.

"Only a couple of minutes out now!" Potter, a highly experienced firearms officer, responded.

"Roger that, Potts. The second you reach us, stop and quickly get your full kit on, including stun grenades; this could become an instantaneous hostage rescue!"

"All received John, ETA..............two minutes!" He replied.

"Bloody hell Peter, we need them in there fast, he's already been in there five minutes!" Richards exclaimed inside the Mondeo.

Anaura told him to keep calm before asking the Intel officers what was going on. Williams replied that they couldn't see or hear anything due to the noise that the nigh on horizontal rain was making, and asked whether they should move forwards, to which Anaura replied that they were not to move from their position under any circumstances.

Foster reached the top of the stair case and slowly peered into the illuminated room through the window. Inside the room he could see Bradford and Cooper playing cards but looking less than happy.

"FUCK THIS PAUL! I can't concentrate on this game, where is Robbie? I don't like this, he should be here already! I've got this bad feeling that he's involved in all of this stuff with Nick and Larry!" Bradford exclaimed as he threw down his hand of cards in exasperation.

Foster looked around the rest of the room to assess whether there was anyone else inside as there was still a possibility that the Gang may have hired protection after hearing about the murders of their associates. Bradford and Cooper were definitely alone though. Fosters heart beat began to pound hard as the fight chemicals started to pump their way around his circulatory system. He took three very deep breaths to shake off the effects of the adrenaline that had a strange way of preventing a person from breathing properly, filling them with stage fright inducing anxiety as a result. He gripped the gun tighter in his hand and took one more sharp breath.

The door burst open so hard that it almost came off the hinges with the handle embedding itself into the stud wall as it did. Foster charged into the room as the two men jumped out of their skins and spun around with expressions of terror to see what had just smashed through their door. Foster pulled the trigger of the gun in a rhythmic sequence of two quick shots, followed by a millisecond pause and then a third, a technique designed to cause the maximum amount of fatal trauma to the victim. The three bullets accelerated at high velocity from the barrel, preceded by three eardrum bursting bangs that reverberated off the office walls. The first two 9mm rounds smashed through Cooper's sternum and upper left rib, shattering the bones and sending the fragments pin balling around his chest cavity before severing his spinal cord and slicing through the right aorta of his heart. The third, went straight as an arrow between his eyes, through his skull, into his brain and out the other side. He was dead before he even had chance to focus on who had just burst through the door. His body slumped, leaning off to one side and slid down half a foot down into his chair.

"SHOTS FIRED, SHOTS FIRED INSIDE THE WAREHOUSE." Taggart yelled over the radio.

Anaura swung around to face Richards, who stared back at him with an expression of extreme shock.

"Team leader to OPS Command, we're coming into the industrial site now, ETA one minute!!!" O'Keeffe declared over the air with Allen behind him saying that he could not believe this was for real.

Back inside the warehouse Foster was taking his time to finish the job, almost revelling in the fact that Bradford's death would return everything back to how it was before Op Barrier.

"Please don't, don't do it! I'll make you a very rich man, whatever you're being paid, I'll triple it!" Bradford pleaded in a terrified voice.

"You think this is about money?" Foster said in a manner devoid of emotion as he placed the gun into the centre of

Bradford's forehead and held it there for a thirty seconds before saying "Enjoy Hell!" as he pulled the trigger.

"ANOTHER SHOT FIRED!"

"DRIVE IN THERE IAN!" Anaura yelled.

Before Richards had a chance to put his foot down, the ARVs flew past the Mondeo and tore into the car park, where each of the fully kitted officers jumped out of their cars and covered the door of the building with their HK G36 assault rifles from behind their cars. As they stood in position waiting, the rain came crashing down on their ballistic helmets, playing havoc with their ear defender microphones and causing them to switch on and off as the water splashed over the speakers. O'Keeffe informed OPS Command that they were going to enter which prompted Drayson to grab his radio and yell that no one was to enter the building until he said so. O'Keeffe stood firm and said to others in his team that they should have been going inside straight away.

Drayson's feet began rapidly tapping the floor with nervous energy.

"OPS Command to O.P officers, remove yourselves from clear sight of the warehouse. Anaura keep your team away from the scene too!" The control Inspector ordered, following Drayson's interruption.

Foster charged out of the room, down the metal stair case and into the dark expanse of the warehouse floor that he was now able to fully light up with his torch. There was no need to be invisible or quiet now; now was the time to extract from the scene as quick as humanly possible and to get himself as far away as he could. Then, he would set the car alight and report it stolen to ensure that if anyone had seen it, it would be linked to the spurious thief.

Outside Richards pulled up to the gates of the warehouse where Anaura jumped out, telling the other three to stay where they were, and ran over to the firearms officers stood behind their cars. On seeing him appear, O'Keeffe shouted at him and asked what he thought he was doing. Anaura replied that it was imperative that he spoke to Foster before anyone moved in on him. Just as O'Keeffe was about to drag Anaura away from the area, Foster burst out of the main doors at speed and skidded to a halt as he saw the strobe effect of the ARV's blue light. O'Keeffe swiftly diverted his attention away from Anaura and towards Foster as the four other firearms officers trained their guns at him, barely able to see him through their rain covered masks and weapon sights that were covered with large droplets of water.

"ALRIGHT GUYS!! Everything's sorted now!" Foster said with a smile.

"Drop the weapon mate!" Potter pleaded with him.

"What, what are you talking about? Did he tell you to come here to support me? Really, there's no need, it's all finished, I don't need help now!" Foster said with confusion as he tried to work out why they had come.

O'Keeffe turned to Allen and MacNeil to ask what the hell he talking about as Potter continued to tell him to drop his gun. Anaura grabbed O'Keeffe by the shoulder and told him that he knew what Foster meant and implored him to let him have a go at negotiating a peaceful surrender. O'Keeffe pulled a bewildered expression in response before telling Anaura that there was no way on earth he would allow him talk to Foster when he was still armed. O'Keeffe pushed Anaura out of the way and began talking to Foster.

"Anthony mate, we know how rough things have been for you, but we need you to drop the gun mate and come with us for a chat. No one's going to hurt you, we're your mates aren't we?!" O'Keeffe said.

"I'm on the same team as you, why do I need to drop my gun? Who sent you here anyway? I never asked for support! I'm not having a rough time, things will be back to normal soon!" Foster replied with frustration.

O'Keeffe explained to him that he needed to come with them to get help, a comment which agitated Foster even more and caused him to start shouting at them, again demanding to know who had sent them. O'Keeffe turned to Anaura and asked him to explain what was going on that instance. Anaura replied that he could not yet and asked O'Keeffe once again to let him speak to Foster, who was now pacing up and down in a highly agitated state, prompting his former colleagues to look through their rain covered sights at him in case he made a sudden aggressive move. O'Keeffe looked at Foster's body language and reiterated to Anaura to stay out of it as he was one of theirs. Richards, Valera and Usher looked on at the scene from the Mondeo with nervousness. The tension and fear of the situation was almost tangible.

Just as Foster was finishing another remark about how he didn't need them and wanted them to leave to prevent the operation being compromised, Anaura cut over O'Keeffe and walked in the open gap between the two ARVs to talk to him. Allen attempted to grab him but Anaura dodged him and pushed him away. Realising that they needed to stay focused on Foster, O'Keeffe told Allen to leave Anaura and to concentrate on Foster.

"Alright Anthony, how's it going mate?" Anaura said in a friendly tone.

Foster asked who he was and whether he was part of the operation.

"I'm DI Peter Anaura, Anthony. You probably don't know me but I'm here to provide you with whatever you need. But just so we're clear Anthony what operation are you talking about? Are Bradford and Cooper dead?"

"You don't know about my assignment do you? Well if you don't have the clearance then I'm not telling you anything!" Foster said. His frustrated and cold expression flashing up between the intervals of the blue lights strobe effect and gushing rain.

"Anthony, just tell me; are they dead?"

"Course they are! I'm not a fucking amateur!" Foster barked.

O'Keeffe looked at the other firearms officers in disbelief.

"OK, OK Anthony, can we go inside to check them?"

"No, not yet!" Foster said whilst moving from side to side with unease.

Anaura asked Foster to tell him what he believed he had been told to do and whether there was anyone else involved in the operation. Foster continued to act defiantly, but after some influence and persuasion from Anaura, he began explaining that he was on a secret operation and that he had been ordered to do it

239

by someone high up. He continued that he would not provide the exact details of the assignment as none of them had clearance before once again telling them that they would have to speak to the man! Anaura decided that it was time to try and make Foster see that he had been used by Drayson, and to get him to say his name.

"I know he told you to do this Anthony, and I know you think you're on an 'operation' but you're not mate! He's used you Anthony, he works for the Gang and wanted them silenced because of what they know about him. He's a piece of shit, he's used you to do the things he didn't have the bottle to do himself. It's not your fault, he's had us all fooled for years! Tell me his name and we'll get everything sorted out!" Anaura said with an empathetic tone.

"You're wrong, there is an operation, he told me; why would he lie, he's a command officer?" Foster asked.

The firearms officers looked on with shock as they started to realise that Foster had actually been told to do it by a high ranked officer.

"Anthony, he's played us and he's playing you; we've all been played by the tosser, that's what he does! Put the gun down and let's talk about this somewhere dry shall we?

"He said I would get back in the job if I took on this operation. It's all real, seriously I had the OP order and everything."

"No Anthony. Think about it, why would an honest command officer order you to kill anyone? He's lying! Drop the gun and tell me his name, we'll stop him together!" Anaura said gently.

With his gun down by his side, Foster stopped pacing and began to sob as he shouted back at Anaura that what he was saying could not have been true. Anaura replied that he was sorry he had to tell him the truth but that he needed to in order to help him. Foster sobbed as he looked directly at Anaura and said that if he was right and it was all made up, he would be sent to a mental hospital for the rest of his life! Anaura said that he didn't need to worry about that for the moment and that he just needed to drop the gun and come with them to say who put him up to it. Foster repeated over and over again that it had to be real and that

Anaura was wrong, despite deep down realising that his original doubts may have been right.

"No Anthony, it's the truth mate, he's a criminal! He's the bad guy not you." Anaura said.

Foster stood there silently for a minute. Through the haze of confusion and the jumbled voices in his head, he had two thoughts, one he had compromised the operation and may have ruined his chance of getting back in the Force and two, that if Anaura was right, he would be locked away in a mental hospital without the chance of ever being released after what he had done. The stress began to overflow inside him, clouding his thoughts and judgement even more.

As Anaura and the firearms officers waited for Foster to say something, they heard him begin to talk to himself.

"Come on Anthony, drop the gun and tell me his name, I need to know his name to be able to help you." Anaura pleaded with Foster once more.

Foster looked up at his former police colleagues, the realisation dawning that he had been tricked by Drayson after all and would be going to a mental hospital after he was arrested. With the tears rolling down his cheeks and an anxious feeling developing in his stomach, Foster knew without a doubt that everyone had been right about him from the start; he really was ill.

"This isn't real is it?" He asked Anaura, who shook his head with a caring expression.

"I can't live in a mental hospital, I can't!" Foster said.

Anaura told him again not to worry about that for now and to come somewhere dry with him to discuss who had put him up to it. Foster raised his arm and pointed his gun at Anaura.

BANG, BANG. The first bullet hit Foster in his left shoulder, spinning him on his heels and causing him to drop the gun. The second hit him square in the chest half a second later and sent him crashing to the gravel floor.

"OH GOD NO; NO!!!" Anaura screamed out as he spun round and threw his hands up to his face as if he was in agony whilst the firearms officers ran forwards to begin first aid. Allen and Lewis, who had fired the shots both stood still in total shock, unable to move or speak. O'Keeffe, Arthur and Potter started tearing Foster's shirt off to start treating his wounds. He didn't move or make a sound as Potter and MacNeil worked together as quickly as possible to try and save their friend and former colleague. O'Keeffe stood up and placed his hand over his eyes as he updated over the radio that shots had been fired and that they needed an urgent ambulance for Foster. Richards, Usher and Valera sat frozen in their seats, staring at out of the car's windows in shock.

After O'Keeffe had finished with the radio, MacNeil looked up at him and shook his head slowly as the other firearms officers came over with looks of severe distress across their pale faces as they all suddenly realised what was going on. Foster was dead. Bradford and Cooper could wait.

Potter looked down at Foster's gun that was less than ten feet away and proceeded to throw up as he saw that the safety catch was still on, so it could not have been fired; Foster would have known this! For the first time in many months though, Foster looked like he was at peace.

In his office Drayson jumped to attention and asked for an update on Foster. Through his tears O'Keeffe responded that he and the Gang were all believed to be dead. Drayson confirmed he had received the update in a sympathetic tone, switched off his radio and leant back in his seat with his hands behind his head with a smile of pure corrupt satisfaction. With the Gang all dead and Foster too, there was nothing left to link him to any of it. What had once looked like a grave situation for him had now gone better than he could ever have hoped for. He picked up the glass of whiskey and took it out to the Command kitchen's sink where he poured it away with a huge smile.

"Assistant Chief Constable Robert Drayson! I like the sound of that more and more." Drayson said to himself.

Anaura stormed away from the scene in a rage, swearing and kicking the floor as he walked. What he had just seen would haunt him for the rest of his life, there was no way Drayson was going to get away with this, chief superintendent or not.

"Get out!" He said to the other three detectives in the car.

Valera and Usher jumped out into the pouring rain, with not so much as an utter of protest after seeing Anaura's furious expression.

"What are you going to do Peter?" Richards asked.

"Get out Ian!"

"No Peter, wherever you think you're going or what you're going to do, I'm coming with you!" Richards said without moving from his seat.

Anaura walked around the car to the passenger seat and told Richards to take him to Central District as quickly as possible. Richards replied that if he was going to see Drayson, it was a bad idea and that he needed to cool off first as the trauma of what had just taken place would have been clouding his judgement. Anaura looked at him and then told him to drive. The Mondeo had barely come to a stop in the rear of the Central District Police Station yard before Anaura leapt out and charged towards the rear doors, followed by Richards in hot pursuit who had struggled to get out of the car quickly enough to catch him up.

"Peter, calm down, don't do anything stupid!" Richards said. Anaura did not reply to him or a Response officer who greeted them as they went through the door. Anaura charged up the stairs towards the Command Suite and Drayson's office.

"YOU PIECE OF SHIT!" Anaura said as he stormed into the office where

Drayson had stood up after hearing Richards pleading with Anaura to stop. CRACK. Anaura punched Drayson flush in his face sending him reeling over his desk and on to the floor with a crash. Anaura went to hit Drayson again as he attempted to stand up in a daze until Richards grabbed him, desperately trying to stop his powerful friend from hitting the bastard again.

"WHAT THE FUCK ARE YOU DOING ANAURA, I'LL HAVE YOU ARRESTED FOR THAT!" Drayson yelled out in anger and he climbed to his feet with a bloodied mouth.

"ME ARRESTED, ME, YOU'RE THE ONE WHO'S GETTING ARRESTED MATE! I KNOW WHAT YOU ARE DRAYSON! YOU'LL PAY FOR FOSTER YOU FUCKING BASTARD!!!" Anaura bellowed at him whilst being held tight by Richards.

Although shocked that Anaura had managed to link him to Foster, Drayson told him that he would be out of the job by the morning and prosecuted for what he had just done. Anaura went to go for him again but was just about restrained by Richards again.

"YOU'RE THE ONE WHO'S IN TROUBLE MATE, COME ON!" Anaura yelled.

"For what? What evidence do you have? None I bet! Wild slanderous accusations, that along with that assault will cost you your job, you stupid bastard." Drayson said with a smug expression and a huff.

Anaura shook Richards off him and pointed a finger at Drayson whilst shouting how he would end him, to which Drayson laughed and asked how, opening his arms out inviting Anaura to hit him again. Anaura moved forwards to oblige but was restrained and pulled out of the office by Richards who was shouting at him to calm down. As he was ushered along the corridor away from Drayson's office, he shouted back to him that he was going to prison and that he would put him there himself. As they disappeared out of ear shot, Drayon took a deep breath through his anxiety. Anaura may have known everything but he would be able to prove nothing, especially when he would end up being ejected from the Force for assault, Drayson thought to himself. He reached down and picked up his stuff that had been propelled from his desk and placed them back from where they had come. Drayson wished that he had hit Anaura back, however, he knew full well that the satisfaction that would come from Anaura's arrest would be far more pleasing than a mere retaliation punch.

Anaura and Richards climbed into the Mondeo and began heading back to Shoreton in silence. After travelling for about fifteen minutes, Richards asked him whether it had been worth losing his job for, to which Anaura responded that he couldn't have just sat back and watched Drayson get away with it after Foster had died. Richards shook his head and replied that the Scotland Yard superintendent would have got him when he began

244

piecing everything together. But regardless of whether Drayson was caught out or not, Anaura would almost certainly lose his job. Anaura laughed to himself and replied that he would do again a thousand times over; he would rather lose his job than see a dirty copper get away with murder. They pulled up into the rear yard of the station, just as Anaura started to climb out he paused and sat back down.

"Would you have done the same Ian?" He asked.

"Ha, ha! Yeah of course I would have, but I tend to think things through a bit more than you and I know that it would be better to get the evidence first! Go home and see Laura, it's been a shit night, we'll see what we can do about this Foster and Drayson mess tomorrow, including your up and coming arrest!" Richards replied with a smile.

Ten minutes after leaving the station, Anaura pulled up onto his driveway and opened the door as quietly as he possibly could. He walked straight through the hall and into the kitchen where he removed a bottle of red wine from the wine rack and sat down at their large country style wooden kitchen table. As he poured out a large glass, he reflected on how he had never in his whole career had a shift that had been bad enough to make him drink to forget it had ever happened; without a doubt he now had.

"Peter!? You're back early, I thought you would be sleeping in the office because of the O.P." Laura said as she appeared in her nightie and took a seat in front of him.

Anaura nodded rapidly as the emotions began to well up after seeing her.

"What's the matter? Are you OK?" Laura asked with concern.

He put his knuckles up to his mouth and closed his eyes whilst giving her a nod and trying pulling himself together, although he was always himself in front of Laura; crying had never been his thing. However, a minute later the tears began to flow freely. Laura walked around the table to hug him and asked what had happened to make it such a bad night but he was unable to answer her. After five minutes of continuous crying, he stopped and composed himself.

"Peter? Tell me what's happened? I've never seen you upset

about work like this, I'm really worried about you!" Laura said with an expression of deep concern for her husband.

"Where do I start?!" He said with a huff.

"From where ever you want sweetheart!" She replied.

Anaura took a sip of his wine, looked at Laura through his reddened eyes and began telling her what had happened. Laura's concerned expression suddenly turned to sheer horror as he explained what had happened. After hearing the story, she asked how something like that could have happened in the police, and how Foster could have believed what Drayson had told him was real.

"I guess it's just what happens when someone weak and vulnerable is influenced by someone evil and deranged! I wish I could have done more for Foster" Anaura said.

"Everybody is influenced by somebody Peter. And Foster was influenced by Drayson, you couldn't have ever stopped that or helped him." Laura replied before pouring herself a glass of wine too.

Anaura told Laura that he loved her and she reciprocated, also stating that he would always have her love and support. He smiled back at her before the couple continued to talk through what had happened in the comfort and safety of their home, relationship and a large glass of red wine.

No Winners
Chapter Thirty Six

Drayson switched off his computer after seeing that it had turned one o'clock on his office clock. Although the pain of his swollen lip was bothering him and he still felt a little concerned about how things were going to pan out, he was one hundred percent in a better position than he had been a few months ago. He smiled to himself, the Gang were gone, Foster was gone, and Anaura would soon be gone too; what real evidence could there really be or believed. He cleared his desk and left the office to walk down to his car.

He walked out of the basement doors of the station and towards his car which he had positioned perfectly to drive out of the car park with minimal fuss. He climbed in, started the engine and put his Pink Floyd album on remembering that he had been listening to it the night he had influenced Foster into carrying out his devilish deeds. Drayson looked up to drive away and caught a glimpse of a figure walking his way which he believed was more than likely a response officer finishing a late shift.

BANG, SMASH. Drayson felt as though he had been hit by a freight train as he was violently slammed up against his seat with his brain desperately trying to establish what had just happened through the pain and shock. Drayson struggled to catch his breath as he looked down at his shirt which was becoming saturated from the flowing blood. He looked up through the windscreen to try and see who it was coming towards him, but was unable to due to the now opaque effect of the damaged windscreen. As the shadowy figure drew closer, Drayson tried to muster what little strength he had left to place the car in gear to get away; but he couldn't. The figure appeared at his open car window and as Drayson turned his head to see who his attacker was, the man fired another two shots into the car, causing the darkness of the cabin to illuminate twice with the muzzle flashes of the gun and the quiet car park erupt to life with the ensuing explosive echoes.

"Bradford says hi, bitch!" Poultan hissed as he spat on Drayson's now deceased body and ran off as fast as he could out of the car park and into the darkness of the nearby Kings estate, knowing that when he saw Bradford again he would be made a very, very rich man, and would be able to escape to somewhere hot without an extradition treaty.

Out of breath and well away from the scene, he stopped to call Bradford; but there was no answer..........

The End

Printed in Great Britain
by Amazon